GW00640893

SCORPIO

SCORPIO

Caroline Fox

ANDRE DEUTSCH

First published 1981 by
André Deutsch Limited
105 Great Russell Street London WC1

Copyright © 1981 by Caroline Fox
All rights reserved
Photoset in Garamond by Robcroft Ltd, London
Printed in Great Britain by
Redwood Burn Limited
Trowbridge and Esher

British Library Cataloguing in Publication Data
Fox, Caroline
 Scorpio.
 I. Title
 823'.914[F]   PR6056.0

ISBN 0 233 97371 0

For Eva

One

'OH HUSH, CHLOE! There's a man over there who keeps looking at you. I'm sure he heard what you said.'

'I don't care. I tell you, I wish we'd have a *coup d'état* or something. I'll die of boredom sitting here – I'll suffocate!'

In the Tivoli Gardens off the Rue St Lazare, Napoleon Bonaparte's birthday celebrations dragged on and on. Dancers dressed as nymphs and shepherds cavorted monotonously around the small ornamental lake in the centre of the lawns, just as they did at all the other innumerable State occasions. At regular intervals, along the gravel walk encircling the grass, the bright globes of oil-lamps amongst the orange trees sent the shadows of strollers chasing into the darkness, or cast their glow into one or other of the elaborate arbours festooned with roses and honeysuckle.

It was in such an arbour that the young boy and girl were sitting, conversing in impassioned whispers while the older members of their party sat absorbed in the ballet. And if the dragoons and guards officers strolling in pairs and groups on the gravel path gave more than a passing glance that way, or even paused, it was not to be wondered at. The boy, about seventeen years of age, pale and with soft, light-brown hair, leaning retiringly back into the shadows, was of no immediate interest. But the girl. Sitting on the edge of her chair, her hands clasped round her knees, she was leaning forward into the lamplight, so that its glow was falling full on her dusky, vivid beauty, her dark curls and her red lips set off by the black lace of her gown embroidered with crimson roses, and by the crimson silk sash tied just beneath the firm, creamy swell of her young breasts. She was a year or two older than the boy, and although there was a lingering tomboy wildness and irreverence in her dark eyes and her smile, there was a secretive thoughtfulness too. Her laughter, which had genuine anger in its mockery, faded suddenly, and she relapsed in her chair with a deep sigh. The shadows of thorns from the arbour dappled her face and the bare upper curve of her breasts.

'Oh Chloe, you're becoming stranger every day!' her cousin Philippe said, with a glance at her in which brotherly concern was mingled with a schoolboy's admiration. 'You say such wild things – and then sometimes you don't say a word for hours. What is it you really want?'

'Oh, if I could only explain . . . '

Outside the gardens, where the ragged poor of the Paris streets pressed in open-mouthed crowds against the wrought-iron gates, there was a woman selling thrushes and black-birds in wicker cages. Disturbed by the jostling of the crowd, and the lights, and the wail of the violins in the Tivoli orchestra, one lone bird was singing. Listening, Chloe felt a nameless misery, a fevered restlessness, rise in a lump to her throat.

'I feel like that poor bird,' she murmured. 'Oh, listen to it! Listen! Here we are, scarcely ten years after the Revolution – all that fighting and murder in the name of freedom – and yet listen! Oh, how could they?' She gazed for a moment at the locked gates not far away, where armed militia stood guard, and dirty, half-starved faces gaped in through the ornate wrought-iron screen, thin fingers clutching the bars. 'Still, how can they know any better?' she went on, answering her own question. 'In spite of all that's happened, they're not even free themselves. Oh, free to starve – free to die in these endless wars – '

'Chloe!'

' – Free to lick Bonaparte's boots!'

'Oh Chloe, hush!'

Under the orange trees close by, the anonymous silhouettes of strollers who might have been young officers, or might not, paused, turned, and moved casually away, vanishing into the deep shadows.

'Chloe, remember what General de Bourges told us – and Papa's warned us too,' Philippe whispered in trepidation. 'Everywhere in Paris – in the cafés, in the salons, even at receptions like this – there are spies from the Secret Police.'

'Yes, that's how free we all are, in this wonderful so-called Republic!' Chloe said with a scathing laugh. 'Or rather, that's how free *you* are.' And she added, with a proud lift to her chin, 'But I'm English.'

Close behind her, a spray of roses swung suddenly and stealthily against the trellis of the arbour, as if released by an invisible eavesdropper just beyond the dense screen of leaves and flowers. She drew the foliage quickly aside and looked through the trellis into the darkness, but there seemed to be no one there. Or was that the shadow of a man fleeting swiftly away amongst the orange trees?

'Half-English,' Phillipe corrected her. He seemed to have noticed nothing. 'And legally you're not English at all, since Papa's adopted you. But as you're half-English by blood, there's all the more reason to be careful what you say. So do stop it, Chloe. Why are you being so wild and reckless tonight? It's almost as if you want to get into trouble.'

Chloe sighed deeply, and sprawled back in her chair in silence. Philippe was right, of course. She often teased him for being so scholarly and cautious, so much the future lawyer, but he was usually right. To claim openly that she was English was certainly inviting trouble. It wasn't only that England and France were at war again. Almost every week there was another royalist plot to assassinate Bona-parte, and nearly all the conspirators, when they were caught, confessed that they had been helped by the English.

But wasn't there always trouble? And wouldn't there be more trouble tonight? Nothing as exciting as trouble with

9

the Secret Police, but just the usual, boring, everyday family trouble. She gave a glance of tight-lipped defiance at her uncle and aunt and at General de Bourges – by whose invitation, as usual, they were present – sitting round the mock-rustic table still laden with unfinished ices, marrons glacés and *bonbons à la Bonaparte*. Several times, already, Aunt Eugénie had looked reprovingly in her direction, and Uncle Victor had cleared his throat, and frowned, and drummed his fingers. It was very unlikely that they'd overheard her whispered conversation with Philippe, through their own 'Oohs' and 'Ahs' at the pastoral leaps and pirouettes of the ballet dancers; it wasn't that. But there would be the usual lecture, all the way home, about the way she'd yawned, and sighed, and 'flung herself about', as Aunt Eugénie would put it, instead of sitting there gracefully with her hands in her lap and a docile, fluttering smile fixed on her face – in case Bonaparte looked her way – and instead of being nice to the grey-whiskered General Trophime de Bourges, who wanted to marry her. He was quite a fine figure of a man, she supposed, tall and broad, and resplendent in his gold-braided uniform, and perhaps she ought to have felt flattered at the way he kept one hand resting on the back of her chair, and beetled his brows at any young officers who paused too long beside the arbour. But he was all of forty-five, and his whiskers were turning grey, and as for his name . . . Trophime! It was enough to make you burst out laughing every time you heard it.

Still, Philippe was right. It was pointless to provoke more trouble. Chloe sighed again and stirred, trying to pull herself together and take an interest in the ballet. But a vein was still beating urgently in her throat, like the frantic pulsing of a caged wild bird, and she thought, 'It's true – somehow I must escape.'

Yet what escape was there? Her parents had both died when she was a small child, leaving her no money, and she was entirely dependent on her uncle, a minor government official. So what escape could there ever be from the stuffy,

10

gloomy appartement near the Palais du Luxembourg, and the mornings of *petit point* and music lessons, and the decorous afternoon walks in the public gardens, and the endless banquets and receptions in the evenings? If only she had been a boy! Not a quiet, studious boy like Philippe, but a real, wild boy! Then, at least, she could have run and climbed and shouted, and got into scrapes, and she could even have run away. Or if they could only, now and then, spend a day in the country! – real country, with woods and fields, and wind, and great open skies. But they had no carriage of their own – to maintain one would have cost more than Uncle Victor's whole salary – and besides, even the country near Paris was still infested with brigands from the Revolution. Day after boring day, Bonaparte paraded his thousands of troops at the Caroussel and the Champ de Mars, and made speeches about '*la Victoire*' and '*la Gloire*', yet he couldn't even clear the woods of brigands. No, there was no escape – not even for a day.

As if he'd been pursuing the same train of thought, Philippe murmured, flushing slightly, 'Perhaps you ought to think about, you know, getting married. You'd have a bit more independence then, if that's what you want.'

'*Married?*' Chloe echoed in an explosive whisper, almost leaping off her chair.

'Hush!'

' – Married to old Grey-Whiskers?'

'Oh hush! Hush!'

'Or perhaps you meant the esteemed Monsieur Fish-Face?' Chloe went on, waving her hand towards another of her middle-aged admirers, the senior minister Monsieur Turgeon, who was pacing back and forth on the gravel path near Bonaparte's eagle-crested pavilion at the head of the garden, his hands clasped behind his back, his steps smooth and gliding, and the lamplight gleaming on his cold, pallid face with its almost opaque spectacles. Chloe's eyes moved on over the crowded figures of the inner Court circle within the pavilion: the over-painted women in their semi-transparent dresses of sequinned tulle, violet muslin

11

or gold lamé, festooned with jewels, flowers and trailing ostrich plumes; the stocky, coarse-looking men in their tight military uniforms bedecked with gold brocade, ribbons, stars and crosses. The Marshals of the Empire: all of them middle-aged, all of them men of the people. One was even picking his nose. 'Or perhaps you mean one of those gentlemen over there?' she added, her pulse so rapid with anger and despair that she was almost trembling. 'General Tinker, for instance, or General Tailor, or General Candlestick-Maker?'

'Yes, but with a younger man, of good family – '

'There aren't any! Those who weren't killed in the Terror are living in England, as *émigrés*, or they're hiding on their estates in the provinces, hundreds of miles from Paris.'

'I didn't mean them – I meant the sons of doctors, lawyers, merchants, or bankers . . . But it's true, you're not like us,' Philippe murmured, giving her an admiring glance. 'You're an aristocrat yourself, so you naturally look down – '

'I don't! I don't!' Chloe whispered, seizing his hand in a fiercely loving clasp. 'Not if they're good and kind like you! But they're all in the Army, and they go away for years and years. And if they ever come back . . . ' She gazed at Philippe for a moment: gentle, book-loving Philippe, who in only a year's time would be torn away from his studies and conscripted into Bonaparte's ever-growing Army. 'And if they ever come back, it's only because they've been crippled for life by their wounds. Oh Philippe, don't go! I'll help you run away.'

Philippe smiled his lopsided schoolboy's grimace of a smile, and ran his free hand back through his soft, floppy forelock of pale brown hair, but he only said, 'In any case, now that you've grown up so beautiful, Mama and Papa won't let you marry a nobody. They're determined on your marrying someone close to *him*.'

They both looked in silence at the slight, arrogant figure of Napoleon Bonaparte in the midst of that gaudy throng in the imperial pavilion, with the Empress Josephine beside him. After a moment Philippe turned his eyes away, but Chloe continued to gaze in bitter loathing. Everything was Bonaparte's fault! Everyone knew that he'd never stop now until he'd turned the whole of France, and the whole of Europe, and even the whole of Russia into one endless graveyard littered with looted art-treasures – and to no end but his own personal glory. Oh, why didn't someone manage to assassinate him? Where was the difficulty? The pavilion where he was sitting at this moment, for instance, was in the form of an open arcade, and quite close behind him dark figures could just be distinguished, melting in and out of the deep shadows beneath the orange trees. His Secret Police? But why couldn't someone, just once, slip past them? Why was every conspiracy discovered – every single one – almost as soon as it was formed?

'Never mind – take heart,' Philippe whispered, as the violins in the orchestra soared to a crescendo. 'I do believe it may be finishing. And then, with any luck, the Court will leave, and there'll be real dancing – if Papa isn't too displeased with you to let you stay.'

Bonaparte disapproved of real dancing – minuets and gavottes, and above all the wonderful waltz – probably because he was such a dreadfully bad dancer himself, so it never began until late in the evening, after the Court had retired. Dancing was Chloe's great joy – or it would have been, if only . . .

'Oh, if only there was someone exciting to dance with!' she sighed. She glanced round gloomily at General de Bourges, and at a group of dragoons hovering a few paces away from the arbour, clumsy tradesmen's sons to a man, by the look of them. 'But you can see, Philippe – there isn't a single . . . '

She trailed off. From the deep shadow of the orange trees behind the imperial pavilion, the tall, slim figure of a man emerged for an instant, bent close to the Emperor as if murmuring something to him, then vanished again. For a wild moment Chloe thought – hoped – that he'd stealthily jabbed a dagger into Bonaparte's back; but Bonaparte

13

went on watching the finale of the ballet and calmly sipping his iced drink just as before. Who then could the man have been? Just an aide-de-camp or a Court official bringing a message? But then why had there seemed something arcane – something almost sinister – about him? He had come and gone with such inobtrusive swiftness, and his clothes had been so anonymously dark, unadorned by gold braid, that she would never noticed him if she hadn't happened to glance back that way just then – and if she hadn't caught the flash of his hair, strikingly fair, as fair as an Englishman's, amongst all those other dark or greying heads. An officer, then, in the Secret Police? Chloe's heart, already unaccountably fluttering, sank at the thought. Even in that fleeting glimpse, she had sensed a single-minded ruthlessness in the man, as well as stealth and swiftness. If the officers of the Secret Police were like that, no wonder all the conspiracies against the Emperor failed.

But how could he have vanished so utterly? While the audience applauded the end of the ballet, Chloe's eyes searched the darkness behind the imperial pavilion, and the profound shadows under the orange trees to either side of it, but she caught no further flash, however faint or transient, of that distinctive fair hair. But of course he had only to put on the dark bicorne hat worn by officers of both the Police and the Army, and with his dark clothes he would have become entirely invisible.

She looked about her, still inexplicably disturbed. Perhaps fanned by the clapping of hundreds of hands, or by the rustle of silks and satins as the assembly stood for the Court's departure, the sprays of roses and honeysuckle festooning the arbour seemed to stir surreptitiously. What if the fair-haired man, having made his way round the periphery of the garden, moving swiftly from shadow to shadow, were close to her now, only a few paces away in the darkness beyond the arbour? What if .

'Why Chloe, you're shivering!' Philippe murmured – though there was scarcely any need now to speak in lowered tones, because of the cheers and cries of '*Vive l'Empéreur!*' from the crowd outside the gates as Bonaparte left the garden. 'And you've gone pale, too. Whatever's the matter?'

'I don't know exactly,' Chloe said, running her hands over her bare arms. The man had been quite young – in his early thirties, she'd guessed – and even in that brief glimpse she'd seen that he was arrestingly handsome: as handsome as the fair-haired English noblemen she'd often dreamt of. Yet the thought of him – the thought that he might be somewhere close to her in the darkness – sent another involuntary chill tingling over her.

'Didn't you see that man?' she whispered to Philippe.

'What man?'

'That fair-haired man, who spoke to the Emperor.'

The pavilion was empty, the ballet dancers gone, the last of the Court was bowing slowly out of the garden. Parties and couples were emerging from the arbours, strolling over the lawns, mingling at random around the lake.

'What fair-haired man?'

The orchestra struck up a waltz. Chloe spun wildly round on her toes, gave General de Bourges an absent-mindedly dazzling smile, then flung herself abruptly down in her chair again. Her heart was beating violently – from the surging excitement of the music, but also from panic. She'd said rash things against the Emperor; she'd never really believed in the existence of the Secret Police. But what if, as she stepped from the arbour, a man's hand were to reach out stealthily from the darkness and seize her wrist?

'No dancing for you, madam,' Aunt Eugénie said, with a meaning smile, mindful of General de Bourges' presence. 'You've been yawning all evening – you've had too many late nights as it is.'

'Oh, I agree,' Chloe said, casting about for her silk stole, which she had let fall to the grass beside her chair. She'd be glad to be in General de Bourges' carriage, away from all these sinister shadows. Or was she imagining that someone

15

had been eavesdropping on her conversation with Philippe, and that her every movement was under close surveillance now?

Bending down to pick up her stole for her, Philippe whispered, 'Do you mean that man over there?'

Chloe's eyes flashed up, and with a sinking flutter of her heart she found herself meeting the direct gaze of the fair-haired man. He was standing in the full glow of the lamplight on the gravel path not twenty paces away, amid a group of ladies and cavalry officers. She had never thought to look for him there, out in the open. Yet it was surely the same man. There were the same anonymously dark but well-cut clothes, the same silky fair hair, the same luminous and penetrating gaze – which held hers for a moment, with what seemed a look of secret and all-seeing recognition, before flickering courteously away, back to the faces of the ladies conversing with his officer companions.

Chloe risked another look at the man while General de Bourges placed her stole over her shoulders with stiff gallantry. Was it really the same man? Wondering why a faint doubt had entered her mind, she cursed the brevity of her earlier glimpse in the imperial pavilion, and cursed the light dappling of leaf-shadow half-veiling the man's figure now, making it so difficult for her to be sure. But his hair, which had seemed a white-blond flash under the bright lights of the pavilion, now seemed only a pale honey colour – that colour which, with clear olive skin and hazel or grey-blue eyes, was fairly unusual but not exceptional amongst Frenchmen. And although he was certainly handsome, his fine features betrayed none of the relentless keenness she thought she had seen in them earlier; only the poised alertness of an intelligent and sensitive man. And there was, after all, a subtle gold brocade at the collar and cuffs of his dark blue coat, which she would surely have noticed before. No, it wasn't the same man. Or if it was, she had been quite mistaken in her earlier impression. Above all, in the fineness of his features, his manner towards the ladies he was conversing with, and even just in his stance – both

16

hands resting on the head of an elegant, silver-topped cane – there was the unmistakeable distinction of the aristocrat. And what French aristocrat would be a member of Bonaparte's Secret Police? No, he could only be a cavalry officer like his companions, albeit not in uniform as they were. It was true that a few well-born young officers, usually the younger sons of noblemen, had survived the Terror, if they had been abroad with the Army at the time, behaved with circumspection, and distinguished themselves in battle. No, she had imagined it all.

But why, then, as his eyes met hers again, so that she had to look quickly away, did her skin tingle in another inexplicable shiver?

Her uncle and aunt and General de Bourges were collecting up the last of their things – hats, gloves, Aunt Eugénie's fan – ready to go. Several other parties were emerging from their arbours and beginning to converge slowly on the gates. Twenty paces away, on the gravel walk beneath the lamplight, the young cavalry officers, one after another, were leading the ladies of their choice away into the waltz, until only the fair-haired man was left, chatting now to Monsieur Turgeon, who had passed that way. Strange that it was the fair-haired man, by far the most handsome of his group, who had been left without a partner; strange that none of the young ladies, smiling and laying her hand on his arm . . . But he was gazing at her again! She spun quickly away.

'Chloe, he's going to ask you to dance – I'm sure he is!' Philippe whispered. 'He's going to get Monsieur Turgeon to bring him over here and introduce him, if you can only think of a way to delay us for a few moments.'

Chloe stood as if turned to stone, her mind a blank, while the sweeping rhythm of the waltz seemed to surge all round her. It would have been easy enough to slip off one of her silver bracelets, fling it into the deep shadows at the furthest corner of the arbour, and have General de Bourges and Uncle Victor, misled by Philippe, crawling about on their hands and knees in search of it for ten minutes or so;

17

she'd done such things often enough in the past. But did she really want to dance with the fair-haired man? To be alone with him, held close in his arms?

She risked another glance in his direction, and with difficulty stifled a gasp. After a last, timeless gaze at her – calm and expressionless, yet with what seemed a hint of underlying irony or even mockery in it – the fair-haired man took leave of Monsieur Turgeon, shifted his silver-topped cane to his left hand, turned on his heel, and strolled away towards the gates of the garden, walking with a slight but distinct limp. Within a few moments, he had disappeared in the crowd of departing guests.

So that was why he wasn't in uniform. Wordless, Chloe allowed herself to be ushered out of the arbour and towards the gates, taking General de Bourges' proffered arm. That was why the rest of his party had danced away, leaving him standing alone. She glanced round in puzzlement at the melting shadows beneath the orange trees, deeper shadows seeming to dart swiftly through them, also moving towards the gates. But then he couldn't possibly be a member of the Secret Police. The man who had come and gone so stealthily in the pavilion had surely not been hampered by a disability; he had moved with the smooth speed of a lizard. Why, then, did another shiver thrill through her?

'I trust you haven't caught a chill, my dear,' General de Bourges said, as the converging crowd began to jostle them. 'But there's a nice warm rug in my carriage, and you must wrap – '

The rest of his words were lost as a sudden surge in the crowd at the gates separated them. Alone, Chloe fought to keep her balance as Army officers, Court officials, finely-dressed ladies and rough-clad workmen jostled her on every side. Expensive perfumes mingled with the smells of garlic and sweat. Someone trod on her toe; an ostrich plume swept against her face. Was there a flash of fair hair? Somewhere nearby she could hear General de Bourges anxiously calling her name, but the air was filled with

18

shouts of 'Make way, make way!' and 'Order!' and would have drowned her answer – drowned her stifled cry as she felt a hand stealthily run down her bare arm, encircle her wrist, then close her fingers firmly over a piece of folded paper.

'Ah, there you are, my dear young lady – not hurt, I trust?' General de Bourges panted, shouldering his way back to her side.

Without answering, Chloe looked swifly round. Only the faces of middle-aged Court officials and their wives, and a few senior Army officers and young dragoons surrounded her, already moving more smoothly out through the gates as the crowd thinned and dispersed. Ahead, she could see her uncle and aunt and Philippe stepping up into the waiting carriage. Just inside the gates, hardly three paces from her, the fair-haired man stood calmly, both hands resting on the silver head of his cane, chatting to one of the guards. His grey-blue eyes were already resting on her when she looked his way, as if he'd been watching her, and he gave her a slight but elegant bow, and a faint, mocking smile of private recognition.

In a daze of shock, Chloe passed by on General de Bourges' arm. Clasped tight in her free hand, the folded piece of paper seemed to burn into her palm like a sliver of ice.

Two

It was mercifully dark in the carriage as they jolted southward through the city towards the Seine. Chloe had quickly hidden the piece of paper in her reticule – without reading it, of course; there'd been no chance even to glance at it. In the dark, her reticule clasped tightly closed on her lap, concealed under the folds of the woollen rug which General de Bourges had insisted on wrapping round her, she ought to have felt safe from all possible detection. Yet she started at every approach of galloping hoofs, only breathing more evenly again after they'd passed and faded away into the night. She ought to have thrown the note away, of course; she ought to have dropped it instantly. And she felt strangely guilty at having kept it and hidden it, unsuspected even by Philippe.

Now and then the lamps of another carriage, or the flaring torch or lantern carried by one of a group of pedestrians, or the bright lights of a café, or the wan gleam of a streetlamp, flickered over the interior of the carriage. She and Philippe and Aunt Eugénie were squeezed together in a row, with General de Bourges and Uncle Victor facing them. Desultory conversation about the ballet, and about the Empress Josephine's dress and *coiffure*, and about the other guests, went back and forth. In silence in her corner, Chloe gazed out into the night. As long as General de Bourges was still with them, there would be no family scene about her yawning and languishing all through the ballet; she would be left in peace to think.

Who had slipped that note into her hand? Just some half-starving member of the ragged crowd outside the gates, begging for a few *sous*? Or some tipsy dragoon, dared by his comrades, offering her amorous compliments? It was possible. Yet she remembered the flash of fair hair she thought she'd glimpsed in the midst of the confusion; seemed to feel again the stealthy caress of those fingers down her bare arm, and their steely calm as they closed her hand over the folded paper; seemed to see again that penetrating grey-blue gaze, that mocking little bow, that faint, secret smile, from hardly three paces away from her. And her heart beat faster, for there could hardly be any doubt that the note was from him.

He must be a royalist, then. And this note must be an invitation to join in a conspiracy against Bonaparte. Her heart beat wildly. If it was, would she dare to accept?

Oh, how slowly the carriage was moving! Yet, as she gazed out of the window, everything she saw seemed to be saying to her, 'Yes, accept – in spite of all the dangers!' The district they were passing through, like so many others in Paris, was in the throes of being demolished and rebuilt by Bonaparte. Gone were the honeycombs of narrow streets and pretty little squares which she remembered from her childhood. The carriage was jolting its way through a wilderness of rubble, from which rose great pyramids of new stone and ghostly scaffoldings, where vast, vulgar, pseudo-Roman edifices were to appear, monuments to the glory of the Empire. Bonaparte was ruining Paris, the most beautiful city in Europe, just as he would ruin the whole of the civilized world if he wasn't stopped. Even as they passed the Palais des Tuileries – the residence of Bonaparte himself, and a dazzle of lighted windows from end to end – they had to wind their way through a no-man's-land of debris and scaffolding, stretching the whole length of the palace and its gardens on their north side.

'It'll be the longest street in Paris,' General de Bourges was explaining, with an almost proprietory enthusiasm. 'And as straight as a ruler all the way, with an arcade – you know, like a Roman viaduct – running its whole length. I've heard it's to be called the Rue de Rivoli.'

It was at the Battle of Rivoli, in Italy, that the General had distinguished himself. Plain Monsieur Bourges, son of a grocer, only a few years previously, he had hopes of shortly becoming the Duke of Rivoli. Under Bonaparte, brand new dukes, counts, viscounts and barons had begun to appear almost daily. Already the ribbon and cross of the newly-founded Légion d'honneur hung on the General's broad breast.

The carriage crossed the great open square at the western end of the Jardin des Tuileries. A few years ago it had been called the Place de la Révolution, and the guillotine had stood there. There, King Louis and Marie-Antoinette had been murdered, as well as thousands of others during the Jacobin Terror, 'heads falling,' as people said, 'like apples.' Bonaparte himself had been a Jacobin. But now the guillotine had gone, out to the eastern suburbs of the city, and the great square had been renamed the Place de la Concorde, and the lights of the palace twinkled prettily through the trees in the gardens. But Chloe, for one, had not forgotten.

But what was she thinking of? General de Bourges had begun reminiscing, as ever, about the Italian Campaign. Chloe cursed herself for remaining so lost in thought while the conversation had dwelt on the other guests at the Tivoli. She had to find out what she could about the fair-haired man; and if he had once been an army officer, General de Bourges must surely know him, if only slightly. Yet how could she now turn the General's flank, as it were, and lead the conversation back again, without seeming to, to the Tivoli? Already they were crossing the Seine, and would be rumbling over the cobblestones of the Quai Malaquais, where General de Bourges had his lodgings. Sometimes he came all the way home with them, but just as often, if he had a busy day at the War Office ahead of him, he took leave of them outside his door, generously lending them his carriage to take them the rest of the way. Chloe had begun by fretting at the slowness of the journey, but now she willed the carriage to crawl. It seemed to go only the faster. And meanwhile the Battle of Rivoli went on and on.

'It's true, isn't it, that the Italians are all as dark as blackamoors?' she suddenly broke in desperately, just as the General's forces were storming the ridge. 'A lady of my acquaintance, who has been visiting her kinsfolk in Genoa, told me that some of the gentlemen are fair, and extremely handsome, but I can't believe that's true. After all, even in France fair-haired men are most uncommon.'

'I see you're quite recovered now from your chill,' Uncle Victor said to her, rather drily, and then, to the General: 'Pray do continue, sir. Your account's so graphic, one can almost hear the thunder of the cannon, and see our gallant cavalry sweeping on up . . .'

They passed a streetlamp, and Chloe gave General de Bourges a radiantly admiring smile.

'Ah yes . . . Yes, perhaps in the north of Italy, and in Piedmont, you do see a few tow-haired fellows – but very swarthy, of course, all the same,' General de Bourges answered her, visibly straightening his shoulders. 'I shouldn't have called them handsome.'

'Quite so,' Chloe agreed. 'Not handsome at all. I was reminded of it by the gentleman who bowed to you just as we were leaving the Tivoli, and wondered if perhaps he was some Italian nobleman you'd taken prisoner, or whose life you'd saved, or something.'

'Just fancy! I was certain he bowed to you, Chloe,' Aunt Eugénie said, with an edge to her voice, 'although I know we've never made his acquaintance. Though why a gentleman, even an Italian, should be so presuming – unless he'd been encouraged, of course – I can't imagine. And anyway, I don't think he was an Italian. He looked very French to me.'

'Yes, I too thought it was Mademoiselle Chloe he bowed to,' the General began, puzzled; then he added hastily, 'But of course – as you say – it couldn't have been. And it's true, now I come to think of it, that his face was distantly

familiar. It's just that I can't quite recollect for the moment
. . . Still, I dare say it'll come back to me some other time.'

The carriage rumbled on over the cobblestones of the
Quai Malaquais. Chloe leaned back in her corner, her
fingers tightening on the clasp of her hidden reticule.

'Perhaps he was at Rivoli,' she suggested. 'One of your
staff officers.'

'Ah yes – a junior officer – perhaps! There were so many,
and of course that was seven years ago now. Though
naturally he'd remember me,' the General said. 'Although,
I don't know why, I somehow feel I've seen him more
recently, in some quite different connexion . . . Yet I can't
place him – it's most mysterious. And then, you know, if he
was an army officer, why wasn't he in uniform on our
Emperor's birthday?' He rapped with his short cane on the
panelling of the carriage, and it drew to a halt outside his
door. 'And now, with the greatest regret, but I have several
important appointments early tomorrow morning . . . '

'He limped,' said Chloe.

'Ah, did he? What an observant young lady you are!' the
General murmured absent-mindedly as he climbed down
from the carriage. It seemed to lighten perceptibly on its
springs. 'And of course that would explain . . . De l'Epinay!'
he exclaimed suddenly, pausing beside the carriage door.
'That's who it was – the Comte de l'Epinay! A fine officer,
but I remember now: he was wounded in the foot. Not in
Italy – in Egypt or Syria; I read about it in the gazette. Still,
that was five years ago. I wonder what he's been up to all
this time.'

Everyone in the carriage was leaning silently towards the
still open door.

'The Comte de l'Epinay?' Chloe echoed, speaking half to
herself. 'You mean a real –' Philippe nudged her quickly –'I
mean a *ci-devant* nobleman, a nobleman from before the
Revolution?'

'Yes yes, but he was an excellent officer, and politically
quite sound as far as I remember. A tragedy, that wound!
He'd have been a Lieutenant-Colonel by now, at the very
least. Bonaparte, I know, thought very highly of him.

24

Which makes it all the more strange ... They ought to have given him a post at the War Office, or in the Government. I can't make it out.'

In the light of the streetlamp beside the carriage, General de Bourges put on his black bicorne hat and adjusted his sword, his heavily-built figure bulging in his General's uniform of dark blue gold-braided coat, red sash and white breeches: the uniform which would have looked so dashing on the fair-haired man, the Comte de l'Epinay.

'All the same, there's a reason for it, when a man's career suddenly comes to an end like that,' he added, beetling his brows, perhaps belatedly aware of a too silent interest from the occupants of the carriage. 'Something about his politics, or his private life. Something discreditable, you may be sure. And I keep thinking I've seen him somewhere in the last year or two. Somewhere unexpected, in a bad light – and he didn't bow to me then. But it'll come to me, it'll come to me! And if it doesn't, I'll make a few enquiries.' And then, to his coachman: 'To the Rue Guynemer.'

He stepped back, and amid protestations at his generosity, and cries of farewell, the carriage drove on into the night.

Silence reigned in the carriage as it began to wind its way through the narrow streets of the Latin Quarter. Chloe could guess why her uncle and aunt were so lost in uneasy thought, instead of upbraiding her as usual for her failure to be gracefully charming all evening to their host. They had been counting on her marrying either General de Bourges or Monsieur Turgeon, so as to secure them a permanent place in the new Society of the Empire; and their silent agitation now, it seemed to Chloe, was like that of the dog in the fable, which suddenly glimpses an even bigger and more beautiful bone shimmering in the depths of the river. A *ci-devant* – a real aristocrat of the *Ancien Régime*! Chloe watched the light of the streetlamps, and of a few passing carriages, glide over their anxious faces, and in any other circumstances she might well have laughed aloud.

She gazed out of the window again, hardly seeing the beautiful old streets and squares of the Latin Quarter and the Faubourg St Germain, though it was here that the aristocrats of the *Ancien Régime* had kept their fine houses before the Revolution. They had stood looted and empty for years now, their gilded gates hanging crookedly from their hinges. Yes some, it seemed, had not been empty after all. Here and there were houses where hunted aristocrats had lived in hiding in the attics, plotting to restore the monarchy, and emerging only in disguise at night. Many had been discovered and executed, but perhaps some still remained. Perhaps, during the five years of his mysterious disappearance, the Comte de l'Epinay had been in hiding here too, carefully organizing a *coup d'état* which would succeed.

For there was surely no doubt at all now that he was a royalist. Why else should he have disappeared for five years, sacrificing a brilliant career in Bonaparte's administration? Why else should General de Bourges have that lurking, nameless doubt about him? Chloe's heart beat painfully fast as the carriage left the Faubourg St Germain behind and entered the dull, straight, respectable streets near the Palais du Luxembourg, inhabited almost entirely by minor government officials. Her fingers played nervously with the clasp of her reticule, and she was only distantly aware of the conversation going on in the carriage: merely plans for their visit to the Champ de Mars three days hence, for the anniversary celebrations of one of Bonaparte's victories; whether Monsieur Turgeon, who had invited them, could be counted on to send his carriage to collect them, and what they should wear, and so on and so forth.

At last the carriage came to a halt outside their door in the Rue Guynemer overlooking the Jardin du Luxembourg. Chloe managed to descend calmly to the pavement, and then to walk slowly up the three flights of wide stairs with the others to their appartement. But as soon as the maid had opened the door to them, she muttered something about having a headache and needing her sal volatile, and

26

flew to her room, seizing a lighted candle from a candelabrum in the salon on her way.

Once in her bedroom, she slammed the door behind her and leaned back against it, fumbling for the note in her reticule. What if it were only an ill-scrawled begging letter after all, or a silly *billet-doux* from some drunken dragoon? She set the candle down in a candlestick on the cabinet beside the door, and unfolded the note with trembling hands. The paper was of fine quality; the handwriting firm, precise and elegant, although she saw at once that there was no signature, not even an initial. She moved closer to the candle. For a moment the words danced before her eyes; then she read: *You seem as fearless as you are beautiful, and excite our interest as well as our admiration. So, if you are for the Crown, and peace with England, embroider a fleur-de-lis on your handkerchief and drop it at the Champ de Mars. You will be given an assignment – but be warned that you risk your life.*

Three

THERE WAS A WHISPER and a light tap at the door just behind
her. Chloe felt as if she were returning slowly from some
immense dark distance, with no knowledge of how long
she had been standing there, the note still in her hand.

'Chloe! Are you all right? Can I come in?'

Instinctively, though the voice had only been Philippe's,
Chloe quickly folded up the note again and tucked it down
inside the front of her gown, between her breasts; then she
silently opened the door.

'No staying up till all hours talking, you two!' called a
lazy voice, followed by a yawn, from Aunt Eugénie and
Uncle Victor's bedroom at the far end of the narrow
corridor; then their door closed.

'Chloe, whatever is it?' Philippe asked, staring at her,
after she'd soundlessly shut and locked her bedroom door
behind him; and she saw, as she passed the mirror, that her
eyes seemed larger and darker than ever in the luminously
pale glow of her face.

'I'll tell you in a moment.'

She moved at random about her room, her step rapid
and restless, suddenly unable to keep still. Should she
confide in Philippe, or should she fob him off with some
fictitious tale? During their childhood, she had often
mocked mercilessly at his native caution, flung his precious
books on the floor, and even locked him in dark cupboards
'to teach him to be braver'. They were the wrong way
round: it was she who should have been the boy; everyone
had always said so. But now he was a goodlooking youth,

half a head taller than she was, and he would soon have lost the last of his schoolboy awkwardness. And there was firmness in his character as well as sympathy and thoughtfulness, while she . . . He was right, she was ruled more and more by her own strange, wild moods. And she had to talk to someone, and who else was there?

'Read this,' she said, retrieving the note and handing it to him.

He flushed slightly as he took it from her, because of where it had been concealed, but even in the candlelight she could see the colour drain swiftly from his face as he read it.

'The devil! The clever, calculating devil!' he exclaimed angrily when he'd finished, and made an instinctive move to screw the note up in his hand.

'Who?' Chloe asked, snatching the note back from him and darting out of reach.

'That fair-haired fellow – what's his name, de l'Epinay. It was him, wasn't it?'

'I think so,' Chloe admitted warily, backing further away. She had expected some extreme reaction from Philippe – shock, or fear – but not this uncharacteristic anger. 'Someone gave it to me in the crowd by the gates of the Tivoli, and he was near . . . But why do you call him that – a devil, and everything?'

'Because he's playing on your feelings. I suppose he overheard the things you were saying, and watched you from somewhere in the shadows . . . I didn't like the way he looked at you – I was going to tell you that anyway. Oh, I can see that he's very handsome, and he's an aristocrat and all that, but you wait and see. When Papa's made some enquiries – and General de Bourges too, perhaps – there'll be something turned up that isn't to de l'Epinay's credit. Women, or gambling debts, or something. Oh, I can see that you're very taken with him, but I could tell, somehow, just from the way he looked at you . . . And that letter. It's almost a love-letter, the way it's worded, but all he really wants is just to make use of you.'

Chloe backed away until she was sitting on the edge of

29

her bed, playing with one of the silk tassels of its rose-patterned canopy and eyeing her cousin thoughtfully. She had never seen him with such flashing eyes, such firm lips, such squared shoulders. Only the soft mop of his hair, and his habitual, awkward gesture of pushing it back from his brow, betrayed the seventeen-year-old schoolboy she knew. Could he possibly be jealous?

'Well, I think I see what you mean about the way he looked at me,' she murmured diplomatically. 'And I admit that he made me shiver a bit too, until I'd understood . . . But can't you see – he was looking at me as a fellow royalist, a fellow conspirator, and that explains everything. And after all, Philippe, you're a royalist too. We've always agreed about that.'

'In a way,' Philippe conceded reluctantly. 'And yet, the more I think about it . . . '

'You're never going over to Bonaparte!'

'No no. He's becoming a tyrant. And the Jacobins are even worse – nothing but thieves and murderers. And yet – it's enough to make one despair, sometimes – even the royalists, the more I learn about them . . . '

He fell silent for a moment, and Chloe watched him pacing thoughtfully up and down. By a curious quirk, it was he who looked English, while she . . . She glanced at the miniatures of her parents on the wall beside the fireplace. She was the living image of her French mother, and bore no resemblance at all to her fair-haired English father, son of a great landowner, Lord Culverwood. She sighed. Her father's family had never accepted his marriage to the daughter of a mere French doctor, and because of the Revolution and the war with England, she had grown up as plain Chloe Lenoir, taking her uncle's name. Idly, while Philippe continued to pace back and forth, she picked up a pencil and a notepad from her bedside table, and began scrawling over and over again, as she often did, *Chloe Culverwood. Chloe Culverwood Lenoir. Chloe Lenoir Culverwood . . . '*

'You're bound to see it differently,' Philippe said finally, 'because you're descended from the English aristocracy, and you're always reading and thinking about it. And of course they reformed themselves long ago, and have a tradition of service to their country, and moderation in their style of living. But it wasn't like that here before the Revolution. You've never walked through the back-streets of the Faubourg St Germain, and seen the filthy slums where the servants of the French aristocracy had to live, while their masters enjoyed a life of frivolous and irresponsible luxury – sleeping till midday, taking all afternoon to dress, and spending the whole night playing cards and entertaining their numerous mistresses. It was they who provoked the Revolution, living like that while the common people starved. And they've learnt nothing, not even from fifteen years of living in England. All they want to achieve, with their conspiracies, is to get back their wealth and their privileges, and never mind if the rest of the country starves. They don't care about France at all – only about themselves. That's obvious from the methods they use. Remember that explosion about four years ago in the Rue Niçaise, when they tried to blow up Bonaparte's carriage on his way to the Opera. It was a crowded street, and over a hundred innocent people were killed or injured. Worse than that, the explosives were in a farm cart, and they paid a child, a twelve-year-old girl, a few *sous* to stand there holding the horse's head while they ran off to safety, and of course she was blown to pieces. Perhaps that's the kind of "assignment" de l'Epinay and his friends have in mind for you.'

'They're not all like that,' Chloe protested, with an involuntary shiver.

'No, of course not. Some of them wanted reform, and tried to work with the revolutionaries. But most of those went to the guillotine during the Terror, or they've fled to England or America.'

'But perhaps some of them have been in hiding here in Paris,' Chloe said, smoothing the letter out on her lap and fingering its fine paper. 'Good royalists, I mean, who want to save France from Bonaparte, and bring back a reformed monarchy. If that were so, you'd be in favour of them, wouldn't you?'

31

'Yes, I would. In that way I'm still as much a royalist as ever. But – '

'And you know Bonaparte has all the news-sheets censored. Probably we only hear about the bad royalists who get caught, and we never hear about the good ones. There may be lots of them.'

'I hope so,' Philippe said. 'But de l'Epinay isn't one of them.'

'Oh, how can you be so sure?' Chloe burst out angrily, leaping up off the bed and moving restlessly about the room again. 'You only saw him for a moment. Aren't you being a little . . . well, prejudiced?'

'He looked arrogant, and he looked cynical – as if he thought himself above the law,' Philippe said sharply. 'And that letter's too full of compliments and gallantries. Very elegantly phrased, of course, but there's a frivolous, dishonourable undertone – can't you see that? – which is typical of an *ancien-régime* aristocrat's attitude towards women. I tell you, he's just playing on your feelings, and if you trusted him your life wouldn't be worth two *sous*.'

Chloe paused before the mirror. In the candlelight, framed by a dark arbour of shadows, her own image, in her black lace dress embroidered with crimson roses, gazed back at her, dusky, proud and passionate. 'As fearless as you are beautiful,' the letter had said. She swung round to face Philippe with a teasing smile, her hands on her hips, and said lightly, ' – Because he'll want me to hold some cart-horse's head, you mean? I hardly think . . . Oh, Philippe, don't be silly! He'll just want me to wheedle military secrets out of General de Bourges, that's all. It's obvious.'

'Do you think that would save you from the Secret Police when the plot's discovered? – as it will be. Every plot's discovered sooner or later; you know that.'

'This one won't be – this one will succeed,' Chloe said, going closer to Philippe and gazing intently into his face, as if by doing so she could instill her own deepening conviction into him. 'You call him arrogant, and cynical, and calculating, but there's a quality about him . . . ' She dwelt on the memory of de l'Epinay's unruffled coolness, the penetrating intelligence of his gaze, his air of secret, single-minded ruthlessness. 'You've made up your mind not to like him, so you use those words, but perhaps we're even talking about the same quality. And I know he'll succeed. After all, he must have been planning his *coup d'état* for years – all the time he's been missing. And he was a first-class army officer – General de Bourges said so – and so he's used to planning strategy very carefully, and to commanding other men. And he even spoke to Bonaparte, and to Monsieur Turgeon. How clever he must be, to make them trust him! And even General de Bourges suspected nothing, until now . . . '

She trailed off in a sudden chill of realization. She had been playing persuasively with the lapel of Philippe's coat, but now she seized it urgently, whispering, 'Listen! If General de Bourges makes enquiries about him – and Uncle Victor too . . . Oh, what a fool I was to make the General jealous like that! And de l'Epinay doesn't know. I must warn him – and it's three whole days till that parade at the Champ de Mars. Oh, what am I to do?'

She began to turn away distractedly, but Philippe caught her suddenly by the arms. 'Chloe, Chloe!' he whispered, and she could feel that his hands were trembling. 'You're talking as if . . . You don't know anything about de l'Epinay, except that he represents every kind of danger, including the danger of death. And yet you're talking as if you've made up your mind to fall in with his intrigues.'

Had she? Startled, Chloe turned slowly away and looked round at the warm, vivid colours and the familiar disorder of her room with new eyes, as if she were waking from a dream. She had decided nothing while she had been alone after first reading the note, and had only thought to share her mesmerization with Philippe. Yet it seemed to be true: something deep within her, while they had been arguing, had made its own decision – one which would change her life entirely, and perhaps even end it. She looked round as if she was seeing her room for the first and the last time; and not only her room but her own self too: the girl she had always been. Not only the looking-glass itself, but the rose-patterned hangings of the rumpled bed, the crimson curtains at the window, and the carpet with its pattern of leaves, birds and more roses, strewn with silver bracelets and silk ribbons, all seemed to have become mirrors, offering her shadowy glimpses of herself – her past self, and her future self – in the flickering glow of the low-burning candle. It was as if some secret force within her, only expressed until now in a random wilfulness, and in restless, wild, prickly moods, had suddenly come into its own, and she was powerless to resist the course it chose to take.

'I shall want to see him again and talk to him, to make sure . . . ' she said slowly, aware that she was talking as if she were a sleepwalker. 'And then . . . if I'm right . . . yes.'

'But why, Chloe, *why?*' Philippe asked in anguish. 'If your parents had been killed in the Revolution I'd understand it. But why do you want to risk your life?'

Why indeed? It certainly wasn't just because de l'Epinay attracted her; the sight of him had only awakened something in her which had always been there. But what was it?

The candle flickered low again in a faint stir of air from the open window, and she picked it up in its silver holder and shielded its small flame with her palm. Then, lost in thought, she moved slowly round the room, as if the wavering light, wandering over the wallpaper and the furniture, might suddenly illuminate an answer to her question.

She paused before the miniatures of her parents. Her beautiful, dark, sensuous, almost voluptuous mother; her tall, slim, fair-haired father with his visionary eyes. They'd been very much in love, so she'd been told. Yet they should never have had a child; that had often been said too. They had frequently left her in the care of her nurse, or with Uncle Victor and Aunt Eugénie, to go roaming away to the Alps, or to the great dark forests of Germany, or amongst the classical ruins of Italy and Greece, or the Ionian islands.

34

And it had been amongst those distant islands, caught in a sudden Mediterranean storm, that they had been drowned, when Chloe had only been four years old – too young even to remember them.

What had they been searching for in those high mountains, those impenetrable forests, those ruins and those far away islands? What was the inner quest, the undying restlessness, which they had bequeathed to her?

The glow of the candle moved slowly on along the wall, while Philippe watched and waited in silence.

All Chloe's parents had left her, in the way of worldly goods, were the numerous sketches and paintings her father had made during those distant travels; he had been a gifted artist. Yet her favourite of all – which the flame of the candle illuminated now – was not of any of those exotic places, but of the Lake District in England, where her father had been born. The scene was of a stretch of water at dawn, cradled by misty fells, and from the reeds in the foreground a great flock of birds was rising, winging away until the furthest of them were only faint smudges against the endless sky, fading until they became one with the dim light itself, then vanishing.

'Free!' she whispered, setting down the candle and going swiftly to the open window. 'Philippe, if I can't be free, I might as well be dead anyway. So I've nothing at all to lose.'

'I don't understand. What do you mean – free?'

Chloe gazed out of the window at the high, pointed railings of the Jardin du Luxembourg. 'I mean free to breathe, and to run . . . ' To run like the wind through the sighing trees of some vast, wild forest, yes, but it was more than that. 'And free to feel . . . ' Oh, there were no words for it: but to yield to some deep power within her, greater than death itself, which would make her one with the trees and the earth and the sky. 'It's hard to find words for it,' she said, turning back to the candlelit room, and to Philippe. 'But I mean free to live deeply, to live life to the full. That's worth dying for.'

Philippe said nothing. The candle was flickering lower

and lower, guttering in its pool of melted wax, and the shadows in the room were growing larger and darker, spreading across the ceiling. The note! Perhaps Uncle Victor and General de Bourges would be unable to find out anything about de l'Epinay, or de l'Epinay would be already on his guard against their investigations, but the note – she had to burn it! And the candle was going out – there was no time to plead with herself. 'Quick!' she whispered, seizing the note from where she'd left it on the bed, seizing the candle, and running to the fireplace. With the candle's last dying flicker, she set fire to one corner of the fine-grained paper. There wasn't even a chance to read the message through one last time.

Philippe came and knelt beside her before the hearth, as she gazed mesmerized through the black bars of the grate as the flames flared up, and the paper scorched and curled. 'Chloe,' he whispered. 'What if he isn't a royalist at all?'

'Whatever do you mean?'

'I don't know exactly. I just feel, somehow, that he isn't what he seems. That he might be – I don't know – just an unprincipled adventurer, with no real belief in anything. Chloe, what if all this is simply a clever device to meet you alone somewhere, and try to make you his mistress? – without caring a fig for your ideals, or these deep feelings you've talked about?'

Chloe watched as, one by one, the words 'beautiful' and 'excite' were engulfed by the flames, and then 'peace', and 'England', and 'fleur-de-lis'.

'Then I'd probably kill him,' she said.

'But even if he is a real royalist, he'll expect you to become his mistress, as likely as not. All those *ci-devant* aristocrats are the same.'

'He might not. He might even feel . . . ' Gazing into the dying flames, Chloe visualized de l'Epinay's face again, and remembered that she had glimpsed sensitivity in it too, as well as coolness and irony. If she herself felt something more than a passing attraction – a recognition of some mysterious, long-concealed dream-image which had always been there, in the darkest recesses of her own being – then perhaps he too, deep within himself . . . And when would such a man ever have time for conventional courtship – for calling-cards, and polite conversation, and chaperoned strolls in the public gardens? If for no other reason, she had to join him in his conspiracy, for otherwise . . . As the last of the flames died lower, it was as if she could see his elusive figure merging again with the shadows of the orange-trees, and vanishing for ever from her sight.

'But Chloe, remember the Secret Police!' Philippe whispered desperately. 'I think Papa knows more about it than he's ever told us. If I can get him to talk about it, will you at least listen, before you commit yourself?'

Chloe said nothing. A last pale flame flared up, throwing the shadow of the grate in great black bars over the room; then the flame died, and the room was plunged into darkness. The memory of the orange-trees still glimmered for a moment in her mind, and she shivered suddenly, wondering why the image of them seemed to promise not freedom, but a captivity far deeper and more inescapable than any she had yet known.

The dark-panelled dining-room seemed gloomier than ever, although it was scarcely two o'clock in the afternoon. Since the evening at the Tivoli three days before, the weather had clouded over, and now a steady rain was falling, barring the already deeply-embrasured windows with its dismal bead curtain. The Lenoir family sat at the long table in a silence broken only by the cold chink of soup-spoons.

'Oh, it's really too aggravating for words!' Aunt Eugénie sighed finally, as the monotonous drumming of the wind-less downpour increased until its sound seemed to fill the room. 'If it doesn't clear soon, the Champ de Mars will simply be a sea of mud again tomorrow, and there'll be nothing to look at but umbrellas, just like the last time. I can't understand why there always has to be a cloudburst or a blizzard whenever our dear Emperor celebrates one of his victories.'

Facing each other across the middle of the long, narrow table, Chloe and Philippe were both careful not to look up and meet each other's eyes.

'And after all that trouble we've gone to over your new dress too, Chloe dear!' Aunt Eugénie continued. A tall, regal figure at the foot of the table, crowned by a wreath of carefully tweaked light brown curls, she gave Chloe an unusually fond smile. 'Still, it'll do for another day, and you'll look very nice in your yellow.'

Chloe had risen noticeably in favour during the past two days, since her uncle had returned from an official meeting at the Tuileries with information about the Comte de l'Epinay, discreetly gleaned from one of his colleagues. The matter hadn't been discussed in front of her, of course, but she and Philippe had stood soundlessly in the passage with their ears to the salon door, and had overheard everything. De l'Epinay was rich; he had a château and extensive estates in the Forest of Fontainebleau, some forty miles south of Paris; he was not married; and there was no known stain on his character. His matrimonial pedigree included, as they always seemed to, a catalogue of all the Society beauties with whom his name had been linked at one time or another, and there were plenty, though none of these associations was at all recent. Uncle Victor's informant had only wondered, like General de Bourges, why a man of de l'Epinay's abilities should have retired so completely from public life and from Society, to live alone – as it was supposed he did – in his deeply secluded château; perhaps brooding over the abrupt end to his brilliant military career. Though his estate was less than half a day's journey from Paris, it seemed years since anyone had seen him. Although Uncle Victor's colleague had half-remembered unexpectedly glimpsing him somewhere, or a man very like him, if he could only recall . . .

Chloe looked up from her soup with a start, but it was only a handful of hail rattling suddenly against the windows.

In any case, there seemed no reason to fear for de l'Epinay. Aunt Eugénie's approving smile a moment ago was the surest guarantee that nothing further had been discovered about him.

'A fine thing if the wheat-crop's ruined again,' Aunt Eugénie remarked. 'There'll be more rioting outside the bakers' shops this winter.'

'Oh, the Police will stop that – won't they, Papa?' said Philippe, with only the briefest glance at Chloe. 'I mean the Secret Police. I've heard that they keep a close watch on the Jacobins as well as on the royalists, and the ringleaders would just be quietly removed before any riots could start.'

Uncle Victor, at the head of the table, dabbed at his lips carefully with his napkin, as he always did before speaking during a meal; then he murmured, 'I dare say.'

Philippe's spoon clattered impatiently against the side of his bowl; it wasn't the first time that he'd tried, in vain, to get his father to talk about the Secret Police. Even Chloe drummed her fingers lightly on the tablecloth. But such discretion was all too typical of Uncle Victor. She thought with scorn of his political career. Before the Revolution, when he had been a minor official at Versailles, he had been a royalist, of course, though a discreet one, because of the growing unrest in the country. And then, during the Revolution, he had been a discreet Jacobin. And now, of course, he was a discreet Bonapartist. A slim, dark, dapper little man, with curiously neutral facial expressions, he had a positive talent for discretion, for fading into the crowd. But as a result, though it was true that he'd never been guillotined, it was also true that he had never risen above the minor government post he had started in.

'Oh, do you really believe all that melodrama about the Secret Police?' she said to Philippe, with a yawn, feeling that it was time she gave him a bit of help. 'In my opinion, it doesn't really exist – it's just a piece of silly sabre-rattling on the part of the government, to try to hide how ineffectual they really are.'

Uncle Victor put down his spoon slowly, and dabbed his lips again, pressing his napkin to them carefully several times, as if he were kissing it. 'Not at all, my dear,' he murmured finally. 'And I advise you not to make little jokes of that nature outside these walls – or even within them, as we have a servant. The Secret Police most certainly does exist, and its agents and informers are everywhere. Once they have reason to suspect someone of the slightest anti-Bonapartist sentiments – and a jibe at the government and its officers is a jibe against the Emperor himself, of course – then that person is watched all the time. Watched without even knowing it. Watched, for all he or she knows, by his or her own servants.'

'And then, when he or she comes out with a second little joke,' Chloe said, pretending to laugh, though the room seemed to have grown perceptibly darker as well as colder, 'then this same he or she gets "quietly removed", as Philippe put it – is that true too?'

'You're exaggerating a little, as usual, my dear, but yes: to all intents and purposes, something of that nature does transpire.'

'You mean expire, surely?' Chloe corrected him politely. 'If people are "quietly removed", they don't just disappear into some ledger, or some page of ministerial prose. They get chopped, or shot, or something.'

Uncle Victor shrugged evasively, returning to his soup. 'Who knows? No one knows where they're taken, or what happens to them. No doubt they're interrogated, since they always betray their accomplices. And then they simply vanish.'

' – Interrogated?'

'So we must assume.'

' – Our afore-mentioned he or she?'

'We must assume so.'

'So they torture women!' Chloe exclaimed, flinging down her spoon. 'A fine thing! No wonder you didn't want to talk about it!'

Philippe glanced quickly up at her from his soup. She

40

pretended both anger and laughter, but under the table her fingers trembled as she laced her handkerchief through them: the handkerchief on which she had secretly embroidered a fleur-de-lis.

'My dear, I simply don't know,' Uncle Victor said soothingly. 'As you're well aware, officially there *is* no Secret Police. As a matter of fact, in all my years of working in the government, I've never even seen a document referring to it, or heard it openly discussed. Nor do I know the identity of a single one of its agents or officers. And it's generally believed that only a small handful of men, even within the Secret Police, know the real identity of their own chief.'

There was a silence. The ormolu clock ticked softly on the white marble mantelpiece. Silver soup-spoons chinked.

'But everyone knows his name,' Aunt Eugénie objected. 'You told me it yourself.' She took another dainty sip of her soup, then added, 'You said it was Scorpio.'

'Scorpio!'

The word escaped Chloe's lips involuntarily, in a shivery whisper.

'That's just his code-name,' Uncle Victor said patiently. 'It protects his real identity, so that he's free to move about easily and mix with people. Some say it's our Foreign Minister, Prince Talleyrand, but I hardly think it would be someone so conspicuous. It might be anyone. Perhaps it's the quiet little man in the next office to mine at the Palais du Luxembourg.' He gave a little laugh, then added, 'Perhaps he thinks it's me.'

'But why should he need his real identity kept such a secret?' Chloe asked, with another shiver.

'Because he's irreplaceable – he's a master mind,' said Uncle Victor, his naturally pale face almost ghostly in the room's gloom. 'No one has ever escaped him. If his identity were discovered, and he were assassinated – as he almost certainly would be – then the security of the whole Empire would be at risk.' And then he added, with a little smile, 'And besides, the secrecy frightens people.'

41

Another silence fell. The room seemed darker than ever to Chloe, and the white porcelain on the table, the silver candelabra on the sideboard, and the white marble fireplace, glinted cruel and cold. Scorpio: the Chief of the Secret Police, whom no one had ever escaped ... She gazed round at the funereal dark panelling, the potted palms, the uniform dining-room chairs with their *petit point* seats and backs, lined up with bureaucratic precision down each side of the long narrow table. Outside the windless rain still fell, barring the windows. And somewhere out there, in Paris or Fontainebleau, was de l'Epinay, making his plans for their encounter tomorrow. She ran her handkerchief slowly through her fingers again, their trembling stilled. To escape, to see him again, was worth any risk.

Four

'ALLOW ME, CHÈRE MADEMOISELLE,' said Monsieur Turgeon, doffing his black top hat and offering Chloe his arm as she descended from his carriage, which, sure enough, he'd sent all the way to the Rue Guynemer to fetch them. And he added, by way of greeting to the rest of the Lenoir family, in the peculiar nasal tone he always spoke in, 'A splendid day!'

Aunt Eugénie's fears had been quite unfounded: the Champ de Mars was canopied by a sky of almost cloudless blue. Only a few wispy mares'-tails, very high up, made the expanse of sky seem even wider, and now and then a light breeze set all the ladies' dresses billowing, and made the windmills turn briskly on the far side of the open plain, beside the great encircling curve of the river. On Monsieur Turgeon's arm, her embroidered handkerchief in her free hand, Chloe caught her breath in exhilaration, just at the fresh air and the open space. For a moment she almost forgot the perilous but longed-for encounter which awaited her.

In a group, they began to stroll slowly towards the Military Academy, several hundred yards away, where the crowd was densest. All Paris seemed to be there, as well as thousands of parading troops and cavalry, in their varied and richly coloured uniforms. On the raised parade ground of the Military Academy – the only building on the whole plain, apart from the windmills – Bonaparte, framed by the façade with its massive dome and tall Corinthian columns, could be seen, wearing a red and gold uniform and

43

mounted on a white horse, his Imperial Guard, with their
dark green uniforms and black horses, surrounding him.
There was the bright flash of a sword in his hand, and then
the deafening thunder of guns. Military bands struck up
the Marseillaise.

'Oh, I do like a really good victory celebration!' Aunt
Eugénie exclaimed enthusiastically, while Uncle Victor
hummed *"Aux armes, citoyens! Aux armes, citoyens!"* discreetly
under his breath. Philippe, who was pale enough for Aunt
Eugénie to have commented on it, walked behind them in
silence.

'Actually, we're just a minute or two late,' Monsieur
Turgeon murmured, taking out his fob-watch and glancing
at it. 'I doubt if we'll get close enough now to hear the
Emperor's speech.'

In spite of this hint of reproach, Chloe hung back a little
on his arm, affecting a languorous, dallying manner, and
obliging them all to walk slowly. It wasn't only that the
Emperor's speech would be full of the usual boring
reminiscences about the battle being commemorated,
followed by the usual promises of further victories and
further *'gloire'* in the future. She shrank from becoming
engulfed in the crowd with all its idle chatter and artificial
scents, and from being hemmed in on all sides by columns
of marching troops and galloping platoons of cavalry,
blotting out the fresh air and the view. And besides, how
would de l'Epinay be able to find her there? Surely she
would be more conspicuous – but not too conspicuous –
here amongst the other parties of strollers under the trees
at the edge of the great field?

She looked round, still exhilarated for the moment in
spite of everything. Here, beyond the western outskirts of
the city, the view was immense. Across the Seine, beyond
the little farming villages of Chaillot and Passy, she could
see the seemingly endless wooded expanse of the half-wild
Bois de Boulogne; and behind, when she looked back, she
could see the whole of Paris surrounded by its old city wall,
with its dark domes and the twin towers of the cathedral of

Notre Dame rising above the grey jumble of rooftops. To the north, the distant village of Montmartre was visible on its high hilltop, with the spire of a small Gothic church rising into the sky. The scene was only marred by the dust-storms swirling above those districts of the city which were being demolished and rebuilt. She had heard that they made the neighbouring streets and squares almost uninhabitable.

There seemed to be a new area of demolition or building not far away across the Seine to the north-west. Clouds of dust were rising in flurries from the crown of a low hill there, beyond the little ornamental wood called the Champs-Elysées, which marked the western boundary of the city on that side of the river. Flocks of sheep, harried by the dust, were running hither and thither over the bare heathland.

'There's to be a new triumphal arch up there,' Monsieur Turgeon informed her, following the direction of her gaze. 'Very big, and rather in the Egyptian style – I saw the plans for it only yesterday.'

'But that's right out in the country!' Chloe objected with a laugh. 'Still, won't the sheep feel grand, running back and forth beneath it!'

Philippe flashed her a warning glance, but Monsieur Turgeon only gave one of his polite, thin-lipped smiles and began to explain that there would be a triumphal avenue, of course, leading from the new arch to the Place de la Concorde. Glancing at him, but scarcely listening as he described how long, wide and perfectly straight the new avenue would be, Chloe suddenly felt a slight shiver run through her. The Emperor's speech was over, and she watched General de Bourges ride sedately past at the head of a column of marching infantry, as the troops began to parade back and forth over the field. She had always preferred the General, as far as she felt any preference at all between her two influential but middle-aged suitors, dismissing the tall, pale, bonelessly slender Monsieur Turgeon as creepily fishlike, or sometimes like nothing so much as a long stalk of cold asparagus. But had she ever really looked at him before? His eyes, behind his thick spectacles, certainly looked like pale grey pebbles; but wasn't their pallor inhumanly cold – cold and perhaps very calculating behind their glassy politeness? He was said to be an extremely astute politician, very close to Bonaparte, although what his exact duties were no one seemed able to say. And why, on State occasions, did he so often pace back and forth on his own, with that curiously smooth, gliding step he had: near Bonaparte's Court party but not part of it, yet not mingling with the crowd of other guests either? Could she be walking, at this very moment, on the arm of Scorpio himself, the anonymous and dreaded Chief of the Secret Police, who tortured women? She almost snatched her arm away, but managed to contain herself. No, surely he was too bloodless, too bookish. Yet hadn't Uncle Victor said that Scorpio might be some apparently insignificant official? But no. Monsieur Turgeon still lived with his elderly mother, and played whist with her on his free evenings; it wasn't possible.

Yet anything was possible; she was learning that.

They were getting too near the crowds again, and she cried out girlishly, 'Oh, my new dress!' and backed away towards a shady grove of lindens as a platoon of hussars galloped madly past, wheeled round, then galloped madly back again, brandishing their sabres – though in fact they had been standing well clear of the flying lumps of turf thrown up by the horses' hoofs. Her dress was in a deep rose-coloured silk, striped with a subtly lighter rose, and with a wine-coloured sash tied in a bow just beneath her breasts – a hard-won compromise with the pink and white Aunt Eugénie had wanted her to have, because they were the Emperor's favourite colours for women – and she began to wonder if she would be easily visible in the shade of the trees. But then, after another glance at Monsieur Turgeon's cold, bland eyes, she longed to shrink back altogether into invisibility. Surely, if he were really Scorpio, those pebble eyes would miss nothing when de l'Epinay approached her – not the briefest exchange of glances, never mind the dropping and retrieving of a handkerchief? But perhaps de l'Epinay, too, suspected that Monsieur Turgeon might be Scorpio, and that was why he was keeping away. Why else hadn't he appeared by now? She could see that her aunt and uncle, though for different reasons, of course, were also glancing distractedly about, disappointed at his absence. After all – they must be thinking – he knew Monsieur Turgeon; it was a perfect opportunity for him to make their acquaintance. Chloe remembered de l'Epinay standing chatting with Monsieur Turgeon near the shadows of the orange-trees at the Tivoli. Daring of him, if he suspected Monsieur Turgeon of being Scorpio, but perhaps there was design in it. Casual chatting, the lulling of idle words; and then pacing up and down with him, so that one day, as they paced together through a pool of deep shadow, there would be the swift flash of a knife – '

'Why, Turgeon!' said a soft voice, just behind her. 'What a pleasant surprise!'

They all swung round – it seemed to Chloe that Monsieur Turgeon started slightly – to see a tall, elegant figure standing there in the deep shade, both hands resting on the silver head of his cane. He seemed to be watching them with a faint, mocking smile, and as the leaf-shadows stirred in the wind his hair flashed very fair.

'A surprise indeed,' Monsieur Turgeon replied expressionlessly, but Chloe, her hand still linked through his arm, could feel his sudden tension. Was it plain annoyance, or was it suspicion? Or was it even fear? 'I thought you'd gone back to Fontainebleau,' he added, looking away rather pointedly, and seeming to become absorbed in the military parade. 'Perhaps if you're still in Paris tomorrow . . . '

'Tomorrow who knows? Today various affairs – not without a certain interest – detain me,' said the figure in the shadows, laughing as if at some private joke. Then, still smiling, he stepped forward into the sunlight, and gave the Lenoir family a gallant bow.

'The Comte de l'Epinay,' murmured Monsieur Turgeon with a thin-lipped smile, obliged by etiquette to make introductions.

As de l'Epinay bowed again to her uncle and aunt, Chloe studied him quickly and covertly, and she saw that Philippe was watching him too. In the shadow he had seemed sinister again, but now that he was standing in full sunlight, and so close, that impression was dispelled entirely – or almost entirely. He seemed very much the debonair French aristocrat, finely dressed in a pearl-grey suit with a blue and silver waistcoat, and very handsome with his honey-coloured hair, clear olive skin and darkish grey-blue eyes. His gaze was attentive, his manner faultlessly courteous. There was only an air of private gaiety about him, which gave him a certain cavalier dash. Was he secretly laughing at all of them? Or – Chloe watched him bowing gracefully over Aunt Eugénie's hand – was it the cool gaiety of a man who was at that very moment risking his life?

His eyes at last met hers, their grey-blue alert and warm with what might have been a secret question, or might just have been a deepening private amusement; she couldn't tell. Their gaze dwelt for an instant – so, tingling, it seemed to her – on the neckline of her dress as he bowed; then he lifted her hand to his lips with a murmured, *'Enchanté!'* But her embroidered handkerchief! Thinking that he couldn't possibly expect her to drop it now, under the very eyes of Monsieur Turgeon, she'd had the presence of mind to tuck it quickly inside the short puffed sleeve of her dress; to put it in her reticule would have required both hands, and drawn too much attention to it. But the dress had been run up in a great panic by Aunt Eugénie's dressmaker, and the cuff of the sleeve was a little too loose; with horror, as de l'Epinay bowed over her hand, she felt the handkerchief slip free, and then it fluttered to the ground.

Philippe turned paler still. Aunt Eugénie shot her a frown of exasperation. Monsieur Turgeon stared expressionlessly through his opaque spectacles. De l'Epinay bent swiftly, retrieved the handkerchief, and offered it back to Chloe with a gallant flourish. He was still smiling, still perfectly composed. But although the embroidered fleur-de-lis had been briefly visible as the handkerchief touched the ground, she saw that it was carefully concealed now by his fingertips as he returned the handkerchief to her.

'The privilege of beautiful women,' he said lightly. 'To be late for everything, and to keep dropping things.'

'I can't think why you put it up your sleeve at all, Chloe,' Aunt Eugénie said reprovingly, though she was obviously mollified by the compliment Chloe had just been paid.

'I keep thinking I'm going to sneeze,' Chloe explained. 'It's all this dust.'

'What dust? After all that rain yesterday, the ground's nicely – '

'I mean the dust over there, where they're building all those triumphal arches and things – just the sight of it. It makes me want to sneeze.'

De l'Epinay started laughing again. He seemed remarkably unconcerned about Monsieur Turgeon, although the senior minister's icy, thin-lipped silence surely expressed something more than disapproval, jealousy, or professional suspicion: something almost like hatred.

'Well, you're not going to sneeze,' said Aunt Eugénie. 'Put that handkerchief away in your reticule, before you – '

'Ah, but suppose she did sneeze, after all?' said de l'Epinay, still laughing. 'You fear, perhaps, that she'll drop her handkerchief again? So do I.' His eyes briefly met Chloe's. 'I fear she'll drop it the moment I've taken leave of you, and make some other gentleman's day the sweeter.'

Chloe understood. No message could pass between them in Monsieur Turgeon's presence; it was too dangerous. Someone else, someone entirely unknown to Monsieur Turgeon, would make contact with her, and de l'Epinay was telling her to drop her handkerchief again, but not until he'd signalled to her to do so by taking his leave of them. It began to seem certain that Monsieur Turgeon was either Scorpio, or one of Scorpio's lieutenants. But if de l'Epinay was under suspicion, why hadn't he already been arrested? Perhaps he was just too clever; perhaps the Secret Police, for all their pervasive and anonymous surveillance, were unable to catch him out.

Chloe glanced uneasily round, while Uncle Victor, feigning ignorance, asked de l'Epinay politely, 'Don't you live in Paris then, sir? Did I hear Monsieur Turgeon mention Fontainebleau?'

'I do have a house in the Faubourg St Germain, though it's sadly neglected, I'm afraid, now that I've no family,' de l'Epinay said. Chloe saw that he too was keeping a keen veiled watch on the passers-by. Yet his eyes continually returned to dwell on her for long moments, their colour deepening to a thoughtful dark blue, as if he was seeing into her, or through her, or visualizing her in some quite different situation.

'Whatever's the matter?' Aunt Eugénie asked Philippe, as he gave the linden tree beside them a violent kick. 'You're as white as a sheet, too. Don't say you're going down with one of your migraines.'

De l'Epinay gave Philippe a swift glance, his eyes suddenly a cool light grey; then he continued casually to Uncle Victor, 'Fontainebleau isn't far, I grant you, but I have a contract to sell the Emperor a great many oaks to build his new fleet, and it all seems to take so much overseeing, I seldom have time – '

'Speaking of beautiful women, there's Manon de Malebois herself,' Monsieur Turgeon interrupted suddenly. His thin lips twisted into a smile, and his pale eyes gleamed, as the famous beauty he had named came strolling past, accompanied by two gentlemen. Chloe gave her a brief, covert look. She had figured significantly in the catalogue of de l'Epinay's past liaisons – it was said that he had been deeply in love with her – and although that had been at least five years ago, Chloe's heart gave a sickening flutter. Svelte and very sensuous-looking, her vivid auburn hair and creamy skin admirably set off by her dark green dress trimmed with gold, the Vicomtesse de Malebois was certainly still very beautiful, even if there was now a taint of scandal about her. Five years ago, after de l'Epinay had been wounded, she had abruptly married another of Bonaparte's most promising young *ci-devant* officers. But, he having proved more interested in gaming than in promotion, she was now openly the mistress of a certain field-marshal. It seemed to Chloe that de l'Epinay's face became rather too cool and set, perhaps with a deep, enduring bitterness at her rejection of him, as her tawny, cat-like eyes slid sidelong over their group in passing. 'Why, if it isn't our old friend Lucien de l'Epinay, come back from the grave!' she exclaimed with a sudden peal of laughter. Then she added, with a glance at his cane, and his lame foot, ' – or at any rate half-way back!'

De l'Epinay gave her a curt bow before she strolled on, still laughing with her companions. For a moment his features were like chiselled stone, and his hands rested like chiselled stone on the head of his cane. Covertly studying him again, Chloe felt a stirring of intrigued pity. It was as if his mockingly insouciant poise was only a mask, and for an instant she glimpsed what lay behind it: the lonely courage of a man who had lost everything. From what he'd said a moment ago about his house in the Faubourg St Germain, it seemed all too likely that he'd lost his entire family, and perhaps his friends too, during the Terror. And his unlucky wound had cost him both his military career and the woman he'd loved. Perhaps that was why he seemed so coolly indifferent to danger: because he had nothing left to lose.

Or was that indifference too deep, too far-reaching? Still looking at him, at the chillingly clear grey of his eyes as he glanced after the Vicomtesse de Malebois' receding figure, Chloe felt a sudden shiver. It was as if she had glimpsed a curious and depthless absence of all feeling in him.

Monsieur Turgeon, meanwhile, still had a lingering smile on his face. No, he wasn't Scorpio, Chloe thought contemptuously. He was just petty and warped enough to wish to be someone like that. She said lightly, following the direction of his gaze, 'Yes, she gets more like a tiger-skin every day – teeth and all – doesn't she? You ought to try wiping your feet on her too, like so many other gentlemen.'

Monsieur Turgeon's smile vanished abruptly. De l'Epinay, who had quickly recovered his poise, gave a laugh which seemed genuine, and said gallantly to Chloe, 'Who are you talking about? I didn't see any other beautiful woman.' His eyes were a warm grey-blue again as they met hers. Lucien: she knew his first name now. Perhaps she had only imagined the terrible, fathomless indifference she'd thought she'd glimpsed in him.

But now she saw his eyes sharpen fleetingly in a look of recognition, quickly and stealthily veiled, as he glanced over her shoulder. With an effort, she checked the impulse to turn round.

'Well, with the greatest regret, I must take leave of you now,' he said easily. The briefest look of understanding passed between them, then he turned to her uncle and aunt and Philippe with another elegant bow.

Chloe glanced swiftly round while farewell pleasantries were being exchanged. ' . . . If you're ever passing by the Palais du Luxembourg,' Uncle Victor was saying. 'Our humble abode . . . ' She could see only strollers moving slowly in and out of the shadows: the same chattering, fashionably dressed parties, the same occasional single gentleman or pair of gentlemen, smoking cigars as they sauntered, or lifting their hats to passing acquaintances. Yet amongst them, somewhere, looking just like all the others, was an accomplice of de l'Epinay's; perhaps even two or three. She laced her handkerchief surreptitiously through her fingers again. What if agents of the Secret Police – even Scorpio himself – were amongst the strollers too, watching every move?

' – Until then!' de l'Epinay said, with a last brief bow; then he turned and limped away, disappearing rapidly amongst the crowds of strollers and the deep, stirring shadows of the lindens.

52

Monsieur Turgeon proffered his arm again, a little stiffly, and Chloe took it, if only to avoid walking beside the white-faced and inwardly fuming Philippe. She knew what he was thinking: that de l'Epinay's unconcealed attraction to her was the only motive for his stratagems, and that it would end in his trying to seduce her. But Philippe was wrong; he was blinded by jealousy. She glanced at him. He was really suffering, she could see, and she wished she could reassure him.

They strolled on, away from the direction de l'Epinay had taken. After a moment, Chloe stealthily let her handkerchief fall from her fingers, without glancing back.

Strollers passed them in both directions. Leaf-shadows flickered over half-glimpsed faces with incurious, sidelong eyes. Chloe could feel her heart beating hard, in time with the elapsing seconds. 'If you'd care for some ices ... ' Monsieur Turgeon was saying.

'Mademoiselle!'

The voice came from behind them. Chloe forced herself not to look round.

' ... Or perhaps some sugared almonds,' Monsieur Turgeon continued.

'Mademoiselle! Mademoiselle, your handkerchief!'

Chloe swung slowly round, and found herself facing a small, colourless man with grey hair and a well-cut but almost threadbare suit of clothes. 'You dropped your handkerchief,' he said, smiling timidly, and gasping a little as he spoke, as if from the exertion of overtaking her.

'Oh ... thank you very much,' she murmured, and thought, with a sinking heart, 'It's the wrong man! A complete stranger – a complete nonentity – has picked it up! And I can't possibly drop it a third time.' And then she realized with a shock, as she took the handkerchief from him, that it wasn't the one she'd dropped. And her fingers felt the crackle of paper folded or sewn into it.

'Oh – thank you!' she said again, startled; but with a barely audible murmur of, 'Not at all, not at all,' the man had already turned away, and within a moment he had vanished into the crowd. Already she couldn't even clearly recollect his features.

'Chloe, whatever's the matter with you today?' exclaimed Aunt Eugénie. 'And who was that gentleman? He looked like a counting-house clerk, or something, but I didn't really see him properly.'

'Neither did I,' Chloe said, closing the handkerchief quickly into her reticule. 'Perhaps some iced lemonade, or orange-flower water ... ' she went on, to Monsieur Turgeon, to change the subject; then she trailed off. Deep amongst the shifting linden-shadows, only twenty paces away, she saw a flash of fair hair, a pearl-grey suit, a silver-headed cane. Unseen, de l'Epinay must have been watching the whole encounter. Still only half-visible, he smiled, and beckoned to her with a slight movement of his forefinger, his hand scarcely leaving the head of his cane. Then he stepped out into the clear sunlight.

'Oh, there's the Comte de l'Epinay again!' Chloe exclaimed gaily. 'I fear he wants to scold me, but I'll just run and explain ... '

She gathered up her skirts and began to run towards him. No one tried to stop her. But, once sure of that, she slowed to a walk. Something about the way he'd smiled, and still more the way he'd beckoned her to him, piqued her slightly, she wasn't sure why. But the feeling persisted, and she stopped when she was still several paces from him, and stood nonchalantly opening and twirling her wine-coloured parasol, so that he was obliged to limp forward to meet her. As he did so, a small, grey-haired man emerged for a moment from the shadows nearby. The two men's eyes met without a flicker of recognition; but as the grey-haired man turned away, Chloe thought she glimpsed a look of hatred on his face, before he vanished into the crowd and the shadows again. Why did de l'Epinay arouse such violent antipathy, not only in Monsieur Turgeon, but even in his fellow royalists?'

'Votre serviteur!' he murmured, with an ironic little flourish, as he reached her. 'So far so good. As a budding conspirator, Mademoiselle Lenoir – '

'Miss Culverwood,' Chloe corrected him, twirling her parasol so that it narrowly missed his eye, and he had to step back a pace. She had been introduced to him as Uncle Victor's niece, and perhaps he had overheard something of her history at the Tivoli, but it seemed as well to underline the point. 'Perhaps you don't know that I'm the daughter of an English nobleman?'

'Are you putting me in my place?' he said, with a laugh. 'How delightful! If only we had more time! But listen, that's just precisely ... ' He glanced swiftly round as a group of strollers momentarily screened them from the Lenoir family's view, then stepped back into the shadows, the suddenly urgent intensity of his manner drawing her with him. 'Listen, this whole affair is much more dangerous than you can possibly realize. And it seems a pity ... ' His eyes, warm and very blue, contemplated her for a moment. 'I must talk to you before you commit yourself any further. If I called on your family, could you arrange for us to be alone, just for ten minutes or so?'

Chloe thought of the cramped appartement, and the avidity of Aunt Eugénie's eyes, which had never left de l'Epinay's face all the time he'd been conversing with them earlier, and above all Philippe's jealous suspicions. Unless, after all, his suspicions ...

'No,' she said, her heart beginning to beat faster.

'So I assumed. Think again, quickly: is there anywhere I could meet you, alone?'

Chloe felt herself turn cold all over. Could Philippe have been right after all? Careful to show nothing of her feelings, she casually studied de l'Epinay's face.

' – Without my cousin?'

'Yes, absolutely without your cousin. I'll explain why when I see you.'

His face betrayed nothing but the same keen, single-minded urgency, and she couldn't be sure of anything. But perhaps it was quite usual, amongst conspirators, for conventions between the sexes to be set aside. And after all, if she thought the better of it later, on reflexion, she could simply fail to appear at their rendez-vous.

'The palmhouse at the Palais du Luxembourg,' she said. During her childhood, and even quite recently, Uncle Victor had sometimes let her wander there on her own while he was working: somewhere where she could be alone amongst living plants, even though they too were imprisoned. Though the gardens were open to the public, the palmhouse was not. It formed a wing of the palace itself, and was only accessible from within, through the government offices. Seeing a difficulty, she asked, 'But how will you be able to – ?'

'Quite easily – don't worry. Tomorrow?'

'Yes, but – '

'Tomorrow, then. At what time?'

'The afternoon's easiest. About three o'clock. But – '

'Three, then.' He smiled, kissed her hand, and began to back away. She guessed that the group of strollers screening them had passed, and that they were visible again to her family. Turning her head, she saw that Philippe was approaching. Monsieur Turgeon, it was curious, was again staring opaquely at the military parade, apparently oblivious – too oblivious? – of everything.

'Listen,' she began. 'Is Monsieur Turgeon – ?'

'I'll explain everything tomorrow.'

'But – '

'Tomorrow.'

He backed away, deeper into shadow. She watched the dim dapples of sunlight play through the leaves over the fair gleam of his hair, his enigmatic grey-blue eyes, and his faint, secret smile; then he was gone.

'What did he want? What did he say to you?' Philippe hissed between his teeth, as they walked back together to rejoin the others.

'He was just warning me ... ' She glanced towards Monsieur Turgeon, and added, 'I'll tell you later.'

She fell silent, biting her lip in trepidation. Philippe was her only protection; yet if she went to meet de l'Epinay alone tomorrow, he was the last person she could tell: he would move heaven and earth to prevent it. And would she go? Perhaps she would have to, despite the deep misgivings de l'Epinay had stirred in her – misgivings not only about his intentions towards her, but other more obscure misgivings, which she couldn't yet put a name to. But perhaps seeing him alone was the only way to find out.

Five

SCARCELY ANY SUNLIGHT penetrated through the dense tropical foliage in the palmhouse, and the shadows were deep and green, although outside it was a perfect summer's afternoon. Waiting, Chloe surreptitiously lifted a spray of moist fronds and looked out at the public gardens. The glittering gravel walks, very straight between the bright beds of geraniums, somehow seemed diminished in scale and far away, as if she were looking at another world. There were a few elderly folk sitting on the iron chairs under the trees, and a few nursemaids in uniform. A little boy and a little girl were running back and forth along one of the gravel paths, bowling their hoops. Their mouths were open, as if they were screaming, but no sound penetrated the thick glass.

She let the concealing leaves swing back slowly and heavily into place. She had chosen their rendez-vous well. She was entirely alone in the whole long palmhouse – she had walked its dim, tunnel-like length from end to end without glimpsing even the figure of a gardener – and nothing could be seen or heard from the outside. She wondered how de l'Epinay would manage to effect his entrance. By pretending business with a government official, perhaps – the whole palace was given over to government offices – or by bribing an attendant. He wasn't late. It was she, in her anxiety not to be prevented from coming, who had arrived a little early.

Uncle Victor had fallen in easily enough with her request. A solitary hour or two in the palmhouse was often her reward for being 'good', and although he and Aunt

Eugénie were still maintaining, or pretending to maintain, a certain reserve on the subject of de l'Epinay, they had been smiling on her more fondly than ever. Aunt Eugénie had even called her 'my blessing.' And now Uncle Victor was at a meeting which promised to last all afternoon; Aunt Eugénie was resting as usual after the midday meal; Philippe was at a lecture in the Latin Quarter. Everything had gone very smoothly.

Even Philippe's suspicions about de l'Epinay's intentions, though they still made him terse and pale, had been put in abeyance – or rather eclipsed – by the note Chloe had received at the Champ de Mars. He had been sure that it would contain further gallantries, this time more openly amorous, and probably some dishonourable proposition. But when they'd unsewn it from the handkerchief together last night in Chloe's bedroom, the message, though written in the same neat, elegant hand as before, and on the same fine paper, had proved to be as unadorned as it was brief. It had simply read: *'Pour this on the curtains at the Tuileries ball. Vive le Roi.'* 'This' was a liquid, so pale a yellow as to be almost colourless, contained in a tiny glass phial. They hadn't opened it, guessing that it was phosphorus, which ignited within seconds of coming into contact with the air. 'You're never going to do it?' Philippe had whispered at last. Chloe had said nothing.

She took the phial out of her reticule now, and looked at it lying in the palm of her hand in the arcane, greenish dusk. To set fire to a ballroom! It had seemed daring and exciting at first. But – as Philippe had been quick to remind her – the ballroom would be filled with hundreds of people, who might die in the flames if the fire took hold, or who might trample one another to death in the panic. In what way would that serve the royalist cause? And why her? Why couldn't de l'Epinay do it himself? True, he had seemed to have second thoughts about it, and had said that to work for the royalists was more dangerous than she knew; true, he had promised to explain everything. But she remembered the terrible detachment in his eyes when he'd

59

glanced after Manon de Malebois. And she remembered his secret, enigmatic smile after she'd agreed to meet him here alone. The little phial lying in her palm, catching the green, unnatural light, suddenly seemed a distillation of some pervasive and nameless evil, to which she had become unwittingly in thrall.

She started. There had been a just audible click, as of a door being very stealthily opened and closed, or of a cane tapping the floor. She spun round and gazed into the deep shadows, so dense they were almost black in places, but with flashes like fair hair where the sun slashed through the dark, tropical fronds. Click! This time the sound was much closer, but she was quick enough to see its cause: condensation oozing to the tip of a large rubbery leaf and dripping on to the green mosaic floor.

But surely it must be three o'clock now, or even a little later? She hadn't heard the chimes of any nearby church clock, but then no sound penetrated here, not even birdsong. Nothing broke the deep silence but the occasional drip of moisture, or the faint sigh of a leaf stirring as the weight of condensation left it – swaying back into place with a slow, groping movement, like a carnivorous plant blindly in search of prey.

She half opened her reticule – of sage green, embroidered with marguerites and darker green leaves, to match her dress – then continued to hold the phial in her hand a moment longer, undecided. Should she leave now, quickly, before de l'Epinay arrived, and never see him again – try to forget him, and all that he had seemed to promise? She shivered. It was as if already – whatever he was, whatever he wanted of her – she would no longer be able to break free of him.

She started again, and closed the phial quickly into her reticule. A few paces away, a cluster of leaves like a giant black hand was waving slowly and rhythmically to and fro, as if someone had brushed against it. But a pool of water on the mosaic floor beneath it was quivering, as if a large drop of condensation had just dripped into it. She let out her breath very slowly, so that her heart-beat would return to normal.

'Good afternoon,' murmured a soft voice, just behind her.

Chloe whirled round, to see a gleam of fair hair, the glint of a smile of secret amusement, in the deep shadows only a pace or two away.

'You're mad!' she flared up, her fear turning into genuine anger. 'I might have screamed.'

'And if you had? No one would have heard,' he said, laughing softly as he emerged from the dark foliage half screening him. Disturbed by his passage, a fringe of palm-leaves, like stealthy fingertips, lightly brushed Chloe's bare arm. 'And besides, you didn't scream,' he continued, circling her, still half in shadow. 'You have beautifully cool nerves.'

'How long have you been here?' Chloe snapped, provoked to fury, she didn't know why, by this smooth compliment.

'Only a few minutes.'

She glanced the length of the shadowy palmhouse – perhaps two hundred paces from where they were standing to the door he must have entered by – and said disbelievingly, 'But how did you get so close – right past me – without my noticing?'

'I've had years of practise.'

He stood still, facing her, still in shadow, his hands resting on the silver head of his cane. He was wearing a dark, greenish-blue suit, with a turquoise waistcoat only subtly embroidered with silver, and turquoise links at his shirt-cuffs: colours he must have chosen to aid his invisibility. The turquoise made his eyes seem lighter and bluer, even in the shadows; but as always, when he was in shadow, they seemed to have a calculating expression, which made her want to shiver. Beside him, the warped trunk of some tropical plant, black and lustrous, twined upwards like a snake.

'I think you just like frightening people,' Chloe said.

There was a curious flicker of a look in his eyes, which

she couldn't have named; it was quickly veiled. Then he laughed, and said, 'How cross you are with me, Mademoiselle – ah no, my apologies: Miss Culverwood. But you must make allowances. Five years of living in a kind of underworld have given me some peculiar habits, I dare say, and made me something less than a perfect gentleman, if I ever was one. And besides – ' he stirred so that a splash of sunlight fell on him – 'how could I be sure that you really would come here alone?'

As ever, when he emerged into the light, the sinister aura about him was almost entirely dispelled. Dwelling on the warm, clear tones of his honey-coloured hair and light olive skin, and on the sensitivity of his lips, Chloe thought, 'It's surely true – and hasn't he just said so himself, in his joking way? – that it's only the clandestine life he's forced to lead which gives him that amoral and devious air.' She was almost sure of it. And after the *coup d'état* he was planning – after it was all over, and he could return to normal life . . . There was only a lingering hint of private amusement in his eyes, for all that their colour had deepened to a warm blue as he stood contemplating her, to make her less than certain.

But that faint irony, that air of taking nothing seriously, was enough to remind her of the potentially murderous task he'd so negligently set her. She took the little phial out of her reticule again and held it out to him, saying, 'I'm not sure that I want to do this – unless you can explain.'

'Ah yes – business!' he murmured, rousing himself from his contemplation of her, and taking the phial. He held it up to the light for a moment, and she noticed for the first time a faint, polished indentation on one of his fingers, which could only have been made by a signet-ring he was no longer wearing. Then he agreed, 'Dangerous stuff. The main thing is not to spill any of it on your own clothes.'

'It isn't that I mind starting a fire,' Chloe explained. 'That could be fun. And I'm perfectly willing to set fire to Bonaparte or anyone who works for him, or I wouldn't be here now. But at the Tuileries ball there'll be hundreds of innocent people, who might get hurt or even burnt to death.' She was watching his face closely as she spoke, praying that he would disprove Philippe's criticisms of the royalists. But for some reason he only seemed more amused than ever. 'I can't see the point in starting a fire there anyway,' she continued, more sharply, 'or why you should want me to do it. There must be lots of other ways I can help – by getting State secrets out of Monsieur Turgeon or General de Bourges, for instance. I thought that was what would be required of me.'

'Of course, of course – it will be,' de l'Epinay said soothingly, but he was still laughing. 'And don't you know that a soldier should never question his orders? However, since you ask, the fire's only to be a diversion, to occupy the guards while some important documents are stolen from Bonaparte's study. It won't get out of hand.'

'How can you be sure?'

'I'm sure,' he answered laconically, and for once the level, calculating look in his eyes was strangely reassuring.

'But why me?' she persisted. 'Why do you want me to do such a thing?'

'Well, it's in the nature of an initiation ceremony,' de l'Epinay said, beginning to pace idly amongst the slanting, hairy stems of the palm-trees again. 'First of all, it implicates you too deeply for you to withdraw, or turn informer, or change sides – and you mustn't be surprised at that. It's the usual practice, and perfectly reasonable. And then it's also a test of your sincerity, and of your courage and ability to dissemble. You'll be watched, of course. Afterwards – if you're successful – you'll be contacted again, and given a more serious assignment.'

He had returned the phial to her a few moments before, and she turned it over uneasily in her hand, watching the translucent liquid turn from pale yellow to green as it caught the light, still mysteriously evil. 'And after I've committed myself, and can't draw back,' she said, 'how can I be sure that you won't ask me to do something worse one day? Something that really does involve killing innocent people?'

He was silent for a moment, still pacing. 'You can be sure that I shan't ask you to,' he said finally. 'But I can't answer for the others. That was precisely what I wanted to warn you about. They're quite capable of giving you the kind of assignment you mention, or even one which might be likely to cause your own death – although of course they wouldn't tell you that. You can withdraw now – that's one solution.' He paced on in a wide, casual circle round her, passing behind her. 'The other solution – which is a little dangerous perhaps, but which I should prefer – is that you confer with me before carrying out any task they set you. And we'll contrive to draw its sting somehow, if it has one. Especially,' he added with a laugh, 'if they ask you to poison me, which isn't impossible.'

'You? Why?' she asked, swinging round to face him.

He shrugged. 'Internal rivalries.'

If only Philippe could hear de l'Epinay now, Chloe thought, her heart beating faster. It was becoming clearer every moment that he was the kind of royalist Philippe admired, perhaps fighting a solitary battle against his more extremist confederates.

'I'll do that – I'll do as you suggest,' she said, putting the phial decisively back in her reticule.

He lifted a dark cluster of leaves spiking the green dusk between them, and smiled. 'Good girl,' he murmured.

'But how will I be able to tell you what they've asked me to do? Shall I see you every day?'

'We'll talk about that presently,' he said, still in an almost caressive murmur. The fringe of leaves brushed her bare arm again as he let them fall, moving away from her.

'Was that why you made contact with me in the first place?' Chloe asked. 'Because you guessed I'd be on your side, not on theirs?'

'Made contact with you?' De l'Epinay was almost invisible in the green dusk.

'At the Tivoli.'

'Ah.' There was a brief silence. 'That wasn't me. They didn't even know I was there, at first, but I overheard them talking about you, and decided to investigate.' There was a soft laugh in the shadows. 'It's caused no end of bad feeling, my cutting in like this.'

' – It wasn't you who gave me that note, in the crowd by the gates?'

'No. That was the Marquis de Grismont.'

'The Marquis de Grismont?' Chloe echoed, puzzled. She knew the name: one of the most illustrious of the *Ancien Régime*, whose bearer had owned several châteaux and vast feudal estates before the Revolution.

'Yes, it was he who gave you the second note yesterday at the Champ de Mars.'

'That was the Marquis de Grismont?' Chloe exclaimed disbelievingly, remembering the colourless little man whom her aunt had likened to a counting-house clerk. She watched de l'Epinay's elegant and handsome figure, briefly visible as he paced through a flicker of sunlight and deep shadow, and was more glad than ever that he, at least, looked like a true aristocrat and a royalist. 'But the Marquis de Grismont's an *émigré* – he's in England,' she said, still scarcely believing him.

'So everyone supposes. But in fact he was smuggled across the Channel more than a year ago, and he's been in hiding in the Faubourg St Germain. And don't be deceived by his appearance, or by his playing messenger-boy, which he only does because he's so unnoticeable. He may look like a frightened rabbit, but he's utterly ruthless. He always was. I could tell you a few stories about him, before the Revolution – the things that used to happen in his châteaux. Of course he was rich and powerful then. And now that he's lost everything – he was half-destitute in England – he'll stop at nothing.'

'And it was he who wrote me that first note!' Chloe said, half to herself, remembering the mood of anguish and desolation in which she'd burnt it.

'Or de Malebois. Was it very full of gallantries?'

'Yes, it was rather. But you surely – ?'

'Then it was probably composed by de Malebois. He's

65

very taken with you. I trust you burnt it?'

'Yes of course. But you surely don't mean the Vicomte de Malebois? – the man who . . . '

'I do indeed.'

Visible again in a splash of sunlight, de l'Epinay was clearly amused at her deepening bewilderment and her confusion. The Vicomte de Malebois, who had married the woman he himself had been in love with! Yet the two men had been conspiring so effectively together that the beautiful Manon – to judge from her remark at the Champ de Mars yesterday – hadn't even known of de l'Epinay's pervasive presence. True, she was no longer living with her husband. And it all surely proved, at least, that de l'Epinay could have no secret, lingering interest in his former mistress . . . Chloe turned away, obscurely troubled: by the memory of his glance of infinite indifference, or even of contempt, at the Champ de Mars; by the fact that he had collaborated so easily with his former rival; by his amusement now. Hadn't Philippe warned her that an attitude of frivolity and cynicism towards women was usual amongst *ci-devant* aristocrats – perhaps even amongst the best of them?

'But is he any real use?' she asked, mostly to cover up her discountenanced silence, but picturing the Vicomte de Malebois, whom she had often seen at the Tuileries. A dark, handsome rake of a man, he had been famed for his recklessly daring cavalry charges in battle, it was true; but he was equally famed for his gambling debts, his duels and his love-affairs, which were said to take up so much of his time and attention that Bonaparte could no longer entrust a military command to him, and had made him one of his equerries.

'He's brave,' de l'Epinay conceded. 'And de Grismont manages to keep him in check – and also to influence his ideas, unfortunately. But there's a surprisingly vindictive streak in his nature, so don't underestimate him. It's he, by the way, who'll be stealing secret documents at the Tuileries while you divert the palace guards, and it's he who'll make contact with you there later during the evening.'

'But won't you be there?'

'No.'

'Oh . . . Because you don't want to be seen too often in Society?'

He didn't answer for a moment, and was still. But the rhythm of his slow pacing seemed to continue in Chloe's memory: curiously arresting in its grace, despite his limp . . . His limp! She bit her lip. Of course he wouldn't want to attend a ball – and perhaps have to watch her dance with the Vicomte de Malebois, who was the best waltzer in Paris.

'That doesn't signify,' de l'Epinay said negligently, still motionless several paces away from her. 'In fact it's part of the plan that I should be seen more often in Society, from now on.'

He hadn't really answered her question, and she wondered, with a secret thrill, if he wasn't more deeply affected by women than his manner suggested.

'It's just that I have a prior engagement,' he added quickly, as if he'd realized his mistake.

'I only asked because my uncle – ' she began, just as quickly; then she felt the colour rising in her cheeks, and swung away. 'Because my uncle's been making enquiries about you.'

'Naturally,' he said, sounding amused again.

'And General de Bourges.'

'*Tiens!* What fatherly altruism on his part!' He started pacing again, and added lightly, 'They won't find out anything.'

'Yes, but several people thought they'd seen you some-where – somewhere strange, in the dark, but they can't quite remember where. What if they do remember?'

He had begun to move in a wide circle round her again. For an instant, lifting a spray of long fronds out of his path, he seemed to become very still. Then he let the leaves swing back behind him and paced on, asking casually, 'Who thought they remembered this?'

'General de Bourges. I'm not sure who else. Just some colleague of my uncle's at the Tuileries.'

He nodded, but said nothing.

'And I saw you too, come to that,' Chloe said. 'Perhaps I'd have forgotten, or I wouldn't have been sure it was you, if I hadn't seen you again a little later under the lamplight. At the Tivoli, I mean.' He had circled round almost behind her now, and she turned to look at him as she added, 'I saw you speak to the Emperor, and you looked quite different, somehow.'

Though he was unexpectedly close behind her, and very still again, he was scarcely visible in the half-darkness, except for the level light grey-blue of his eyes.

'I was one of his aides-de-camp, in Egypt,' he said eventually. 'When I find myself near him, I'm obliged to pay my respects. Besides, he's always plaguing me for his wretched timber.'

'But why are you selling it to him?' she asked, wondering what it was that made her want to shiver. Perhaps just the memory of her first glimpse of him in the imperial pavilion, when he had looked so like an assassin.

'It's an excellent cover. It allows me to disappear for quite long periods, and also to approach Bonaparte very closely.'

Chloe remembered Turgeon pacing glidingly back and forth near the imperial pavilion at the Tivoli. Something was still making her feel strangely shivery.

'Why does Monsieur Turgeon hate you?' she asked.

'Hate me?' Circling slowly on, de l'Epinay passed between her and the sun piercing through the palm-leaves, and paused there. 'You underestimate yourself, my child,' he said, after a moment. 'I should have thought the answer was obvious.'

'Ah,' she said, not entirely convinced. 'For a while, I quite thought he was Scorpio.'

'Scorpio?'

De l'Epinay remained motionless, a dark and unreadable silhouette. Then he stirred, and murmured, 'How do you come to know that name?'

'My uncle told me.'

'Ah yes.' De l'Epinay circled on, away from the light, and she could see his honey-coloured hair again, and his grey-blue eyes and fine, aristocratic features. 'No, I don't somehow think he's Scorpio,' he said, with a smile, 'though I dare say he'd like to be.'

'And doesn't anyone know who is?'

'Amongst the royalists, you mean? No.' He laughed, and added, 'Of course not. Otherwise he'd be a dead man.'

'But doesn't the success of the conspiracy depend on finding him out?'

'Absolutely.'

'So everyone's looking for him?'

'Yes.'

'And when is it planned for – the *coup d'état?*'

'In the autumn. More men and arms have to be smuggled across from England yet – just the last consignment. It has to be before Bonaparte's coronation, you see. His declaring himself Emperor earlier this year ... Well, that was bad enough. But there's still much popular resentment at his rise to power. However, let him once be crowned by the Pope, at Notre Dame in December, and all that resentment will turn to holy awe, people being what they are.'

'In the next two or three months, then!' Chloe said, looking round at the dense tropical foliage enclosing them, then up at the arched, complex structure of the palmhouse itself, so like a cage. 'And then we'll all be free! And you,' she added, resting her eyes on him. 'You won't have to live in an underworld any more.'

There was another curious, elusive flicker of expression in his eyes as he watched her from the shadows; then he said lightly, 'Oh, but it rather suits me, you know: my underworld. When this is over, I dare say I'll just go in search of another conspiracy.'

Lost in disquieted speculation, she realized suddenly that his eyes were dwelling on her, so dark and blue that she caught her breath and turned away. 'Is it part of the plan that you should kill Bonaparte?' she asked, swinging round to face him.

He shrugged. 'Or de Malebois. We're the only two who can get close to him unchallenged.'

Chloe turned away again. His shrug and his tone of voice had been almost dismissive, but she thought she understood now. Bonaparte was always surrounded by guards. It was scarcely possible that de l'Epinay – and it was sure to be de l'Epinay, because he was so much the better man – could stab him, and not be killed himself an instant later.

'Why didn't you want Philippe – my cousin – to come with me?' she burst out. 'You're just the kind of man he admires most.'

'That wasn't the impression I received.'

Still turned away, she could hear amusement in de l'Epinay's voice again, and she said nothing more. Something else, some undertone of subtle suggestion, made her heart begin to beat fast.

'I do advise you to stop confiding in him, by the way,' de l'Epinay added. 'His face betrays his feelings far too much for safety. If de Grismont and the others notice, you'll be in trouble.'

'But he may have to accompany me sometimes,' Chloe objected. 'I'd never persuade my uncle to let me go about Paris on my own.'

The leaves stirred in the half-darkness close behind her, and de l'Epinay said softly, 'But why don't you just move out?'

Chloe's heart beat wildly, but she told herself, 'It can't be true – I'm misunderstanding him.' After a moment she asked distantly, 'Whatever do you mean?'

'But you're so – so dizzyingly beautiful . . .' he murmured, still more softly, and something – perhaps a leaf, perhaps a fingertip – very lightly traced the line of her neck and her bare shoulder. 'Why do you even ask? I'll give you a house, a carriage, servants, money . . . You'll be your own mistress entirely. All I ask in return is that you have no lover but me, as long as the arrangement lasts.'

Chloe turned slowly to face him. The impulse to slap him across the face and run from the palmhouse – out of his life for ever – passed through her mind and was gone, too trivial an action to express what she felt. A wonderful, deep, cool calm descended on her, and she only stood contemplating him in a motionless silence.

'And now you're a thousand times more beautiful than before,' de l'Epinay murmured, a little breathlessly. The sun slanted down gold, in stripes, through the deep green foliage surrounding them. He ran his fingers in a restless, involuntary movement over a spray of leaves close to her face, and moistened his lips; but instinct, or experience, made him let his hand fall, and he stepped back a pace, adopting a stance as deferential as it was elegant.

'You're very quiet,' he observed, with a little laugh. 'Yet I can't believe that a young woman of your intelligence and spirit can fail to perceive . . . Still, I needn't spell it out for you. But perhaps you need time to think about it. You needn't give me your answer now.'

'I wasn't going to,' Chloe said.

'I see!' he murmured, with another laugh. 'Still, I shall ask you again, after a decent interval. You don't expect me to offer you marriage, do you, on such a short acquaintance? And besides – ' there was a brief expression of wariness and hardness in his eyes – 'I've no intention whatsoever of marrying. I value my freedom too much.'

Chloe said nothing. In her deep calm, she could see a certain sophisticated logic in his proposal. Many women in the past, with the same natural advantages as herself, and faced with the same intolerable social limitations, had hesitated, then gone on to a life of freedom, passion, luxury and social brilliance; many more would in the future. Some, like the Empress Josephine, crowned their careers with fairy-tale marriages. And what was there to set in the scales against choosing such a life? Not the middle-class respectability which her uncle and aunt had tried to instill in her. Not religion, for she had grown up during a time when there had been none. There was only the same deep feeling which she had tried to communicate to Philippe: that sense of a oneness to life and death, which a great, mutual and lifelong love might fulfil, but which would be violated by anything less. Even with de l'Epinay, though her heart bled at the prospect of losing him. Nor would she explain herself to him, for fear of his cynicism. It was a curious and ironic coincidence that he gave the same name to that cynicism – freedom – as she gave to a deep faith in life.

'No, I don't expect anything of you,' she answered him finally. 'I just have other plans entirely.'

She turned to go.

' – What other plans?' he asked casually, stepping into her path.

'I must go,' she said with a smile, eluding him.

'But we've made no arrangements to contact each other.'

'You could send me a message via de Malebois.'

He was silent. She had intended no mischief by her last remark, but when she glanced back at him from the doorway, he was still standing motionless in the half-shadow, watching her with eyes like grey-blue ice.

Six

'HE'S GETTING DIVORCED, they say,' Aunt Eugénie murmured behind her ostrich-feather fan, following the direction of Chloe's eyes to the dancing figure of the Vicomte de Malebois. Slim and spruce in his dark green cavalry officer's uniform, he was leading the opening quadrille of the ball, with all the gay grace and panache in his twirls, stamps and hand-claps that he had long been famed for when parading on the Caroussel or riding in tournaments at the Champ de Mars. He had only glanced once towards Chloe, his fine dark eyes briefly meeting hers without a trace of expression; and Aunt Eugénie's remark, Chloe knew, was really a comment on the Comte de l'Epinay's failure to call on them during the past several days, or even to leave his card, and on his absence now. Yet it was difficult not to gaze in a kind of thrall at the Vicomte de Malebois, if only because the brilliance of his dancing – proud as a Spaniard, fiery as a Cossack – enlivened so the otherwise interminable monotony of the quadrille, with its repeated geometrical figures performed with such military precision back and forth across the great expanse of gleamingly polished floor.

Chloe gazed beyond the dancers – eight couples selected to open the ball by imperial decree – at the ornate white and gold marble of the vast ballroom, with its fluted pilasters, and its pier-glasses mirroring the dazzle of the great chandeliers with their thousands of candles, and its painted ceiling of pink clouds floating in a heaven of soaring blue. Here, once, the kings and queens of France had led the dance, gliding with all their courtiers like swans in pavanes and minuets. Now Bonaparte sprawled scowling, his arms crossed, on the throne at the far end of the ballroom, while his multitude of guests – almost all the men in military uniform; almost all the ladies in gowns of pink or white – stood wearily to attention around the edges of the floor. All the tall windows were open on to the balcony and the formal gardens below, and the late summer night was so warm and still that scarcely a candle flickered; yet no one dared wander out to breathe the air's fragrance. No one dared pace inobtrusively back and forth. No one dared engage even in a whispered conversation. And meanwhile the quadrille went on and on.

The long, dark blue velvet curtains at the windows stirred faintly, once, in a languid movement of the air, then were still again.

On the pretext of resting her hand modestly on the low neckline of her vivid scarlet ball-gown, which was lavishly trimmed with rosettes and loops and streamers of black and gold ribbon and black fringes, like the dress of a gipsy dancer, Chloe made sure that the tiny phial of phosphorus was still secure in its place of concealment between her breasts. The baroque grandeur of the palace ballroom; the rich beauty of the gold-brocaded curtains; the great crowd of distinguished guests; the light-hearted dancing of the Vicomte de Malebois: all conspired to give the scene, and her coming part in it, a dreamlike unreality. Yet she only felt the more deeply calm for that.

She glanced sidelong at Philippe. Though very slender, he was tall and manly-looking in his student's blue coat and snuff-coloured breeches, and only someone who knew him as well as she did could have detected that slight increase in his natural gravity and pallor. It had been enough to point out to him that his visible agitation and hostility towards de l'Epinay were endangering all of them. She hadn't dared tell him of her meeting with de l'Epinay in the palmhouse, though she had lain for hours afterwards on her bed, as though pinioned, staring up at the crimson canopy in a state of frozen shock, anger and bitter disillusionment. She hadn't even felt very tempted to enlighten Philippe about de l'Epinay's position as a moderate royalist amongst extremists. Probably it was true; yet the more she dwelt on their interview in the palmhouse, the more an inexplicable uneasiness crept over her, as if there had been some unseen element of deception in everything he'd said and done. It would be a relief to meet some of the other royalist leaders, and form her own impressions.

'And what liars men are – they're as bad as women!' she thought, as she watched de Malebois again. De l'Epinay had warned her that there was a vindictive streak in the dashing cavalry officer, but after several minutes of covertly studying him, Chloe was convinced that the worst defects of character which could be read in those gay, darkly handsome features were irresponsible recklessness and a touch of vanity. De Malebois was dazzling, but he was surely too shallow to be vindictive. She supposed that he must be about the same age as de l'Epinay, about thirty-three; yet it seemed to her that he was still a devil-may-care boy rather than a man, with his unruly black curls, his flashing eyes, and his teasing smile; that he had never really grown up.

'All the same, perhaps I'll pretend to myself that I'm a little in love with him – just to amuse and distract myself, just to forget,' Chloe thought, checking her gaze from wandering searchingly over the throng of guests, especially in the more shadowy recesses of the ballroom. She knew de l'Epinay wouldn't be there, and her own continual, involuntary, restless searching for a glimpse of him filled her with angry misery. At first – nearly a week ago now –she had wondered, with a wild throb of hope, if his disappearance was due to an access of jealous pique, and thus betrayed a deeper interest in her than he'd pretended. But day after day had passed without a word from him. True, until she had talked with de Malebois later this evening, there was no reason – no political reason – for de l'Epinay to contact her. But after all those lingering blue gazes, those whispered words of desire ... Perhaps he was punishing her. Or perhaps, finding that she wasn't to be possessed instantly and effortlessly, just for the asking, he had lost interest. Hadn't she suspected all along that while beautiful women might arouse his desire, in passing, he secretly felt nothing more than indifference and contempt?

'But I'll pay him back, when I see him!' she promised herself, swirling round on her toes and running her fingers over her bare arms and her flushed cheeks in a crisis of humiliated fury. She found herself gazing straight at the Vicomte de Malebois, and carelessly flashed him a flirtatious smile. After all, though she wasn't supposed to know yet that he was a royalist, there was no harm in a little dalliance. He gave her a startled smile in return, then turned back to his partner with a look of private, lingering speculation. Perhaps the same thought had occurred to him.

But what about General de Bourges? Chloe glanced swiftly round and up at his tall, imposing figure standing just behind her shoulder, to gauge his mood. He was no dancer himself, and knew it; but sometimes, at a ball, showing an almost fatherly indulgence, he was agreeable to her waltzing with one or two of his younger and more reliable aides-de-camp. He would have made a kind husband, she thought, tucking her hand impulsively under his arm, and feeling an inexplicable lump in her throat. But if she were to flirt openly with the Vicomte de Malebois? That would surely be a different matter. Yet, as she glanced up at the General again, she reflected – not for the first time that evening – that something seemed very amiss with him. He had been a little late calling for them in his carriage, which was most unusual, and had repeatedly muttered something about 'a slight contretemps – most unfortunate', though without ever saying what it was that had detained him. And now he was staring glassily straight in front of him, the lines of his face sagging so that he looked like an old man, and he hadn't patted her hand or given any other sign of having noticed her affectionate gesture. There was

76

a letter with a tattered edge protruding slightly from one of the pockets of his coat, which was also very unlike his usual punctilious attention to his uniform, and she thought, 'He's had a shock – bad news of some kind,' and gave his arm a little squeeze, but still there was no response.

The quadrille ended at last in a round of polite applause. Bonaparte, who never stayed for longer than the first dance, even at a ball in his own palace, flung himself from his throne and stomped out of the ballroom without ceremony, followed by his entourage, leaving his guests stupidly bowing and curtseying to an empty doorway. A clock chimed nine in the frozen pause of disbelief and relief. Then there was a quiet hum of violins tuning up in the orchestra, and subdued murmurs of conversation here and there. Two plump, rosy little girls in pink dresses dashed out on to the polished floor, squealed, and ran back again. A trio of young dragoons swaggered out on to the balcony and lit cigars. And in another moment everyone was talking, laughing, shouting, the violins were humming loudly, and groups of officers and their ladies were spilling out across the great empty floor. People who had been invisible before, screened by other people or standing in shadowy alcoves, became visible. A dozen young subalterns began to converge on the corner where Chloe was standing, and the Vicomte de Malebois strolled past, paused, and turned, drumming his fingers lightly on the hilt of his sword, but she couldn't prevent herself from swiftly scanning the crowd again. Her heart almost stopped at the sight of several men here and there in anonymous dark coats and breeches, leaning singly, or in twos and threes, in alcoves, or pacing casually amongst the other guests. Were they merely palace officials, or had someone betrayed the plot? And there were so many! At a single sweep of her gaze she could count . . .

The image of de l'Epinay, as she had last seen him – a gleam of fair hair in the shadows; eyes like grey-blue ice – had become so imprinted on her memory, so deeply a part of her thoughts and dreams, that she must have gazed at

him for a full second or more before it began to dawn on
her that he was really there: very still in the shadows, and
watching her with the same icy intensity as in the palmhouse, though whether it was a look of jealous fury or of
chilling contempt she still couldn't say. Or was it a mental
mirage after all, a trick of the light? For the instant that he
was still visible, he seemed to be standing in a dark alcove
on the opposite side of the ballroom, where there were no
alcoves but only a row of windows. Yet he couldn't have
been out on the balcony, for she had glimpsed a half-
curtained doorway behind him. But the pier-glass between
two of the windows – of course! He had been behind her.
She spun round, but there was no one there.

'Good evening, General. Won't you introduce me to
your charming friends?' said a soft, drawling voice.

Chloe spun back again to see the Vicomte de Malebois
step through the throng of young subalterns as if they
weren't there, and stand before General de Bourges,
bowing gracefully and smiling.

'Ah yes, of course – delighted!' General de Bourges
stammered, seeming to half wake with a start from his
glassy trance. His hand strayed involuntarily to the letter in
his coat pocket, and Chloe thought she glimpsed a look of
guilt, or even fear, in his dazed eyes. 'He's in some terrible
trouble,' she thought. Could that letter contain an anonymous threat, or perhaps even blackmail?

The orchestra quietly throbbed out the first thrilling
beats of a waltz.

'Enchanté!' de Malebois murmured, bowing low over
Chloe's hand; and then, beginning to glide backwards
without releasing her fingers, drawing her with him:
'Would you care . . . ?'

'Good evening,' said another soft, drawling voice, this
time heart-flutteringly familiar, just behind Chloe's
shoulder. She turned to see de l'Epinay, handsomer than
ever in a midnight blue velvet coat and breeches with silver
buttons and a silver waistcoat, holding out his hand with a
compellingly blue gaze, so that she was obliged to withdraw

78

her fingers from de Malebois' clasp and offer them to be kissed. Etiquette, anyway, made it impossible for her now to dance away with de Malebois, at any rate for several minutes. 'But he's jealous!' she thought gleefully, as de l'Epinay's cool lips brushed her fingers. 'He meant to stay away tonight, but he couldn't. And he can't bear that I should waltz with the Vicomte de Malebois.' Yet her own fast-beating heart reminded her of the torment of the past several days without word from him, and she told herself, 'All the same, I'll pay him out – I'll make him suffer too!'

De Malebois began pacing gracefully back and forth before her, in time to the music, so that the subalterns had to shuffle away to one side and the other to make room for him, treading on one another's toes. A smile was still playing about his lips, but his dark eyes were unexpectedly level.

'Urgent business has detained me, else I'd have called on you,' de l'Epinay said, addressing Aunt Eugénie, but releasing Chloe's hand slowly and caressively. 'I've thought of it every day, I can assure you.' He too was smiling, but his eyes, too, were very level as well as very blue as he added, glancing at Chloe, 'The Palais du Luxembourg holds some exquisite memories for me – as well as some regrets – and I dream of finding myself there again, and reliving such enchantment. Without the regrets, of course.'

Chloe withdrew her fingers swiftly from his, but not before the thrill of his caress had seemed to steal through every cell of her body. What had he meant? While he continued to exchange courtesies with her aunt and uncle, she glanced sidelong at him, trying to decide. Had he meant that he had been haunted by impassioned visions of her, breaking through his guard, taking him unawares, or just that he had been teased by the recurring and idle whim to possess her? That he regretted making her that dishonourable proposal? Or that he merely regretted her declining it? She was unable to say, and could only remain uneasily intrigued at his ambiguity.

'I was at Rivoli, sir, but of course that's a long time ago,' de l'Epinay was saying to General de Bourges; then he concluded his courtesies by exchanging a curt nod with de Malebois.

'Oh, do you . . ? Oh, yes of course you know each other – how silly of me!' Aunt Eugénie said, fanning herself rapidly. She had certainly indulged in the most ambitious dreams of Chloe's fame and fortune, yet she could hardly have anticipated this embarrassment of riches. Half the eyes in the ballroom were on them – not least those of the exotic Manon, watching them with affected indifference from the midst of another crowd of officers near one of the windows.

'We were in Egypt together, as well as at Rivoli,' said de l'Epinay, with a gentle smile.

'Yes of course. How too silly for words.'

Still gliding back and forth, de Malebois smiled too, letting his glance travel in passing over de l'Epinay's cane and his lame foot. 'He is vindictive after all – de l'Epinay was telling the truth,' Chloe realized. 'And it's just because he is so shallow. He hasn't the intelligence or the character to be anything else, when he's crossed.'

'. . . All the same, I keep thinking I've seen you some-where,' General de Bourges said to de l'Epinay, speaking almost like an old man whose mind was wandering, vague yet obsessed, and he fixed de l'Epinay with a furtively appealing gaze, as if in the hope that he might prove to be an influential friend.

'Perhaps in a corridor at the War Office,' de l'Epinay suggested, meeting the General's gaze. 'I've had some business there – rather confidential – in connexion with the new fleet.' His voice and his smile were more gentle than ever, and even quietly soothing, as if he'd perceived that the General was in some desperate trouble. Yet he swung rather abruptly away, and with a shock Chloe glimpsed a strange, remote bleakness in his eyes, which in no way matched his manner, and which sent a shiver through her. What was it about him? And why, in spite of the chiselled sensitivity of his features, and the gay charm of his social poise, did she keep glimpsing that terrible absence of real feeling in him?

Yet it was as if the General's wretched state, or his desperately appealing gaze, had affected de l'Epinay after all, in some curious way. Up till that moment, he had effortlessly dominated the whole encounter; but now, for a fatal instant, he seemed translated to some other realm of thought, chill and abstract, and a silence fell. The violins soared. Seizing his chance, the Vicomte de Malebois bowed to Chloe and held out his hand with a smile, murmuring, 'If you would do me the honour ... '

' – Yes, it is rather warm, isn't it?' de l'Epinay said quickly, as Aunt Eugénie fanned herself more rapidly than ever. 'Almost too warm even for conversation, though there's so much I want to know about you. For instance – ' he was smiling, but his gaze seemed to transfix Chloe with its sudden urgent intensity – 'do you still have that tickle in your nose? Perhaps you'd care – ' his gesture of invitation briefly included Philippe – 'for a stroll out on the balcony?'

There was a deathly silence. Both de l'Epinay and de Malebois stood deferentially awaiting Chloe's decision, and she was aware that now everyone in the ballroom was watching the three of them, and that beneath the sweeping, pulsing rhythm of the waltz all murmurs of conversation had died away. In the few timeless, dreamlike seconds that passed, she was irrelevantly aware of the curious similarity between her two new suitors, if they could be called that: both aristocrats from head to foot; both about thirty-three; both tall, and of the same lean, graceful, military build; and with nothing to choose between them for handsomeness, except that one was dark and the other fair, as if they were one man and his image in a shadowy mirror. But while de Malebois was swaying in time to the waltz, a confident smile on his lips, de l'Epinay was as still as a statue, leaning on his cane and watching her with a secret, daring look of challenge in his eyes, as if to say, 'Very well, I insulted you – and now I'm entirely at your mercy.' As indeed he was, for in her choice between them

81

lay social triumph for one and social disaster for the other. Oh, how clever he was, as well as brave! He knew she was furious with him, yet offered her a revenge too devastating for her to take, and thereby disarmed her. And yet if she chose him, not only had he demolished his rival at one stroke, publicly and for ever; he had forced her to admit to him, and to everyone in the ballroom, that she was his.

Well, she would rather die than admit such a thing. Yet she couldn't risk losing him either. 'I'm deeply obliged to you both,' she murmured with a smile, having hesitated as long as she dared. And then, spinning round with a laugh she couldn't suppress, and seizing Philippe's hand, she added, 'But I promised the first waltz to my cousin.' And as she and Philippe danced away she called back over her shoulder, 'Still, never mind – we've the whole evening before us.'

Fortunately it was a slow waltz.

'Hold me properly – everyone's looking at us – and for heaven's sake don't tread on my toes!' Chloe hissed. She had given Philippe endless waltzing lessons during the past few months, round and round her bedroom floor and round the dining-room table, and had almost despaired of him. But now he rose splendidly to the occasion, and they revolved round the ballroom amongst the other dancers not only without mishap but gracefully. Chloe even felt proud of her cousin's grave good looks.

'Tell me what's happening – how they've taken it,' she whispered, as soon as they were a few revolutions away across the floor. 'I daren't look that way myself, else they'll think I care.'

'De Malebois seems to be in a fearful huff,' Philippe reported after a moment's appraisal. 'He's stalking off looking daggers at you, and at de l'Epinay, and everyone. And I say, you know, you did smile at him during the quadrille – I saw you – and he did get there first, so – '

'Yes yes, but what about de l'Epinay? What's he doing? How does he look?'

'He's still talking to Mama and Papa and General de Bourges – what's the matter with the General, do you think? – and he keeps laughing to himself, I don't know why.'

Chloe was silent. It was true, of course, that the episode had still been a private triumph for him. He had asked her to become his mistress, and he had disappeared without explanation for nearly a week, and she ought to have snubbed him. And he had probably seen her smile of invitation to de Malebois. He was bound to interpret what had happened as a sign that she was far from indifferent towards him.

'And now he's gone,' Philippe added.

'Gone! Where?'

'I didn't see.'

Chloe scanned the ballroom with a semblance of casualness as they danced on. Aunt Eugénie and Uncle Victor were still in the same corner, side by side, like a pair of wax dolls with fixed smiles on their faces. Beside them, General de Bourges was furtively searching the face of every passing man. But de l'Epinay had vanished. There was only the shadowy alcove where Chloe had first glimpsed him reflected in the pier-glass, empty again now but for its half-curtained doorway leading through into Bonaparte's private appartments.

Her eyes travelled on over the crowds of watching guests around the edge of the great polished floor. Many eyes were still following her, and whispers were being exchanged behind fans. Once she found herself meeting the gaze of a portly old lady loaded with diamonds: not a gaze of sidelong, speculative envy, like those of most of the other women in the ballroom, but a beadily calm appraisal. Could she be another royalist, watching to ensure that the curtains were skilfully and successfully set on fire? Startled, Chloe flashed a glance round the whole ballroom. How many other royalists, entirely anonymous amongst the crowds of guests – ?

'During the next quadrille.'

The murmured words had been so soft, and so close to her ear, she might almost have imagined them; so casual, they might have been a mere snatch of innocuous passing conversation. Only Philippe's slight increase of pallor assured her otherwise. She didn't dare turn her head, but covertly scanned all the other waltzing couples near them as they continued to revolve smoothly on. De Malebois was standing alone on the far side of the ballroom, watching her with level black eyes. And there was nothing whatever about any of the nearby waltzers to suggest that they might be royalists, or might have whispered that message to her.

The next quadrille! That meant the next dance, for at every ball given by Bonaparte quadrilles and waltzes alternated throughout the evening with military regularity. So soon, then! Chloe couldn't prevent her heart from fluttering. So soon – and de l'Epinay, her only ally apart from Philippe, had vanished. And de Malebois . . . She had made an enemy of him. And the ballroom was teeming with dark-coated figures now, lurking inobtrusively in the shadowy alcoves and arcades behind the brilliantly-dressed crowds of guests. There seemed twice as many as before. Everywhere she looked . . .

Her heart fluttered wildly once more, then subsided with relief, as she glimpsed a gleam of fair hair far back in those shadows. Across the ballroom, over Philippe's shoulder, she could see de l'Epinay limping nonchalantly along the length of one of the dark arcades, passing pairs and trios of the dark-coated men without the slightest sign of concern. Once he even nodded slightly, as if acknowledging a deferential greeting from one of them. Perhaps, after all, they were only palace attendants. Then Philippe swung her on round, and she lost sight of de l'Epinay. A moment later she glimpsed him again, pausing to exchange a brief word with Monsieur Turgeon, who had appeared beside one of the curtained doors to Bonaparte's private appartments; then, the next time she looked, he had vanished once more.

But he was still there somewhere, behind the scenes; nothing would go wrong. Chloe breathed evenly and held her head high – the more so as they were just dancing past the window-recess where Manon de Malebois was holding court.

'. . . Yes, yes, I dare say, but she'll run to fat before she's twenty-five,' a feminine drawl carried clearly after them. 'These pretty village girls are all the same, you know. I can't imagine why the Emperor allows . . . '

'Did you hear that?' Philippe hissed in a furious whisper, as soon as they were safely out of earshot. 'I can't help hoping you didn't, but if you did – '

'I did, but don't worry,' Chloe murmured calmly, eyeing the hem of Manon de Malebois' gold lamé gown, which was resting against the draped curtain of the window behind her. 'I somehow think she'll have cause to regret it.'

The violins soared higher than ever, as if the waltz was about to end. Chloe espied a recessed window in a shadowy corner, which was open on to the balcony, but where no one happened to be standing. 'Don't dance on any further,' she whispered to Philippe. 'Waltz round just here, on the same spot.' And a moment later, as the music ended in a burst of applause, she seized his hand, waved gaily to her aunt and uncle on the opposite side of the ballroom, and drew him quickly out on to the dark balcony.

For a moment, still dazzled by the chandeliers within, she thought there was no one there. Then the urn-grown roses and honeysuckle stirred faintly in the deep shadow, with a wave of amorous scent, and the light from the ballroom gleamed subtly on de l'Epinay's fair hair, and caught the flash of his smile.

'Good evening once again,' he murmured, still leaning negligently against the balustrade, with the dim fairy-lights in the trees of the palace gardens below forming a magic background to his silhouette. And then, indicating the rest of the long balcony with a wave of his hand, he said to Philippe in a soft, courteous, but unmistakeably level tone, 'Walk that way, if you please, young man. We've urgent matters to discuss.'

Philippe hesitated, glancing at the depth of shadow in that fragrant arbour at the corner of the balcony, then stood his ground. 'I hardly think – '

'Do as I tell you!' de l'Epinay said in a curt whisper, his eyes suddenly like ice again, even in the shadows. He stirred, only slightly, but as stealthily as a tiger, and Philippe took an involuntary step back, glancing uncertainly at Chloe. She gave him a just perceptible nod, and he turned on his heel and walked slowly and furiously away amongst the couples and groups of guests taking the air further along the balcony.

'What's happening? Has the plot been betrayed?' Chloe began, alarmed at de l'Epinay's manner. But he only drew her back swiftly into the arbour and kissed her hand, then turned it over and kissed her palm and each of her fingertips in rapid succession, murmuring, 'Ah, ah!' between kisses, like a man who had been dying of thirst.

Chloe's head swam with intoxication, but she managed to wrest her hand away. She hadn't yet avenged either his insults or his neglect, and yet here he was doing exactly as he pleased with her! 'What is it?' she whispered angrily. 'What do you want?'

'I should have thought that was evident,' he murmured, laughing under his breath. He ran his fingertip lightly and swiftly over the line of her bare shoulder, then stepped back and rested both hands with elegant correctness on the head of his cane. For a moment they gazed at each other silently in the half-darkness; then he murmured casually, 'Pestilential girl! To be perfectly frank, I've spent the last few days trying to forget you, as I don't care to be trifled with. But without success, as you see – I can't seem to stop thinking about you.' He stirred, though without attempting to touch her, and moistened his lips. Then he asked softly, no longer smiling at all, 'Won't you reconsider my offer?'

'There isn't the slightest – '

'Don't answer!' he said quickly. 'Not just yet. Let me explain ... ' He began to pace, graceful even in the confined space of the arbour, circling her. 'After all, you've led a rather sheltered life, really,' he continued, in a smooth murmur. 'Perhaps you think I'm being a little too mercenary. But you must understand that what I offer you . . . well, you should look on that merely as a corollary. An act of chivalry, if you like, between friends – saving you from the dragon of social obscurity – but not of course the essence of the matter. I mean . . . ' Behind her, he brushed against a spray of roses, which enveloped them in a wave of headiness. She felt a light caress, this time of his lips, trace the line of her shoulder and neck again, coming to rest close to her ear, and he whispered, 'I mean that I'll adore you.'

'" – For as long as the arrangement lasts?"' Chloe said, managing to keep her voice level.

'Of course, of course. But let's not spoil this moment with any vulgar imperial measurements.' He was laughing, but his hand was a little unsteady as he began to turn her gently to face him, murmuring, 'Come – say yes.'

Chloe stepped back out of his reach and leant against the balustrade, hoping he couldn't see how she was trembling. 'I'll thank you not to joke with me,' she whispered, more fiercely than she felt.

'Joke with you? But I do . . . ' His face was still passionate for a moment as he returned her gaze, but even in the shadows she could see something in his eyes taking flight from her, travelling far, far away, perhaps involuntarily. He glanced away along the balcony, then back to her, and stirred restlessly, as if equally divided between the desire to escape and the desire to possess her. 'But I am . . . I am, as a matter of fact, extremely taken with you,' he concluded evasively. It was a visible effort for him, but he continued to meet her gaze; then he repeated softly, 'Say yes.'

'No,' Chloe said.

For an instant he gazed expressionlessly at her; then he murmured, 'I see!' with a dry little smile, and swung away. The orchestra struck up a quadrille. Amongst the loiterers further along the balcony, Philippe turned and stood looking their way. De l'Epinay took Chloe's hand and kissed it, with a *ci-devant's* easy, face-saving elegance, difficult not to like him for; and said lightly, 'Ah well, better luck next time! And now to business.' He moved a pace or two along the balcony, to where he was still in deep shadow but could see into the ballroom, and murmured after a moment, 'Good – there's de Malebois on his way.'

From beside him, Chloe saw the Vicomte de Malebois pause casually by one of the doors leading to the imperial private apartments, stand watching the dancers for a moment, then slip coolly through and out of sight. It seemed strange that the door wasn't guarded. True, there were two dark-coated figures standing only a few paces away, but they were deep in conversation, and didn't glance round. Nor, by chance, did any of the others stationed at frequent intervals round the edge of the ballroom.

But there were so many of them – some only a pace or two away from the windows, albeit with their backs turned. Chloe glanced at de l'Epinay beside her, intrigued by his unruffled calm. 'Aren't you afeared of so many Secret Police – that someone may have alerted them?' she whispered.

He remained silent for a moment, a motionless dark figure in the shadows; then he murmured, without looking at her, 'If you mean those men in dark coats, they're just palace guards – all the better to put the fire out and prevent a panic. Whatever made you think they were Secret Police?'

'I don't know. I just felt they were.'

He glanced at her in the half-darkness, then said lightly, 'Ah – feminine intuition! Usually sound, but sometimes mistaken. You're a little too exercized, forgive my saying so, by that whole subject, which has been greatly exaggerated by rumours.'

'But you said yourself that Scorpio . . . that the success of the whole conspiracy depended on his being identified and killed.'

88

He was silent again for a moment, his face unreadable in the shadows; then he said negligently, 'Perhaps. But he's only one man, after all. I'd forget about him, if I were you.' He took her hand suddenly, and added, 'But what cold little fingers! Come – give me the phial, and I'll do it for you. No one will see.'

'No!' Chloe flared up, withdrawing her hand. 'If you're not afeared, nor am I!'

He gave her a brief smile in the half-darkness, perhaps of apology, or perhaps of approval, or of both; then he said, 'Well then, it's almost time ... but listen.' His voice dropped to a suddenly urgent whisper. 'I shall have to leave shortly, to keep a rather tiresome appointment –' his eyes, catching the light from the ballroom, seemed strangely bleak again for an instant – 'So we may well not have another chance to talk this evening. But I suspect that there's to be a meeting of several of the royalist leaders tomorrow, in the Faubourg St Germain, to which you'll probably be invited, and to which I, for various reasons, shall not. There's a plan afoot to blow up the foyer of the Opera, for instance, and they know I'll oppose it. I shall do my best to be present at the meeting even without an invitation, but if I'm detained perhaps you'd better meet me at the Luxembourg palmhouse again the day after. Shall we say three o'clock?'

Chloe bit her lip, not answering for a moment, the memory of his deeply persuasive caresses all too vivid to her mind and senses. Would she be able to resist another time?

'I'll need information from you,' he said gently. 'And I'll need it urgently enough to give you my word, if I must . . .'

Chloe nodded her assent. After all, he was an aristocrat: his word was his bond. And while he was unconventional in many ways, he might still have taken even an instant's hesitation on her part as a mortal insult. And she guessed, too, that in any crisis his work would always come first with him. The levelness of his eyes as he'd made his promise had told her that.

'And don't trifle any more with de Malebois,' he said, in a tone which made her swing back to face him again. 'You won't find him as chivalrous as I am – in any sense – if you're ever alone with him. And if he ever lays a finger on you without your consent, I'll call him out – and you can tell him I said so.'

Chloe gazed back at him, measuring him. He had told the truth about de Malebois before, she remembered. But beneath that debonair exterior, what a dangerously jealous man he was! It gave her the sharpest possible weapon against him – but so terribly sharp that she might be well advised to use it with the greatest caution. But meanwhile he was arrogating to himself the right of a protector, and the quadrille was well advanced into the first of its set of five movements. She gave him a mockingly docile curtsey, and stepped away.

'Where are you going?' he whispered sharply.

Her chosen window was half way along the balcony, beyond a group of cigar-smoking dragoons. She turned a few paces away and whispered back, 'Where do you think?'

'But what's wrong with this window? There's no one here.'

'Wait and see.'

He glanced past her, to where there was a shimmer of gold lamé beside a dark blue velvet curtain. Perhaps, pacing the balcony earlier, waiting for her to emerge with Philippe, he had heard Manon de Malebois' clear, drawled words. At any rate, seeming to hide a smile, he only murmured, 'As you will.'

She moved swiftly on, silent-footed in her silk slippers. *'Bonsoir, belle dame!'* mumbled one of the tipsy young dragoons, swaying precariously as he swung round after her, then bending as slowly and cautiously as an old man to retrieve the cigar he'd dropped. None of them looked much older than Philippe – just lonely schoolboys far from home – and they'd probably get the blame, but it couldn't be helped. 'Quick, loosen the stopper for me,' she whispered to Philippe, stealthily extracting the phial from its hiding-place as he stepped forward to join her.

They leaned for a moment, deathly still, against the balustrade only three paces from the open window where Manon de Malebois was holding court, a crowd of be-ribboned and be-medalled field-marshals and generals to each side of her. Every back was turned, and the music of the quadrille drowned out even the murmur of conversation. The hem of the gold lamé dress still rested against the drape of the curtain. Further along the balcony Chloe could still see the faint gleam of de l'Epinay's hair, as he waited motionless in the shadows where she had left him.

'After this there'll be no turning back,' she thought, and was glad that she was sharing the moment with Philippe. She gave his hand a quick squeeze – his fingers were icy cold, her own warm and steady – then crept forward.

It was all so easy. Still no head turned, and the phosphorus soaked into the velvet curtain as she carefully poured it. She allowed only the last few drops to fall on the gold lamé – just enough to ruin the dress, she hoped – then walked with a swift but casual step back along the balcony towards de l'Epinay. Catching her up, Philippe took the empty phial from her after they'd passed the dragoons, and flung it far out into the palace gardens.

'Excellent,' de l'Epinay murmured as they reached him, and the three of them sauntered nonchalantly back into the ballroom.

Nothing happened.

'If this is another of your silly jokes . . .' Chloe began in a fierce whisper to de l'Epinay.

'It can take a minute or two – that's the beauty of it,' he murmured reassuringly, resting his hands on the head of his cane and watching the dancers with apparently absorbed attention. 'And anyway, look now.'

There was a greenish-white flicker, like summer lightning, in the window behind the Vicomtesse de Malebois, followed by a lazy curl of smoke, as from a cigar. Then suddenly the whole curtain burst into a great sheet of flame. Women screamed, men shouted, chairs were overturned, a cello in the orchestra fell to the floor with a harmonious boom, and the crowd surged towards the doors to the main staircase, showing the whites of their widened eyes. Chloe saw one of the little girls in pink dresses trip and fall headlong, disappearing beneath a forest of running legs. She gasped and stepped forward, but de l'Epinay restrained her, murmuring, 'Don't worry – nothing will go wrong.' He still seemed infinitely calm, albeit watchfully level-eyed, though smoke from the burning curtain was beginning to swirl round them. And Chloe saw that every door and window leading out of the ballroom had been quickly closed, and that polite-faced, dark-clad men were preventing anyone from leaving, while others moved discreetly about amongst the crowd, dividing it into small and manageable groups. One of them helped the little girl to her feet unhurt. There was a thunder of approaching footsteps in adjacent corridors – the moment, perhaps, that de Malebois had been waiting for, lurking in some obscure alcove or ante-room – and more palace guards in dark red and gold uniforms rushed in, armed with buckets and pumps. There were shouts of 'Stand back, please!' while buckets of water were thrown, and the still flaming curtain was jerked down from its ornate valance. A gilded plaster eagle crashed to the floor in a cloud of dust.

'I did it! I did it all!' Chloe thought, feeling herself sparkling with excitement and pride, now that the danger seemed over.

De l'Epinay gave her a brief, dizzyingly blue gaze, then kissed her hand, murmuring, 'Well, now I must take leave of you. I espy a lady in distress over there, and can't refrain from going to her aid, knight-errant that I am. Till tomorrow, then, or the day after.'

He limped away towards the mêlée by the window, where the uniformed palace guards were still stamping on the smouldering curtain and shouting instructions to one another. Only a few paces away, Manon de Malebois stood contemplating the ballroom with an amused smile, her hand on her dazzlingly-sheathed and shapely hip, while her venerable field-marshal bent and flapped his handkerchief at the back of her gown, as if dusting off plaster from the fallen eagle. But clouds of smoke were beginning to rise, and her smile was becoming fixed. Beside her, a palace guard stood staring, mesmerized, a brimming bucket of water in his hand. Chloe didn't see exactly what happened, because of the converging crowd. But there was a deluging splash of water and a scream, and she caught a glimpse of the Vicomtesse standing dripping from the waist down, while de l'Epinay was laughing so much that he had to lean on his cane for support. Chloe couldn't hear what the bedraggled Manon was hissing at him, but his drawled answer, as he gave her an elegant bow and backed away, carried clearly across the intervening space: 'Perhaps you scarcely notice such trifles nowadays, Madame, but you were on fire. And besides, I shouldn't fret too much about the water – the effect's wonderfully slimming.'

The field-marshal stepped quickly forward with his gloved hand raised, but one of his attendant generals just as quickly linked arms with him and walked him on round in a smooth, conversational circle. De l'Epinay waited for a moment with a polite smile, then disappeared into the smoke and the crowd of onlookers.

Even after the doors and windows had been opened again, and the smoke had thinned and drifted away, Chloe could no longer see him anywhere. Tapestry screens were placed round the mess of water, plaster and burnt velvet on the floor. Manon de Malebois, enveloped in a military cloak, swept from the ballroom with her retinue. Bonaparte appeared briefly in a doorway, coatless and with his cravat loosened, stared round at the crowd with gimlet eyes, spat on the parquet, then strode out again. The orchestra struck up a fast waltz, and the dark-clad figures melted away as if they had never been. Only two or three of the guards in red and gold uniforms still milled about on the balcony, poking about here and there with their swords, and exchanging aimless recriminations with the young dragoons. The Vicomte de Malebois reappeared coolly in an alcove with a curtained doorway, and began to make his way round the ballroom towards her. Once she thought she glimpsed de l'Epinay in a similar alcove, reflected in a mirror and therefore behind her, but when she turned her head there was no one there.

'If I might now finally have the honour . . . '

With an ironic little smile playing about his lips, de Malebois bowed before her and held out his hand. She took it, and was whirled wonderfully away into the waltz like a leaf or a feather in a storm.

'*Vive le Roi,*' he murmured in her ear, after a timelessness.

'*Et la Reine,*' Chloe murmured back, feeling that it was as good an answer as any.

He laughed, his teeth flashing very white in his hand-some, olive-skinned face, and she thought, 'He isn't such a villain really – at any rate not when he's getting his own way.' He was holding her too close, but how else could a man and woman waltz together like one wild, elemental being? And besides, de l'Epinay had gone.

'You seem to have done very well,' de Malebois observed, after a while of more heavenly whirling. 'Brave, too. The place was so swarming with Secret Police I feared you might cry off.'

'Secret Police?' Chloe whispered, turning suddenly cold.

'All those fellows in dark coats and breeches. Didn't you realize? There's always a few about, but there were so many tonight I wondered if we'd been betrayed. Still, it seems not.'

Chloe was silent as they whirled on. Had de l'Epinay kept the truth from her, so as to calm her fears? Or was de Malebois mistaken? After all, no arrests had been made. Perhaps de Malebois was even lying, wanting to impress her with his own daring. That seemed by far the most likely explanation, and she maintained a diplomatically neutral silence, pretending to be lost to the world in the waltz, and then no longer pretending.

'This is marvellous,' she heard him say as they spun on. 'You're not only brave and beautiful – weren't you glad to get my letter? – but you waltz like some wild, wonderful creature from one's dreams . . . I only wish we could dance all night, but alas, I must leave all too soon – I've some documents to pass on. Still, there'll be other nights, won't there? – and meanwhile we'd like to see you tomorrow.' He whispered an address in the Faubourg St Germain, then added, 'At eight in the evening, if that suits you.'

Chloe bit her lip, wondering how it was to be managed. 'I'll have to bring my cousin,' she warned. 'I'll need him as an escort.'

'Yes yes, we realize that's necessary, for the time being, but of course he'll have to wait outside.' Then de Malebois smiled, and said softly, 'So you haven't succumbed to de l'Epinay? How original of you. He always prides himself on getting his game at the first shot.'

Chloe smiled back, and said, 'I'm no one's game.'

'Very wise,' de Malebois complimented her, as he swept her round more irresistibly than ever, until she felt as if her feet were scarcely touching the ground. 'Especially in his case. He never has less than three mistresses at a time, you know – because there's safety in numbers, as he puts it.'

Liar, liar, liar! Chloe thought, though she felt pierced to the heart. De l'Epinay's confident and precipitate wooing, and his wariness of any threat to his freedom, made it all too likely that de Malebois was telling the truth. 'Then I'll never get him!' she thought in despair; but she managed to say, with an indifferent shrug, 'That's no concern of mine.'

'And by the way,' de Malebois added casually, 'Don't mention tomorrow's rendez-vous to him, if you happen to see him – not even if he asks. We think he may be an informer, or a double agent, or something. We'll be discussing that tomorrow. I'd keep well away from him, if I were you. If we're right in our suspicions, anyone closely associated with him will naturally share his fate.'

Liar! Chloe thought again, and she tried to dismiss the familiar but inexplicable shiver which tingled through her. It was just that the other royalists were bound to be suspicious of de l'Epinay, because he was less extreme than

95

they were. And de Malebois was just jealous. And it was difficult not to be caught up in his tissue of lies, not to fall under his spell, when he was holding her so persuasively close to his hard, lean, virile body, alive with rhythm, and whirling her round with such deftness and grace – a communion far more intimate, by an irony, than any she had known or could allow herself to know with de l'Epinay, whom she loved. And if it had only been de l'Epinay holding her so close in his arms now, she would never have felt that shadow of a doubt.

Perhaps misinterpreting her subdued silence, de Malebois said generously, 'Poor Lucien! Before he was wounded, he used to waltz – oh, like the devil himself! What a bitter pill to swallow!' And then he laughed.

Containing her anger, Chloe looked round casually at the swirling, spinning ballroom, and asked, 'Why – is he still here now?'

'How should I know?'

It was true that it was difficult to see anything but a flashing blur of faces, diamonds, chandeliers, dark alcoves and bright mirrors. Was that him – that fair gleam, that figure leaning in the shadows like a man in pain? Or was that cold glitter the ice of his gaze? Perhaps he wasn't there at all; yet to her he was, for he was everywhere, and in her heart she was waltzing only with him. 'And it's done now, and there's no turning back,' she thought, exulting, and feeling as if she were soaring away for ever amongst the clouds and angels in the painted sky above. 'And somehow I'll win, and I'll have him. And whatever happens now, I'm free!'

General de Bourges, it transpired, also had to leave early, and Chloe made no objection to their all leaving with him. She'd seen no sign of de l'Epinay anywhere when the waltz had ended.

The General still seemed dreadfully agitated, and kept taking his letter out of his coat pocket, then stuffing it back again with trembling fingers. Half way down the main staircase of the palace, on a half-shadowed turning between the glow of two chandeliers, he dropped it without noticing. Philippe, who was walking behind, picked it up, and Chloe saw him turn as white as a ghost.

Casually she slipped back to walk at his side, and without a word he showed her. The black wax seal of the letter was broken, of course, but when the two halves came together they formed the deep imprint of a scorpion poised to sting.

Scorpio! The sinister black insignia seemed to writhe before Chloe's horrified gaze. Was the letter a command for the General to give himself up to the Secret Police? But whatever could he have done to deserve such a fate?

' ... And you haven't forgotten about the Opera on Friday, have you?' Aunt Eugénie was reminding him archly, as the guards in their red and gold uniforms bowed deeply at the top of the steps, and the General's carriage drew up.

'Oh no! No indeed! No, no!'

'He's going to vanish,' Chloe thought, in numb disbelief, 'And he knows it.'

Outside in the Cour des Princes, dark-clad figures stood in the shadows, and along the future Rue de Rivoli the scaffolding was black against the night sky.

'I think you dropped this, sir.'

'Ah, did I? Ah, thank you, young man,' General de Bourges muttered vaguely. Then he looked round, straightened his shoulders with an effort at military pride, and said, 'I'll take leave of you here, if I may. But do take the carriage. I have an appointment – most unfortunate and tiresome – only a few yards from here.'

'Only a few yards? Really?'

'Yes ... just here, as a matter of fact.'

Chloe wondered if she'd imagined it, or whether the dark-clad figures had really moved a little closer. It was like a terrible dream, but there seemed to be nothing she could do. 'Goodnight, General,' she said, as he handed her up into the carriage, and on an impulse she kissed his cheek.

'Goodnight, and thank you.' And then she saw his eyes glisten with tears, and turned quickly away.

Facing each other in the carriage as it rumbled away over the cobblestones, Chloe and Philippe exchanged many glances under the light of passing lamps. The black seal on the letter; the way General de Bourges had scanned the face of every likely man throughout the evening; his nocturnal appointment in the Cour des Princes. . . It all led to one conclusion. Scorpio had been at the ball.

Seven

'I NEEDN'T TELL YOU what I'm beginning to suspect,' Philippe said.

It was ten minutes to eight the next evening, and they were sitting in the Café des Artistes in the Faubourg St Germain, only a stone's throw from the house where Chloe had been summoned to meet the Vicomte de Malebois and his confederates.

Philippe's words, uttered in a low voice even though they were sitting in a quiet corner, were the first to break the long, frozen silence which had fallen between them ever since they had left the Tuileries the night before.

'You're prejudiced,' Chloe whispered back, though she herself had been trying all last night and all today to dismiss the shivers of intuition which kept creeping over her. 'You've never liked the Comte de l'Epinay, and you're ready to suspect him of anything and everything, no matter how fantastical. It could have been one of a hundred other people.'

Like Philippe, she was leaning forward and gazing into her coffee, so that their heads were almost touching across the table. To the other occupants of the café – a few small groups of bearded or long-haired gentlemen wearing loose corduroy jackets and bright kerchiefs knotted at their throats like peasants – they must have looked like a pair of young lovers snatching an illicit interlude together. It was as well, for now they were being left undisturbed. At first, though Chloe had kept the hood of her pelisse close round her face, she had attracted many admiring connoisseurs' glances, and Philippe had even had to scowl fiercely at a young fellow who had started sketching her portrait on the back of his menu.

'De l'Epinay left early – only a little while before we did,' Philippe reasoned.

'So did the Vicomte de Malebois. So, for all we know, did dozens of other people.'

'But de Malebois had a good reason – he had his stolen documents to pass on, you told me.'

Chloe said nothing, remembering that de l'Epinay had only said that he had 'a rather tiresome appointment', without specifying anything of its nature. And she remembered, too, with a chill, how remote and unfeeling his eyes had looked as he'd spoken. And hadn't they held the same look when he'd been conversing with General de Bourges earlier in the evening? The possibility was so unreal she felt as if she was dreaming, yet it did exist: the General's arcane rendez-vous in the Cour des Princes could have been with de l'Epinay.

Still gazing into her coffee, she dwelt, too, on the memory of those dark-clad figures lurking in the shadows of the Cour des Princes. More palace guards? Surely not. And de l'Epinay's smooth assurance to her that they were, up in the ballroom earlier, now seemed ominous, another piece sliding into place in a sinister mosaic.

'And besides,' Philippe continued, in a whisper, 'General de Bourges can hardly have been a royalist or a Jacobin – he was hoping to be made the Duke of Rivoli at any moment. There seems only one reason why he should have been arrested – he and that colleague of Papa's at the Tuileries – and that reason points straight at de l'Epinay.'

'What do you mean?' Chloe whispered back, though she knew perfectly well. Not only had the news-sheets that morning reported that General de Bourges had vanished; one of the officials at the Tuileries, with whom Uncle Victor had been friendly, and of whom he had made enquiries about de l'Epinay, had also disappeared.

'Two men half-remember seeing de l'Epinay somewhere,

in mysterious circumstances,' Philippe whispered, 'and two men suddenly vanish. It seems rather too much of a coincidence.'

Silent, with glazed, only half-seeing eyes, Chloe looked away across the tiled floor of the café with its sprinkling of sawdust, and round at the booths of red leather seats topped by brass hand-rails, and the marble tables on their ornate wrought-iron pedestals. The light of the setting sun streamed in through the open doorway, and the murals above the booths seemed gay and vital, yet also melancholy, though she took in only a random detail here and there: an olive grove; a field of corn; a meadow tapestried with flowers; a beautiful, half-naked, laughing nymph leaning from a gold chariot drawn by black horses . . . She started and shivered suddenly as one of the artists at another table drew out his fob-watch, and an amber seal flashed as it dangled from the chain. Nearly all gentlemen wore such seals on their fob-chains, yet all day she'd flinched each time she'd seen one, even Uncle Victor's. Had de l'Epinay worn one? She closed her eyes, visualizing him, trying to remember, but all she could see was his handsome, half-laughing elegance – and the laughter fading, and the blue of his eyes becoming dark and passionate as he'd come close to kissing her . . .

'This is wicked – wicked and silly!' she whispered in anguish, turning back to Philippe. 'We're just upset about General de Bourges, and the seal on that letter, and there must be some other explanation for it all. And de l'Epinay's risking his life for his country, and he's – he's . . . Well, he's an aristocrat for a start, so it can't be possible!'

'So is Prince Talleyrand, and he's Bonaparte's Foreign Minister. There are always a few men willing to be traitors to their class as well as to their country – men who'll do anything, betray anything, for the sake of money and power.'

'Not de l'Epinay,' Chloe whispered, closing her eyes again. Surely if he were so corrupt, so devoid of ideals or scruples, she would have sensed it? But as if there were a traitor lurking within her own mind, there crept back into her memory that look of infinitely cynical detachment she had sometimes glimpsed in de l'Epinay's gaze. And she recollected, too, that while most of the surviving *ci-devants* were living in penury in England, he had offered her a small fortune if she would become his mistress, as though he were as rich as Croesus. Yet it could all be explained. His wealth could be explained by his having been astute and diplomatic enough to keep on the right side of Bonaparte, and his terrible detachment by his having lost so much, and by his living so close to death. 'Besides,' she argued, opening her eyes again and leaning closer across the table towards Philippe, 'the other royalists must have investigated him – followed him, spied on him, perhaps even set traps for him – long ago. They're not fools. It's true that they seem rather suspicious of him at the moment, but that's probably just rivalry, or because he disagrees with their extremism. After all, he's been working with them for years. He and the Vicomte de Malebois were brother officers at Rivoli, seven years ago, as well as in Egypt. And we've scarcely met him three times, and we've no experience of these affairs. It's inconceivable that we should be right and they wrong – it just isn't possible.'

'Perhaps not,' Philippe conceded reluctantly, pushing back his soft forelock of light brown hair, and then frowning into his coffee-cup. 'But don't forget what Papa said – that Scorpio was devilishly clever. I agree that the last place anyone would expect to find him is amongst the royalist leadership – but perhaps that's just what he relies on: that the royalists have never thought of looking for him there. And of course it would explain why every plot's discovered . . . And if they're suddenly suspicious now – as we are too – perhaps it's because even the cleverest man makes a mistake in the end.' He glanced up at Chloe, then fiddled idly with his coffee-spoon, adding, 'Especially if something's distracting him.'

Chloe's heart seemed to leap and then flutter in her breast, and she took refuge in finishing her coffee, so as to hide her wild confusion. If Philippe had noticed it too, then surely it might really be true: de l'Epinay might really be falling in love with her, try as he would to resist it. But if so, he was in the most terrible danger of being finally identified and . . . Catching the drift of her own thoughts, she almost choked. If he was really Scorpio – deceiver, traitor, torturer and murderer – she couldn't still care!

'Oh, you're clever too, Philippe – you'll make such a good lawyer,' she said, stifling a gasp, as if she'd been plunged into icy water. 'But it isn't true – it can't be true! After all, he even offered to set fire to that curtain for me, because he thought I was afraid. And he knew that de Malebois was stealing secret documents from Bonaparte's study, and he didn't try to stop him. And none of the royalists was arrested. It can't be him!'

Philippe gazed at her for a moment, then bowed his head, replacing his coffee-spoon in its saucer with a curious gentleness. 'But can't you see?' he murmured. 'He'd have to let things happen sometimes – and after all, what's a curtain? The documents . . . that's harder to explain, I agree. But if he isn't making arrests, it must be because he's gambling with time – because there's still some information he wants, or a few minor royalist agents he hasn't yet identified. Or perhaps there's a consignment of men, arms and money yet to come from England, and he's planning to wait till then before he closes his trap.'

'Oh, you have an answer for everything!' Chloe said in despair.

Philippe smiled rather wanly, without looking up, then continued, 'And don't you see? His going to the ball, and then leaving at the same time as the General: that's his mistake, that's what's made us suspect him.'

'You mean he planned not to go,' Chloe said, her heart all a-flutter again, 'and then he couldn't resist . . . I mean, and then he changed his mind?'

'Perhaps,' Philippe murmured, fingering his coffee-spoon more gently than ever. 'Or perhaps it was because he's like a gambler who's already winning and winning, and it goes to his head and he can't stop, and he risks everything for the sake of one more prize.'

'One more prize?' Chloe said, gazing round distractedly at the painted walls, only half-understanding him.

'Well, that curtain . . . You say he offered to set it on fire for you, but he must be a very astute judge of character, and he must have known you'd refuse. And he was there – he watched you do it. And that puts you in his power. He can make you do anything he likes now.'

For a moment the café seemed to swim round and grow blurred. Almost irrelevantly, Chloe remembered how de l'Epinay had persuaded her to meet him secretly at the palmhouse tomorrow, if he didn't come to the meeting tonight. Her own voice sounding far away to her, she said mechanically, 'You mean he might make me turn informer?'

'That too, I dare say. But you know what I really mean.'

The mural Chloe was still gazing at slowly came back into focus, and she suddenly understood the picture. There was a dark, sinister figure driving the gold chariot, one arm forcefully encircling the beautiful nymph's slim waist. And she wasn't leaning from the chariot to scatter roses and lilies laughingly over the meadow; she was struggling, and helplessly dropping her flowers, and she was screaming, and the horses were galloping into a black, yawning chasm where the earth had opened up. It was the rape of Persephone – Persephone being carried off by Pluto, the King of the Underworld.

Somewhere in the neighbourhood of the café, a church clock chimed eight. Slowly Chloe drew the hood of her pelisse closer round her face, and slipped the looped cord of her reticule over her wrist. 'Don't come with me,' she murmured. 'It's only across the way.'

'But you're not still going?' Philippe said, aghast. 'Chloe, don't you understand? If I'm right, de l'Epinay has the power of life and death over you now, and no law in France can gainsay him. You could just vanish for ever.'

'I know,' Chloe answered, standing up. 'But it's too late not to turn back. If you're right, he can come to the appartement and take me away – he can arrest me anywhere. The only way I can survive is to play him at his own game – and to win.'

'You're in love with him,' Philippe muttered, staring at the table.

'Yes,' Chloe agreed, feeling deathly calm as she looked down at him. 'And that's all the more reason to find out whether you're right or wrong. And I'll only find that out by going on.'

Philippe said nothing more, and Chloe walked away out of the café. She held her head high, but in her mind there was only a trail of crushed roses, and Persephone's screams, and the ground opening up before her.

Eight

THE SUN HAD GONE DOWN behind the tall houses, and the narrow street was already veiled in a soft, purplish-grey dusk. Chloe could see why the royalists had chosen this hour for their meeting, for discreetly dressed human figures would be even less visible now than later, when the streetlamps might single out the pallor of a face, or a lace shirt-cuff, and cast long shadows. Her pelisse was well chosen, she thought: not only because its black lace – through which the subdued rose silk of her dress only subtly glimmered –seemed to merge with the dusk, but also because it made her look so chaste and unapproachable, with its loose hood framing her face like a Spanish mantilla, and its silver clasp at her throat drawing an ebony veil over her *décolleté*. Dramatically chaste, chaste and yet secretly, glowingly fecund, like a Madonna by the painter Raphael: so she'd thought with a brief flash of stealthy triumph, glancing at herself in the mirror earlier, before they'd left home. And if de l'Epinay was there . . . But he wouldn't be there. He probably wouldn't be there.

The street was deserted, save for a single Catholic priest in a black soutane, who was walking away into the twilight. He was the third she'd seen that day. There had been one pacing for a long time in the sunlit Jardin du Luxembourg opposite her window that morning and afternoon, reading his breviary, and another crossing the Place St Germain when they'd got down from the diligence. Since Bonaparte had signed a Concordat with the Pope, and some of the churches had reopened, priests were beginning to be seen again in public places, but to Chloe, who had been only four years old when the Revolution had started, they remained something of a novelty. She glanced again after the retreating black-clad figure, and suddenly wondered . . . Could she have been watched and followed? She half-dismissed the thought, but waited until the priest turned a corner and disappeared before she crossed the street.

There was still no one else in sight. She glanced round once more, to make sure, then slipped quickly through the gap in the half-closed wrought-iron gates, hanging askew on their broken hinges, and found herself in a forecourt even more deeply shadowed than the street outside. But there was still just enough light for her to see how the paving-stones had been heaved up by the weeds growing between them, and to make out the shape of a headless stone nymph reclining at the edge of a fountain's pool, which was dry and full of rubbish and dead leaves. All the ground floor windows of the house were smashed, and not a glimmer of candlelight showed anywhere. There was only her memory of the address she'd been given to tell her that she hadn't come to a completely abandoned ruin.

The front door, at the top of a once graceful double flight of stone steps, looked as if it had been nailed up, and was probably visible from the street in any case, so she looked round for some other and more obscure entrance. In the darkest corner of the forecourt there was the opening of a passage, like the mouth of a black tunnel, which perhaps led through to the stables and the servants' quarters. Suppressing a mental echo of Persephone's screams, she made her way towards it.

Picking her way over the uneven paving-stones in her silk slippers, she must have approached very silently. There was a faint glimmer of dark grey fading daylight at the far end of the tunnel, where it debouched into an inner courtyard, or a stableyard, or a sidestreet: just enough light for her to glimpse two silhouetted figures within the tunnel, one wearing a black soutane. She drew back quietly out of sight, to one side of the tunnel's opening, and heard indistinguishable whispers, and the chink of coins. So she had been spied on – and by an agent of the royalists themselves. She ought to have remembered that many of the clergy were rumoured to be royalist sympathizers. But how careless of them to let her realize. Still, if they saw fit to spy on her, she was under no obligation to betray her knowledge of the fact. Then they would go on using Catholic priests, and she would know when she was being watched.

She waited until she heard one pair of footsteps retreating, then edged soundlessly away along the wall until she was half way back to the wrought-iron gates. Then she stepped out into the open, lifted a loose stone with her toe and sent it clattering across the forecourt, and gave a stifled but clearly audible gasp.

'This way! Over here!' came a whisper from the dark mouth of the tunnel, and she made her way back towards it again with pretended diffidence.

A figure half-detached itself from the gloom within the entrance, and she was able to distinguish the grey hair, blurred features and small stature of the Marquis de Grismont.

'Ah, there you are, my dear young lady,' he whispered. 'We meet again.' The faint grey light from the far end of the tunnel caught his small, uneven teeth as he smiled, but he didn't bow, and took her hand only to draw her in out of the forecourt. The tunnel had a dank, mossy smell.

'I'm afraid I'm a few minutes late,' Chloe began, in a tremulous, docile whisper, 'but the courtyard was so dark, and I . . . '

'Not at all, not at all,' de Grismont murmured, pushing open an unlatched door in the side of the tunnel and ushering her into a narrow, windowless corridor, where the stub of a candle, standing on a shelf in its tarnished silver holder, cast a wan, fitful light over the walls mottled with mildew and the stone-flagged floor. 'The meeting doesn't actually begin till half-past eight, so in fact you're nice and early.' He picked up the candle, and its light gleamed on his features from below as he smiled again. Chloe remembered de l'Epinay's hints about her host's having indulged in some unusual vices before the Revolution, and wondered if they were alone in the whole derelict mansion. A just audible sound, like the faint creak of a leather boot, coming from one of the dark rooms opening off the corridor, made her suspect otherwise, and de Grismont, hearing it too, quickly drew a pistol from his coat pocket and flattened himself against the wall, leaving Chloe to protect herself as she might. After a moment a small black cat emerged from the dark doorway, and arched its back against de Grismont's legs with a soft mew.

'And you must forgive this lack of ceremony, my dear,' the Marquis continued, as if nothing had happened, kicking the cat out into the tunnel and restoring his pistol to his coat pocket. 'Monsieur de Malebois had hoped to meet you in the forecourt and conduct you through the house himself, but unfortunately he was called away on urgent business at the last moment. And nowadays, alas, servants can't be trusted.'

Carrying the candle, he led the way along the corridor, past rooms which must once have been pantries and game-larders, to judge from the bare marble shelves and the great iron hooks hanging from the ceilings, which the candlelight briefly illuminated in passing. Following, Chloe warily noted the discrepancy between the actual time of the meeting and the time given her by de Malebois: that half-hour during which he had planned to 'conduct her through the house', if he hadn't been unexpectedly called away. By whom? A few paces behind de Grismont, she thought she caught another very faint sound, which might have been a sigh, or a rustle of clothing, or almost, almost, a soft laugh. But de Grismont made no sign that he had heard it, and when she glanced round over her shoulder there was nothing to be seen but the profound darkness closing up again behind them.

De Grismont pushed open a moth-eaten green baize door, and even in the faint light of the candle Chloe could ·

see that they were now in an immense main entrance hall. Black and white marble tiles, many of them cracked or broken, stretched far away into the shadows, and above the dark well of the marble staircase the wreckage of a huge chandelier dangled aslant, revolving slowly in some imperceptible draught, like a dead moth suspended from a spider's web. All the windows, as well as the great front door, were boarded up from the inside, so closely that no candlelight could show through.

'We don't use the front door, because it's visible from the street,' de Grismont explained.

'Ah, I see,' Chloe said, as if the thought hadn't occurred to her until then.

He gave her a smile which might have been merely patronizing, or might actually have been derisive – it was difficult to tell, because his features were so blurred and inconclusive – and led the way up the main staircase. Following his small figure dressed in a velvet coat and breeches of faded, threadbare olive green, with greyish lace at his cuffs, Chloe reminded herself of de l'Epinay's warning not to underestimate him. And there was certainly nothing of the timid counting-house clerk, the frightened rabbit, about him now. His words had been decisively spoken, and his eyes cold and sharp. Nor had she forgotten the speed with which he had drawn his pistol, or his ruthless indifference to her safety in what might have been a moment of extreme peril.

They climbed on past the first floor, up and up. Marble cherubs cavorted and tumbled on the bannister, seeming to leer with knowledge of sensual perversity as the candle lit them from below. There was something about de Grismont's manners towards her, Chloe reflected: a brusqueness, an absence of even the most automatic and empty gallantry, which was almost uncouth in an aristocrat . . . Perhaps the vice de l'Epinay had hinted at was of a kind which made it perfectly safe for a woman to be alone with him.

A last flight of stairs, narrow, bare and wooden, brought

them to what must once have been the domestic servants' bedrooms up in the attic. Chloe supposed it must be the safest part of the house. There was a maze of small interconnecting rooms and winding passages, where a royalist in hiding could dodge his pursuers, and there was probably an escape-route leading away over the neighbouring rooftops, as well as other internal staircases and exits into various courtyards and sidestreets. Again, as she followed a few paces behind de Grismont, she thought she heard a faint sigh or rustle in one of the dark rooms they passed, but probably it was only mice in the wainscoting, or pigeons settling down for the night under the eaves outside.

De Grismont ushered her at last into a room rather larger than the others they had passed through, though it had the same low, sloping ceiling and oval-shaped dormer windows, closely boarded up like all the rest. Several doors opened off it, perhaps into cupboards or perhaps into other rooms. There was a threadbare carpet on the floor, a narrow military camp-bed in one corner, an assortment of dilapidated chairs, and a card-table where the remains of a solitary meal – a cold chicken-leg, a few crusts of bread and half a bottle of claret – still stood amongst piles of maps and documents.

'Yes, I live here like some wretched footman,' de Grismont said, as Chloe glanced round the room. 'Still, it won't be for much longer, and then there'll be a few scores to settle – I console myself with that prospect.'

There was an unpleasant glint in his eyes, and Chloe looked away from him. Was it only last night that she had felt so proud and excited at having set fire to that curtain? And yet it had placed her in the power not only of de l'Epinay, who might be Scorpio, but also of this vicious little man and of de Malebois. What did they do to royalist agents who tried to extricate themselves from the conspiracy, or refused to carry out orders they found morally repellent? She was aware that she was still deathly calm; too calm, perhaps, as one may be when all hope is gone. Yet it

111

didn't feel like that. It felt more like the calm which had descended on her when de l'Epinay had first asked her to become his mistress, yet even deeper now: a certainty of what she believed in and would die for if necessary, even though she couldn't put it into easy words; and a cool, depthless anger; and a diamond-hard determination to win.

'I have a rather unusual assignment for you,' de Grismont said, 'which we'll discuss in private – you and I, that is, and Monsieur de Malebois, whom it also concerns. If he doesn't return before the meeting starts, be so good as to find some pretext for delaying your departure afterwards, and we'll discuss it then. There'll be persons present at the meeting itself whom one can't trust in every respect, I regret to say. And now, if you'll excuse me . . . '

He sat down at the card-table, pushed the remnants of his meal to one side and immersed himself in the perusal of some documents. He hadn't invited Chloe to be seated, so she remained standing, and then, after a moment, she began to pace thoughtfully up and down, wondering what her 'unusual assignment' might be, and whether de Grismont's remark about untrustworthy persons meant that de l'Epinay would be present after all. There was a loose floorboard under the carpet which squeaked each time she trod on it.

'Be so good as to stop pacing,' de Grismont murmured finally between his teeth, without glancing up.

'Gladly, if you'll have the manners to invite me to be seated,' Chloe said lightly.

She had paused beside a door at the far end of the room from where de Grismont was sitting. Behind it, perhaps inaudible to de Grismont, the activity of a mouse again sounded eerily like soft laughter. But there was nothing amusing about the vicious glint in de Grismont's eyes as he slowly raised his head and stared at her. 'That was foolhardy of me,' Chloe thought, guessing intuitively that he wasn't merely indifferent to women but secretly hated them, and the more desirable and spirited the woman, the more he'd hate her. She might well have made a permanent and implacable enemy of him. She returned his gaze steadily, but it was almost a relief to hear quick footsteps approaching, and to see the Vicomte de Malebois appear in the doorway.

'That damned de l'Epinay!' he began furiously, before he had even crossed the threshhold. 'I've been all the way to the Tivoli – crossing Paris at a gallop, thinking there must be some serious emergency – only to be given another message saying that he'd been called away, and that it would keep till he next saw me. I could almost swear he knew . . . '

'He didn't, however,' de Grismont said mildly, leafing through his documents. 'There's no way he could have known.'

The two men's eyes met briefly, and Chloe guessed that she had been watched all day for fear that she'd meet de l'Epinay and tell him about the meeting. Yet he'd already known about it, as if he had some other source of information unsuspected by anyone.

'Still, here we are at last!' de Malebois said, giving Chloe a warm smile. His tall, dashing, uniformed figure seemed to fill the shabby room with rapid, graceful movement and sweeping shadows as he approached her and kissed her hand, murmuring, 'You look ravishing! Perfectly ravishing! Doesn't she, Henri?'

De Grismont, still sorting out his documents, affected not to hear, and de Malebois gave Chloe a smile of covert, boyish complicity, as if to say, 'That grisly old woman-hater – take no notice of him!' 'Won't you be seated?' he said aloud, and then, after glancing round: 'Where the devil did you get these chairs, Henri – in some flea-market? Here!' And he swept off his cavalry officer's scarlet-lined cloak, which Chloe supposed he had been wearing to conceal the lavish gold braid on his uniform, and draped it over the nearest chair for her to sit on. 'There – that sets you off wonderfully!' he exclaimed, and added in a whisper, leaning closer to smooth the folds of the cloak out behind

113

her, 'I dreamt about you every minute of last night! Every single minute!'

'If you could spare me a moment of your attention . . . ' de Grismont began drily, laying down his papers in a tidy pile. But there was the sound of several pairs of footsteps approaching, and he only said quickly and quietly to de Malebois, in a tone of contemptuous command rather than of request, 'You'll stay later.'

A group of men crowded into the room, soon followed by others, until there were a score or more present, some conversing together in low tones, while others leaned back quietly in the shadows. Chloe, in her secluded corner, was the only woman amongst them. Some of the men, after giving her startled glances, had bowed to her as they'd come in, and de Malebois, sprawled gracefully at her side, one elbow resting negligently on the back of her chair and his long, lean, muscular legs stretched out, resplendent in their tight green pantaloons and highly polished riding-boots, murmured a few names to her. Others, who sidled in and sat in a bunch behind de Grismont at the far end of the room, didn't bow, and were left unidentified by de Malebois. Chloe looked round the room while de Grismont engaged a man here and there in a brief exchange of questions and answers, and made notes on some of his papers. Their faces partly illuminated by the candlelight, their shadows large on the sloping ceiling, the conspirators seemed a motley collection: army officers in fine uniforms; shabby, pinch-faced aristocrats who were obviously living in hiding; country gentlemen; and rough-looking fellows – especially those grouped behind de Grismont – who were clearly not gentlemen at all. Chloe's attention was particularly caught by two figures, a young man of twenty-five or so and a lad of about fifteen, who were sitting quietly together near the door, apart from the rest of the gathering. De Malebois had murmured the names Marignac and Trévelan earlier, as they'd bowed on entering, and Chloe guessed that they came from deeply royalist and Catholic Brittany, where fidelity to the Crown was rooted in simple piety rather than

114

in political ambition. 'If only they were all like that!' she thought, eyeing their fresh, open faces, their well-cut but unpretentious clothes, and their quiet good manners: the young man, Marignac, sturdily handsome and auburn-haired, and the lad, Trévelan, very dark and slender, like a wild young prince, with features as fine and aristocratic as de l'Epinay's. It seemed to her that the two Bretons had brought with them a genuine faith in something, as enduring as the bare moorlands and the sea they came from – far, far away from Paris, where everyone intrigued for the sake of intriguing or for the sake of money, power and social position, and where wit was valued more highly than sincerity, and where even the priests spied, and took payment for it. The lad Trévelan, in particular, had given her one or two tight-lipped glances, probably assuming that she was de Malebois' mistress, and she wondered bitterly if they knew that they, too, were sometimes spied on by priests, as they almost certainly were.

She had assumed that they were new to the conspiracy, like herself, and was astonished to hear Marignac, questioned in his turn by de Grismont, quietly giving the number of armed men under his command. It seemed as if most of the men in the room were leaders of large royalist factions in their own right, either in Paris itself or in the provinces, and she realized that together they represented many hundreds of armed insurrectionists. 'How could a mere handful of Secret Police outwit and defeat them?' she wondered. And she remembered how de l'Epinay, casually dismissing the threat of Scorpio last night at the Tuileries, had said, 'He's only one man, after all.'

'Have you news of the last shipment of arms and money from England?' de Grismont asked Marignac, and the room fell silent.

'Yes. It's to be landed near La Rochelle, at the next new moon. We're in readiness for it.'

'In ten days' time. And then another week to distribute the arms and levy more men. Which brings us to the twelfth of September. That, then, gentlemen, is the probable date of our *coup d'état.*'

A murmur, subdued but excited, broke out round the room.

De Grismont held out a thick package to Marignac, who rose and went forward to receive it.

'And these are the fully detailed plans for Bonaparte's invasion of England, which were taken from the Tuileries last night. I've checked them very thoroughly, and they comply in every detail with the intelligence we've already received. If you could see them safely into the hands of the British naval commander delivering our supplies . . . '

'I can send them across sooner than that, by fishing-boat,' Marignac said.

'So much the better.'

Watching the sturdy Breton wedge the documents securely down into an inside pocket of his brown coat, Chloe felt her heart leap with hope. De l'Epinay couldn't be Scorpio after all. If he were, he'd never have allowed such vital plans to be stolen and transmitted to the English. Whatever evidence there was against him – and it was all very tenuous and circumstantial – it was entirely cancelled out by this one fact. She had allowed the shock of General de Bourges' arrest, and Philippe's clever but prejudiced reasoning, to mislead her terribly.

'We'll leave for St Malo tonight then,' Marignac added as he returned to his seat beside young Trévelan, and Chloe wondered why, though his tone was casual, his face was suddenly wary.

'You yourself – just as you please,' de Grismont replied sharply. 'But Trévelan has a mission to carry out later this week at the Opera, as you well know.'

The silence in the room was suddenly tense. Marignac glanced watchfully at his young companion, who seemed to have shrunk back further into his chair, then said, in a quiet but firm tone, 'Trévelan has proved himself a good spy and a brave and reliable messenger, but he – '

'Spies, messengers – we've more than enough of them!' de Grismont snapped. 'Your young friend has been with us for a month now, and he's still done nothing of any real account – and you know our rules about that,' he added grimly. The group of rough-looking fellows behind him stirred and smiled. 'Two weeks ago he was given explosives to blow up that statue of Bonaparte in the Place de la Concorde,' de Grismont continued, 'and nothing – '

'The fuse – '

'Oh, the fuse, the fuse!' de Grismont said contemptuously. He took a knife out of his pocket, pressed a catch so that its blade sprang out, and began paring his nails with it. 'And why can't Trévelan speak for himself? Or is he so cowardly that he's lost his voice?'

Too late, Marignac laid a restraining hand on the lad's shoulder. Ashen pale even in the shadows, Trévelan cried out in a clear and almost steady voice, 'There's nothing more cowardly than blowing up the foyer of an opera-house when it's crowded with innocent people, and I won't do it!'

There was a deathly silence. Chloe saw with a painfully beating heart that Marignac was now resting his hand casually on the butt of his pistol. A few other men about the room – a high-ranking naval officer; a young captain of hussars; another sunburnt, clear-eyed country squire – were also idly fingering their holstered pistols or the hilts of their swords.

'The object of blowing up the foyer of the Opera does rather escape me, I must confess,' the naval officer said quickly and smoothly. 'Bonaparte himself won't be there that evening – we have reliable information on that score – and to draw so much attention to ourselves only two weeks before our *coup d'état* . . . '

'That's the whole – ' de Grismont began witheringly.

'What about de l'Epinay, by the way?'

It was Marignac who had spoken, in a quiet, conversational tone, but at once a tense hush fell.

'What about him?' de Grismont snapped.

'Well, assuming that there are good reasons for blowing up the foyer of the Opera, which clearly needs proper

117

discussion,' Marignac said pleasantly, 'de l'Epinay is the obvious man for the task. He knows far more about explosives than anyone present. And by the by,' he continued, still speaking very courteously, 'when I joined forces with the Parisian wing of the royalist movement, it was on the understanding that important decisions would be made jointly by all of us regional leaders – with you, Monsieur de Grismont, as secretary. So Monsieur de l'Epinay assured me. And he has been active in the movement for five years, while you, Monsieur, with every respect, only arrived from England last winter. I should like to know why – '

'There's reason to think he may be working for the other side,' de Grismont said flatly, still playing with his knife.

'So I understood from the message you sent me yesterday, and I've avoided mentioning this meeting to him – like everyone else, here, I deduce – as you requested. Well, no doubt you have evidence in support of this accusation, Monsieur de Grismont, and perhaps we'd better hear it at once and discuss it. Otherwise one might be tempted to believe that it's a mere fiction – a pretext for forcing through policy decisions in his absence which he would almost certainly disagree with.'

There was a murmur of agreement from some of the men in the room, while many others, de Malebois amongst them, were angrily silent. De Grismont stared at Marignac with a cold, ugly glint in his eyes; but Marignac's position was too strong, Chloe guessed: probably the shipment of arms and money from England depended on him.

'We have no concrete evidence against de l'Epinay,' de Grismont admitted reluctantly, idly gouging a small hole in the top of the card-table with the point of his knife. 'But there a growing weight of circumstantial evidence. Just now, for instance, you stated in his favour that he's been active in the royalist movement for several years. So he has, Monsieur Marignac, but where are the men who worked with him? Doesn't it strike you as curious that every time there's a wave of arrests de l'Epinay always escapes detection, and that often he's been the only man who has?'

'So it's a crime to be clever!' Marignac said, with a laugh. 'What else?'

'He was a favourite of Bonaparte's in Egypt.'

'So was Monsieur de Malebois – who also, incidentally, seems to have had a charmed life during the last two or three years.'

De Malebois smiled, recrossed his long legs, and fingered the scarlet lining of his cloak close to Chloe's shoulder.

' – Perhaps even more charmed than de l'Epinay's, since he actually risks it very frequently,' de Grismont replied drily. 'De l'Epinay never seems to do anything tangible at all.'

'Nothing tangible!' Marignac exclaimed impatiently. 'It's he who holds the whole movement together! He controls the contact between the different groups through-out the country; he organizes the distribution of arms and money; he collates all our intelligence, and he investigates all our new recruits. You might as well complain that an army commander is doing "nothing tangible" because he isn't continually off and away leading some glamorous cavalry charge.'

De Malebois recrossed his legs again, with a rather sharper movement.

' – And what else?' Marignac pursued, with a sceptical smile.

'He's been seen several times exchanging words with Honoré Turgeon – '

' – About that timber transaction, no doubt.'

'We've suspected for some time that Turgeon's a senior member of the Secret Police. You know that.'

'Yes, of course I know that,' Marignac said with a weary sigh. 'Suspicion of Turgeon, like suspicion of de l'Epinay himself, seems to circle round and come back to us again every few weeks or so, with monotonous regularity. Last spring someone even suggested that de l'Epinay might be Scorpio. But both men have been watched and followed continuously, and their homes have been searched and their servants bribed, and no shred of real evidence has ever been produced against either of them. So–' he stirred restlessly–'unless you can lay before us some definite clue, or devise some new way of uncovering one . . . '

'We have, as a matter of fact, a promising new approach to the problem of Turgeon,' de Grismont said, looking coldly down the length of the room at Chloe, so that all eyes were turned her way. 'Our young friend there has the dubious privilege of having inspired his affections, which may well lead to his committing some indiscretion . . . '

Was that her 'unusual assignment', Chloe wondered, which de Grismont had been forced to reveal to the whole gathering after all, to strengthen his own hand? Some hint of evasion in de Grismont's eyes made her doubt it. But she began to suspect, with a flutter of her heart, what her secret mission might really be.

' . . . And as for de l'Epinay, we are trying to devise some better way of keeping a check on him,' de Grismont continued, and again Chloe thought she glimpsed an evasive flicker in his eyes, 'but he does present an unusually difficult problem. You say, Monsieur Marignac, that he's been watched and followed continuously, but unfortunately that isn't the case. He's extremely difficult to follow, and he's apt to disappear completely for quite long intervals. No one knows where he goes or what he does, just as no one ever knows what he's really thinking. The truth is, as you graphically described it yourself, Monsieur, de l'Epinay seems to know everything about us, while we seem to know nothing at all about him.'

There was a sudden silence, as if no one, not even Marignac, could think of anything to say.

'Perhaps he *is* Scorpio,' Trévelan burst out.

Everyone looked at the lad, who was leaning back paler than ever in the shadows. Several men laughed, some uneasily, some derisively, while others remained silent. Marignac, after giving the boy an embarrassed glance, murmured, 'Whatever made you say that? De l'Epinay's always been wonderfully – '

'I just feel it.'

'Ah, the famous Celtic second sight!' de Grismont said sneeringly.

Marignac gave him an angry look, then said quietly to the boy, 'It's just his manner – the impression he gives of not believing in anything. I felt it too, at first. But he's – '

'Yes, but I saw him,' Trévelan said, nervously pushing back his dark forelock from his deathly pale brow, in a gesture which reminded Chloe of Philippe, and made her suddenly and inexplicably frightened. 'Last night, in the Cour des Princes. The fire was over, so I left my post in the palace gardens. I thought I'd cut through the Cour des Princes on my way back to our lodgings, and I saw a lot of Secret Police there, so I hid in the shadows. I watched them arrest General de Bourges. And de l'Epinay was there, watching too. It was very dark where he was standing, and he didn't move once or make a sound, but you can't mistake him because of his hair. He didn't see me, and I slipped away – and I can't explain why, but when I saw him I *knew* . . . '

'You should have stayed,' de Grismont said curtly. 'If he's an informer, or a double agent, or whatever he is, he'd probably have spoken to the Secret Police, or even driven away with them, and we'd have the proof we're looking for. As it is – '

'But if he'd seen me . . . '

'As it is,' Marignac cut in decisively, 'what you saw is not only entirely inconclusive, it even proves my point: that de l'Epinay's one of the most useful men we've got. Several people reported that the palace was swarming with Secret Police last night, but only de l'Epinay had the presence of mind to see that they were regrouping out in the Cour des Princes. If they'd arrested Monsieur de Malebois as he came out, or any other of our agents who were present, as they might well have done, he could have alerted the rest of us within minutes. He took a great risk, because they might have seen him, and yet he'll probably never mention the episode to us – since the man they arrested wasn't one of our agents – but that's his way.' He had turned to speak to the gathering at large, but now he looked at Trévelan again, with a persuasive smile, and added, 'Can't you see that?'

'Yes, I suppose . . . '

' – And while you were at your post in the palace gardens, you saw de l'Epinay out on the balcony, watching this young lady' – Marignac bowed towards Chloe – 'setting fire to the curtains, and he made no attempt to stop her. Did he?'

Trévelan stared down uncomfortably at his clasped hands, and shook his head.

Marignac smiled, patted the breast of his brown coat where the invasion plans were concealed, and added, 'And if he's Scorpio, how do I come to be in secure possession of these?'

The lad blushed to the roots of his hair, and said nothing.

' – Which seems to me, gentlemen,' Marignac concluded, turning back to face the rest of the gathering again, 'to be the one and only reliable fact to emerge from this discussion. I have the plans; therefore de l'Epinay cannot be working for the other side.'

There was a general murmur of agreement. Chloe felt her heart-beat begin to subside in relief. Only de Malebois drummed his fingers rapidly on the back of her chair, while de Grismont stabbed the point of his knife into the card-table again.

'That being the case,' Marignac said, in his firm, courteous way, 'I propose that we adjourn this meeting, and all important discussion of strategy, until it's convenient for de l'Epinay to attend.'

There was another murmur of agreement and a stir of movement. Then it died away to a frozen hush as a soft voice said, 'Well, there's no time like the present.' A door close to where Chloe was sitting swung open, to reveal a dark adjoining room. And in the doorway leaned de l'Epinay, a polite smile on his face and a pistol in his hand.

Nine

THE SHADOW WAS VERY DEEP in the door-recess where de l'Epinay was leaning, deadly still, and he was wearing black, so that he was scarcely visible but for the gleam of his fair hair. There was even a black silk scarf at his throat and black gloves on his hands. He gave Trévelan a strange, bleak flicker of a glance. And perhaps because he looked so much as the boy had described him in the Cour des Princes, insisting that he was Scorpio, a perceptible wave of fear went through the room. Even Marignac turned pale.

'What an instructive half-hour!' de l'Epinay remarked softly.

No one answered. The pistol in his hand, and his air of detached amusement, made it seem as if Trévelan might have been right in his intuition. The uncertainty was mesmerizing, and a hint of grim irony in de l'Epinay's smile suggested that he was aware of the fact. Before his keen gaze, men whose hands had flown to their own pistols as the door had swung open relinquished them uneasily. Only de Grismont still played idly with his knife, holding it now by the tip.

'Drop your knife on the floor, please, Monsieur de Grismont.'

After a moment's angry pause, de Grismont let his knife fall.

'And you, Vincent,' de l'Epinay murmured to de Malebois, who was sitting beside the door, his hand still resting on the back of Chloe's chair in an attitude of defiant nonchalance. 'Go and sit with your friends at the far end of the room, where I can keep an eye on you.'

With a swirl of abrupt, graceful, sulky movement, like a panther, de Malebois stood up, stalked down the length of the room with de l'Epinay's pistol trained on him, and flung himself into a vacant chair beside de Grismont. Without deflecting his wary gaze from the assembled company, de l'Epinay held out his hand to Chloe. Suppressing a shivery thrill, she gave him her fingers, and he raised them to his lips, still without looking at her. Like him, she was wearing black gloves – long black lace gloves which reached above her elbows, while his were of black leather – and it was as if the shadow of what he might be, of Scorpio, had come between them.

He released her fingers slowly, surveyed the company once more, then lowered his pistol, murmuring, *'Très bien!* You will forgive my taking such dramatic precautions, gentlemen, but when one enters a meeting of this kind uninvited, certain nervous persons are apt to let fly at one. And how pale you're all looking!' he added, with a teasing laugh. He scanned the room once more, nodding to the naval officer and to the few other men who had spoken in his favour, murmuring, 'Thank you, gentlemen ... And you especially, Marignac – I shan't forget.'

If a wave of fear had enveloped the room at his entrance, now there was a stir of relief. Only de Grismont muttered furiously to the group of rough-looking fellows behind him, 'I said there were to be two guards posted at every entrance to the house, so what the devil – ?'

'I entered the house just before eight o'clock, through the door which you yourself were guarding, Monsieur de Grismont,' de l'Epinay said, with a laugh. 'Really, it'll never do! And don't look daggers at Marignac like that – he didn't tell me of this meeting. No one did. I just couldn't help noticing that two of the gentlemen present, by a coincidence, had ailing kinsfolk to visit this evening. I made further enquiries, and found that by a strange chance everyone seemed to be engaged from half-past eight onward – except for Monsieur de Malebois, who hoped his

124

evening was going to begin at eight o'clock.' He laughed again at de Malebois' visible fury, then added in a tone of quiet contempt, 'You still have much to learn, Monsieur de Grismont.'

De Grismont gave him a look of bitter personal hatred: the same look Chloe had glimpsed on his face at the Champ de Mars, and which it was now easy to understand. But all eyes were on de l'Epinay as he continued smoothly, 'Well, and now to business, gentlemen . . . I've noted, of course, the date of our last shipment of arms and money from England.'

' – And the agents under your command will control their distribution, as usual?' the naval officer asked.

'Naturally.'

Though the chair vacated by de Malebois was just beside him, de l'Epinay was still leaning in the door-recess. Chloe wondered whether it was pride which prevented him from taking de Malebois' place at her side, or whether he was still too much on his guard against de Grismont. He was still holding his pistol casually in his hand, as if he'd forgotten it, and he remained only half-visible in the deep shadow. Perhaps it was just a trick of the wavering candlelight that made Chloe think she'd seen the hint of a private smile on his face as he'd said, 'Naturally,' or perhaps she'd imagined it altogether.

'I agree that you should leave for St Malo tonight, and get those invasion plans to England as soon as possible,' de l'Epinay continued, to Marignac. 'I suggest you leave the moment this meeting's over – it's a very urgent matter.'

Marignac nodded, but glanced uneasily first at Trévelan and then at de Grismont and his brooding supporters.

'Trévelan had better stay in Paris,' de l'Epinay said, with casual persuasiveness, though there was again a curious bleakness in his eyes. 'It's true that he hasn't really proved himself yet – Monsieur de Grismont has a point there.'

'But you surely don't mean . . ?' Marignac began, more uneasily still, while Trévelan shrank back again in his chair.

' – That he should blow up the foyer of the Opera? Why

125

not?' de l'Epinay said with apparent calm. 'Monsieur de Grismont's intention, I assume – am I right, sir? – is that we should organize a wave of explosions in public places during this last fortnight or so before the *coup d'état*, so as to undermine confidence in Bonaparte's régime – '

' – And to make it clear to the rabble that the Court, when it returns from exile, will tolerate no more nonsense,' de Grismont elaborated, looking at de l'Epinay with suspicious interest. 'That retribution will be swift, bloody and – '

'*En effet* – quite so,' de l'Epinay agreed, a trace drily. 'At any rate, an undermining of public confidence in Bonaparte seems essential, so – '

'But the people! Hundreds of people might be killed!' Trévelan cried out, while Marignac and several other of the more moderate royalists looked at de l'Epinay in bewilderment. Chloe too was astonished and horrified. Hadn't de l'Epinay assured her, with apparently deep sincerity, that he was entirely opposed to such indiscriminate violence?

'A few, perhaps,' he answered Trévelan negligently. 'But if we place the explosive under the stairs to the more fashionable boxes, the damage should be mainly confined to Bonaparte's generals and ministers and their wives and mistresses – not a very heartbreaking loss, really. And I say "we" because you clearly need more instruction about placing and detonating explosives. I suggest, as Monsieur Marignac will have left Paris, that you come and stay in my house here in the Faubourg St Germain and allow me to give you some lessons. And it would be best if you came back there with me straight away after this meeting, when Monsieur Marignac leaves for St Malo – there's little enough time to spare.' And he added, with a faint, private, bitter smile as he leant in the deep shadow of the door-recess, ' – If, that is, you've quite overcome your earlier misgivings about me.'

The lad flushed painfully but said nothing. Marignac, who had begun to look thoughtful while de l'Epinay was speaking, murmured a quick and courteous, 'That's extremely kind of you, sir – thank you,' and whispered something rapidly to Trévelan as he bent forward to adjust one of his riding-boots, Trévelan turned very pale, flashed the briefest glance at de Grismont from under his dark eyelashes, then muttered a scarcely audible, 'Yes . . . thank you very much, sir,' to de l'Epinay.

'Good. That's settled, then,' de l'Epinay said, with another smile. 'And now, gentlemen: unless you have any other matters you wish to raise . . . '

The meeting began to break up. Alone in her secluded corner, Chloe sat in a frozen daze, watching the large shadows move across the low, sloping ceiling as the conspirators, singly or in pairs and groups, stood up and left the room. Marignac, after another brief, whispered exchange with Trévelan, was one of the first to go, clapping the lad reassuringly on the shoulder. De l'Epinay, who had crossed the room to de Grismont's table, where he was casually leafing through the Marquis' notes on the numbers and dispositions of the royalist forces, only glanced up with a fleeting smile and a murmur of 'Goodbye, and good luck,' as Marignac left, taking the invasion plans with him. Trévelan leant motionless against the wall, still very pale, his dark, thick-lashed eyes glazed, as if he were seeing into some other and more shadowy world. Was de l'Epinay only pretending to agree to de Grismont's strategy of explosions, and inviting the lad to his house in order to protect him from de Grismont's vengefulness? Marignac had obviously believed so. Perhaps there were agents of de Grismont's at St Malo, or at the royalist-owned inns on the route there, which meant that Marignac couldn't have protected the boy himself. It all seemed entirely plausible; yet Chloe felt a shiver run through her as she looked at Trévelan, as if intuition were telling her that he was doomed: doomed to vanish, like General de Bourges, like anyone else who came too close to knowing that de l'Epinay was Scorpio; and what de l'Epinay had done was to manoeuvre Marignac very skilfully into delivering the boy into his hands. Yet there were the invasion plans; and unless one could explain de l'Epinay's willingness to let them be sent to England . . . But perhaps, outside this very house, or somewhere on the way to St Málo, the Secret Police would be waiting for Marignac . . .

'A penny for your thoughts.'

She glanced up with a start, to see de l'Epinay standing before her, handsomer and more elegant than ever in his black clothes, which wonderfully set off the gleaming fairness of his hair. But his shadow, like a great dark wing, enveloped the ceiling. 'He's beautiful,' Chloe thought, her heart almost failing, 'and he's terribly brave, and as clever as Lucifer – but he's as evil as Lucifer too.'

'Oh . . . there's just so much to absorb,' she said aloud, smiling at him, and thinking, 'He must never suspect that I've guessed.'

De Malebois began to saunter across the room towards them.

'I had hoped to see more of you this evening,' de l'Epinay said to her, 'but other matters have intervened, unfortunately, as you can see. Until soon.' He bowed briefly over her hand, gave her a smile which might have been evasive, or might have been bleakly preoccupied, and turned away. Trévelan, strangely resembling him in the dim candleglow, almost his young, dark replica, followed him like a sleepwalker. A few last members of the gathering drifted away too; the door closed; and Chloe was alone with de Grismont and de Malebois.

'Just make sure de l'Epinay's really gone, there's a good fellow,' de Grismont murmured, and de Malebois took one of the two remaining candles, shone it into each of the adjoining rooms, then went out into the passage. His footsteps faded away through the maze of dark, interconnecting attics in the direction of the stairs. Oppressed by de Grismont's ill-mannered silence, and the shrunken glimmer from the only remaining stump of a candle in the long, low room, Chloe rose uneasily to her feet, adjusted the looped cord of her reticule round her wrist, and smoothed her gloves. De l'Epinay must have overheard de Grismont asking her to stay behind after the meeting with de Malebois; and if he had really gone, abandoning her to the very dangers he'd warned her against – all those dark flights of stairs she'd have to descend, all those dark rooms she'd have to pass, alone with de Malebois – then it would be hard to feel he'd ever really cared . . .

A murmur of voices came from the direction of the stairs, and her heart leapt. But after a moment de Malebois returned alone, and said cheerfully to de Grismont, 'I met Albert at the top of the stairs, just coming up to tell you that de l'Epinay's definitely left the house. He was seen walking away up the street with young Trévelan. I've given orders to keep all the doors closely guarded, in case he tries to come back, so . . . ' He gave Chloe a smile of stealthy charm in the light of the candle he was still carrying. 'Here we are, safe from all interruptions to our little *tête-à-tête*. Won't you be seated?'

'Thank you, no,' Chloe said coolly. 'My cousin's waiting for me outside, and it's late, so I should be obliged not to be kept any longer than necessary.'

She swung on her heel, turning her back on him with studied casualness, but bit her lip in trepidation. She had thought earlier how weak de Malebois was, as well as vain, and had even wondered if she might be able to make use of him in some way by flattering him. But what help would flattery be, on the way down those dark flights of stairs? And as for de l'Epinay: she had to make her heart and her instincts understand that she couldn't take refuge in his protection. Even if he'd been there, he was far more dangerous than de Malebois. She knew what de Malebois wanted of her; but de l'Epinay, if she ever betrayed what she'd guessed by a word, by the merest hint of a facial expression, would probably kill her. Even if he cared for her, in his way – and that was in doubt now – he would have to kill her. And he was so acutely perceptive that her only hope of survival now lay in avoiding him.

' . . . Well, even de l'Epinay can't be in two places at once,' de Grismont was saying drily. 'He's curiously attached to young Trévelan, and of course he knows what will happen to him if that explosion at the Opera doesn't take place.'

How little they'd understood of de l'Epinay's real motives for taking the boy off with him, Chloe realized – if she was right, as she surely was. But then of course only she knew. . .

'Why was General de Bourges arrested?' she asked, turning to face the two men. 'Do you know?'

De Grismont shrugged. 'Our information is that he was misappropriating Army funds. What else can one expect of a mere shopkeeper's son? Why do you ask?'

'I just wondered.'

Yes, only she knew the real reason: that General de Bourges had stumbled too close to the truth about de l'Epinay – like that friend of Uncle Victor's at the Tuileries, like Trévelan. She ought to share her knowledge with de Grismont and de Malebois, of course, and then . . . and they they'd kill de l'Epinay. She turned away again, to hide her face. Could she ever bring herself to betray him?

'You'll have deduced, Mademoiselle, that our suspicions about de l'Epinay remain unallayed, whatever we pretended,' de Grismont said, speaking in a dry, toneless voice and fixing his gaze on a point slightly to one side of her, as if she were a mere servant-girl. De Malebois began to pace gracefully back and forth, passing close to her, and still smiling thoughtfully to himself in spite of her having snubbed him. 'But we need proof,' de Grismont continued, 'and that's where you have a useful role to play.'

Chloe's heart nearly stopped, though she had suspected earlier what her 'unusual assignment' might be. But that had been before she'd become certain that de l'Epinay was Scorpio.

"De l'Epinay's clearly taken a strong fancy to you,' de Grismont went on, looking at her for a moment as if they were discussing some singularly repellent aberration, of which she was the cause. 'And that's very unlike him; very significant. I've always understood that he's avoided serious entanglements with women during the past several years –'

'Society women, anyway,' de Malebois said. 'But as for chambermaids and so on, you know . . . '

'Precisely,' de Grismont cut him short irritably, shuffling his papers. Chloe wondered in passing if his hatred of de l'Epinay wasn't partly a case of sour grapes. 'At all events, Mademoiselle,' he continued, 'you're in a unique position – or you must waste no time in placing yourself therein – to get the proof we need against de l'Epinay. He's bound to drop his guard with you, and let some word slip, or you can go through his pockets while he's asleep. We'll give you something to put in his champagne.'

There was a moment's silence, so deep that Chloe thought the beating of her heart must be audible. Words failed her, and de Malebois too, for some reason, paused in his pacing and stood motionless.

'That's hardly what I understood you to be planning,' he said to de Grismont, with icy politeness, and Chloe was glad to be given a moment in which to collect herself. 'You agreed, the last time we spoke about it, that to keep de l'Epinay on tenterhooks, and to play on his jealousy – '

'True, true, so I did,' de Grismont said indifferently. 'But we've seen this evening how far he still is from losing command of himself, and there's very little time, with that shipment of arms arriving so soon. So our young friend here will have to spy on him very closely, and there's only one way . . . After all, isn't it in the flush of conquest that a man's most likely to betray himself?'

De Malebois turned on his heel in a furious silence, and began to prowl the room again, fuming.

'Besides,' de Grismont added mildly, 'if you provoked him enough, I wouldn't put it past him to call you out.'

'Let him!'

'Yes, but you can't practise your expert sword-play on him, can you, because of his lameness? You'd have to use pistols, and you know what a crack shot he is. He'd simply blow your brains out, if you've got any.'

De Malebois threw himself angrily into a chair by way of answer. His silence seemed to concede the point to de Grismont, which was surprising, for there was no doubt that he was a brave man. But perhaps it was a measure of de l'Epinay's reputation as a marksman. And perhaps that was why Manon de Malebois' field-marshal had been so hastily deflected from challenging him.

'Well?' de Grismont said in a peremptory tone, turning to her.

As once or twice before, a depthless calm seemed to have descended on Chloe, and she had been listening to the two men as if from a great distance – as well she might have, since they had been discussing her as if she were a mere parcel. Many thoughts had passed through her mind, amongst them the hope that this turn of events might at least save her from de Malebois. But from his sombre, brooding silence in the shadows, it seemed all too likely that he'd seize the first opportunity to get his revenge.

'What if I don't care to become de l'Epinay's mistress?' she answered de Grismont coolly, and added for good measure, ' – Or anyone else's.'

'You should have thought of that before you committed yourself to our cause. What else did you expect? Men plan strategy, and fight, while women . . . ' De Grismont gave her a withering stare, then returned to arranging his papers, adding, 'I shall give you three days, and then I shall want regular reports from you. And if I'm not satisfied . . . Well, you can guess how we deal with unsatisfactory agents.'

Chloe was silent. It was only ten days ago that she had looked at herself in her bedroom mirror, and laughed, and said to Philippe, 'I hardly think they'll only want me to hold some cart-horse's head!' yet it seemed like a hundred years. But at least she'd been given a little while – three days – in which to think, and tell herself that she wasn't dreaming, and perhaps devise some means of escape. Meanwhile she must seem to comply.

132

'How am I to make my reports?' she asked.

'To one of our agents – a gipsy who sells lavender on the Pont des Arts. Ask for lilies: that's the password. She in turn will give you any information or directives we may wish to convey to you.'

It was a clever arrangement, Chloe realized. The Pont des Arts, a pretty footbridge recently built by Bonaparte across the Seine by the Palais du Louvre, had become one of the most fashionable viewing-points and meeting-places in Paris. She could pass the lavender-seller three or four times in a day without arousing the slightest suspicion in anyone.

'Oh, and find out anything you can from Turgeon, if the opportunity arises,' de Grismont said, pausing from numbering the pages of his notes. 'And there's this.'

He took a phial from his coat pocket and held it out to her. It was identical in size and shape to the last she'd been given, but contained a reddish-brown liquid, the colour of dried blood.

'What is it?' Chloe asked, holding the phial in her palm, and watching the liquid change from topaz to amber and then to ruby in the candlelight, like blood liquefying again.

'Opium. It has a bitter taste, which de l'Epinay might recognize, so you'd be better advised to sprinkle a few drops on his pillow, close to his face, when he's asleep, or on your handkerchief ... And if you then poured the remainder down his throat, you could be fairly certain of killing him, if the need arose.'

The crimson liquid seemed to wink malevolently at Chloe as the candlelight flickered, and she closed her fingers quickly over it.

'That will be all,' de Grismont added, still absorbed in his notes. De Malebois stirred with stealthy grace in the shadows. 'Oh, and if you need to be escorted down through the house in the dark,' de Grismont murmured, glancing up with a knowing, vindictive little smile, 'I'm sure Monsieur de Malebois will be only too glad to oblige.'

Ten

IT WAS AS BLACK AS THE PIT in the passage as Chloe stepped out
of the room, past de Malebois who was holding the door
open for her with a silent flourish. Then he followed her,
closing the door quietly behind him, and they were alone.

'So sometimes dreams come true, after all!' he murmured,
holding his candle high so as to contemplate her, and
giving her an amorous smile which didn't reach his eyes.
His gaze remained cold and predatory, dark with the vain
malice de l'Epinay had warned her about. And what use was
it to her that his character was weak, when he was so tall,
and with all a cavalry officer's lithe strength in his build?
She supposed that the more he was dominated by other
men – by de Grismont, and de l'Epinay – the more he
vented his malice on women to settle the score.

All the same, she thought, turning away from him
quickly as he smiled again, she must keep calm, and plan.
The candle only lit up a pace or two of bare floorboards and
dingy, peeling walls ahead of her as she walked towards the
stairs, de Malebois following silently, and beyond its dim,
wavering glow everything was engulfed in a total and
unknown blackness, unrelieved by any light from the
streetlamps outside, or even by starlight, since all the
windows were so closely boarded up. It was like a tomb. If
she obeyed the impulse of her racing heart, and ran, it
would only be into that smothering blackness, that invisible
maze of winding passages, cupboards like rooms and
rooms like cupboards, and ruinous staircases with broken
bannisters. Worse still, if de Malebois pursued her the

134

candle might blow out, and then he would grope till he found her in the darkness. So she must think. He wasn't very intelligent, so it might be possible to outwit him somehow. And meanwhile she must betray no impulse to resist, and no fear.

He remained silent, too silent, as they went down the first narrow flight of stairs, and made no attempt even to take her hand. But of course there were at least three more flights to descend; she had forgotten how many. And he must know the house well: where there were rooms with furniture still in them; sofas, or even beds.

She forced herself to unclench her trembling fingers, and became aware that she was still clasping the phial of opium in one of her hands. If she could only think of some pretext for unscrewing the stopper, which might be very tight, and taking out her handkerchief, without arousing his suspicion . . . But it was as if fear had frozen her mind: no idea came to her. And anyway, it was probably just what he was expecting her to do.

'So you're not looking forward to your mission?' he said, with an insinuating smile in his voice, slowing his step as they approached the main staircase. The candlelight gleamed faintly on a curve of white marble balustrade, picking out the smirk of a fat cupid. Below, the stairwell yawned black and bottomless. 'That's a great consolation to me,' de Malebois continued. 'But of course there are far deeper consolations . . . ' His hand stealthily encircled her arm. 'This is an historical old house. Come, let me show you – '

'What's that?' Chloe exclaimed in a sharp whisper of alarm, leaning over the balustrade without attempting to free herself from him.

'What's what?'

'Ssssh! I heard a noise.'

'There's nothing – '

'Ssssh! Listen!'

They listened. The silence was like that of the grave. Chloe supposed it had only been a fancy of her strained nerves, only a vain shred of hope: that sound she'd thought she'd caught, like the sigh of clothing or breathing, like the faint creak of leather, from somewhere not far below. All the same, she said in an urgent, conspiratorial whisper, 'There's someone down there. I can hear breathing.'

'Well, I can't,' de Malebois said, with a laugh, running his fingers caressively up her arm. 'It's just your imagination. Anyone would suppose you were afeared of our being discovered here together.'

Her complicit whispering, and her failure to struggle free of him, had obviously lulled him a little, and his hold on her arm was sinuously persuasive now rather than compelling. 'Well... naturally,' she managed to answer, in a dallying tone. Her mind was still a frozen blank, empty of any subterfuge which might save her, but she daren't provoke him into using force.

'Come in here, then – we'll lock the door,' he murmured, drawing her towards the open doorway of some black room, his face stealthily ardent in the candlelight.

'But it smells musty,' she said, shrinking back on the threshhold, and managing a merely fastidious tone, though she had turned cold all over. Only an intense effort of will stopped her from trembling perceptibly, from screaming, from running headlong down the dark stairs. She should have yielded to de l'Epinay, whatever he was, and then he wouldn't have abandoned her. Anything would have been better than this casual rape. 'And it's cold, too. And I'm hungry. I'd far rather we went to your house, and supped together...' She forced herself to lace her fingers invitingly through his, drawing him back from the room, though she had to turn her face away as she did so. ' ... And everything.'

'So would I, so would I,' de Malebois said, beginning to pull her more insistently into the room. 'But once we've left this house we'll be watched, and – orders are orders – we shan't even be able to waltz together again, never mind –'

'Look! Look there!' Chloe hissed, in another petrifying whisper, pointing towards the stairs.

She startled de Malebois enough for him to loosen his grip on her, and she slipped free. As he followed her towards the head of the stairs, the candlelight shone on a pair of eyes staring at them from just below: a pair of unblinking, disembodied eyes, like blank discs of green glass. There was a faint, squeaky mew.

'There – I told you I heard something!' Chloe said triumphantly, as the small black cat arched its back against her legs. And then, to hide her excitement at the idea which had just struck her, she scooped it up in her arms and stroked it lavishly, murmuring, 'There, then! Come to Mama!'

'It's just a stray, you know, which keeps getting into the house,' de Malebois said, stepping back a pace. 'It's probably full of fleas. Do – '

'Yes, but don't you see? I can try out . . . ' Chloe began. But the first thing was to get away from that terrible black room. She gave the cat's tail a surreptitious tweak, so that it leapt from her arms and fled down the stairs. 'Quick!' she whispered, snatching the candle from de Malebois' hand and making off after the cat as swiftly as she dared.

He overtook her on the turn of the wide marble staircase, catching her arm this time in a vice-like grip. 'What the devil – ' he began furiously.

'Ow, you're hurting me!' she whispered, writhing her arm seductively to and fro, and giving him a promising smile. 'It won't take long.'

'What won't take long?'

'The cat. I want to try this out on it.' She opened her hand to reveal the phial of opium, and forced herself to lean trustingly closer to him, whispering, 'I don't trust him – the Marquis de Grismont – you see. It might be much more dangerous than he says.'

'So much the better.'

'Yes, but I may have to use it on my cousin, or even my aunt and uncle, so as to get away. Here – open it for me, while I . . . ' She handed him the phial, and slipped off again down the stairs faster than ever, shielding the flame with her free hand and calling, 'Puss! Puss!'

Reaching the next landing, she paused and looked around. More black doorways opened off a wide corridor, and the marble statues threw deep, large, half-human shadows, moving as the candle flickered. Its light gleamed on a curve of the white balustrade further down the stairwell, and then, with ghostly dimness, on another curve still further down, descending into an endless darkness. The cat mewed somewhere nearby, and after a moment she saw it emerge from a crevice of shadow between two statues, arching its back against the pedestal of one of them, and watching her with cautious flirtatiousness. She would have to drug the poor creature, she supposed, if she could catch it again, and then, somehow, soak her handkerchief with opium a second time, much more liberally, without de Malebois' noticing. He had followed her down the stairs with a surprisingly casual step, and now stood before her with a smoothly obliging smile on his face, although his eyes, as ever, were only cold and dark. A shiver of some nameless intuition crept over Chloe.

'There!' he said pleasantly, twisting the screw top of the phial half a turn. 'Anything to oblige a lady. Better not open it just yet, though.'

'No . . . Well, you just catch the cat, and I'll get out my handkerchief . . . '

Chloe held out her hand for the phial, but he moved it beyond her reach. 'No, no, *you* catch the cat,' he said, with another suavely charming smile. 'And I – ' he took out his own folded white handkerchief – 'I'll be the apothecary.'

Chloe spun away to hide her face. Had he guessed that she'd been planning to use the opium as a weapon against him? And what did he mean to do now? Another shiver of intuition told her. Helplessly, moving as if in a dream, she went slowly towards the cat, not knowing what else to do. There was no possible escape now, and the irony was too cruel: that she had resisted de l'Epinay, whom she'd at least loved, for the sake of an ideal, only to be subjected to this most total violation. The cat still flirted timidly with her a

138

few paces away, arching its back against the feet of a succession of statues. Meaninglessly she whispered, 'Puss!' and the echo of her whisper in the cold, empty darkness sounded as wretched as the cat's answering mew.

Still arching its back caressively, the cat slipped round the edge of a doorway into one of the dark rooms. Behind her, de Malebois gave a soft laugh.

With pretended casualness, Chloe stood in the doorway, so that the candle shone its low light into the room. Perhaps there would be a vase, or a broken chair – anything that she might try to defend herself with. Her gaze travelled over torn wall-hangings; a four-poster bed in the shadows at the far end – it was a long room – with a bare, stained mattress on it; a wardrobe gaping open, with a few rags tumbling out at its foot; a chest of drawers . . .

An insidious odour, cloying yet bitter, began to steal over her senses. For an instant she imagined that it was emanating from the room – then she spun round with a gasp. De Malebois had crept up silently behind her, and she found herself staring into his black, level eyes, and at the handkerchief in his raised hand. 'Two can play at your little game,' he whispered, no longer smiling at all. 'And besides, it would be such a bore if you kept struggling.'

With an involuntary sob of terror, Chloe fled down the room towards the chest of drawers, where she thought she'd seen . . . But it wasn't. She thought she'd seen something like a pewter candlestick, too broken or bent to have been taken by the looters, but it must have been only a shadow. She turned round and leaned back against the chest of drawers, her limbs as weak as in a nightmare, and watched de Malebois approach her, a calm, cold smile on his face. The handkerchief glimmered very white in his hand as he began to emerge slowly out of the wavering, flickering shadows, entering the circle of candlelight where she was standing. She wanted to scream, but she couldn't. Everything seemed unreal – so unreal that she could only gaze uncomprehendingly as the shadows moved behind him with sudden, violent swiftness, and then, very slowly and silently, he began to fall. He sank to his knees. Then he pitched forward and lay face-down on the floor, utterly still.

Staring down at him, still unable to move, or to understand what had happened, Chloe only gradually became aware of a dark figure standing in the shadows just outside the ring of candlelight. Then slowly she made out the glint of a pistol, still held by its barrel in a black-gloved hand, and a gleam of fair hair. Yet for a moment longer de l'Epinay remained as silent as she did, and as motionless. Then he smoothed back his hair with calm black fingers, and murmured, 'He may be dead. I hit him rather hard.'

Everything still seemed as unreal as a dream to Chloe, yet she wondered distantly if he could really be as unmoved as he seemed. It was strange that he didn't approach her, or even come forward into the candlelight.

The cat appeared from out of the shadows somewhere, and arched its back against de l'Epinay's legs with a welcoming, passionate trill.

'Were you there all the time?' Chloe asked, suddenly angry.

De Malebois stirred, moaned, then lay still again. Bending over him, de l'Epinay didn't answer for a moment; then he said, without looking up, 'Yes, I'm afraid I was. I couldn't make out at first what was happening. It sounded as if . . . as if my intervention might not have been entirely welcome. I'd have left, but I felt I had to be sure.' There was another silence; then he added, still examining de Malebois, 'You've succeeded in making me dislike myself intensely, although I dare say it'll pass.' He released de Malebois' wrist and straightened up, saying in a much lighter tone, 'Well, he has a wonderfully thick skull.'

His eyes met hers, very briefly, for the first time, then flickered quickly away. Chloe had a fleeting intimation of how he might have felt, concealed somewhere in the dark amongst the statues, listening to her apparently wanton whispers to de Malebois: how he might have hated his own aptitude for becoming invisible, and despised himself for

140

the jealous uncertainty which had reduced him to a peeping tom. But this insight was only momentary. Anger returned, although she knew remotely that there was something wrong with her feelings, and that it wasn't really anger which was making her tremble.

'I'm not flattered at what you assumed,' she said sharply. 'You should have known I daren't offer him open resistance.'

'Yes, yes, of course – I do apologize,' he murmured. 'I . . . My judgement was confused.' He bent and stroked the cat, which was reaching up lovingly to him, its forepaws resting on his knee, and added, in an undertone she scarcely caught, 'But after the way you waltzed with him . . . '

'So you did stay a while, then, at the ball!'

'Only a moment. I just happened to catch sight of you as I was leaving.'

Chloe guessed that he had stayed much longer, concealed in an alcove somewhere, watching them in spite of himself, though he would never admit it.

'You encouraged him – you're a flirt,' he said, and she could tell from his voice that he too was angry now, though he still didn't look up. 'Do you wonder that I don't – '

'If you'd stayed properly,' she cut him short furiously, 'and if you'd – if you'd ever been really with me, instead of spying on me, and being so . . . so . . . '

'Spying on you!' he said, straightening up sharply.

' – And being so cynical – you'd have known how I really felt.'

'Cynical!'

Chloe met the blue ice of his gaze, and reminded herself to be careful; not to forget what he was even for an instant. But it was somehow difficult to remember. Her hand, holding the candle, seemed to be trembling more and more, as if of its own volition, and its palpitant light made everything as strange as in a fever: de Malebois' prone form on the floor; the gutted room; the blackness of the house surrounding them like a mausoleum. The only reality was de l'Epinay, dazzlingly handsome in anger – and in something more than anger: passion, perhaps, or pain. His gaze

141

moved to the candle trembling in her hand, then back to her face. 'I had to get Trévelan to safety,' he said unevenly. 'If I hadn't taken him under my protection they might have killed him. I was only gone for a few minutes, and I thought of you every second – every second of that time. And as for my being cynical: if you only knew, these last few days, how little I . . . how much I . . . '

He broke off abruptly, swinging distractedly away.

Chloe nodded, and her eyes filled suddenly with blinding tears. She heard de l'Epinay say, 'You're going to drop that,' and felt him take the candle from her hand and set it down on the chest of drawers behind her; felt the hood of her black lace pelisse brush his face. And then she felt him scoop her powerfully close in his arms, and she was shaking so violently she couldn't tell if he was really shaking too, only that he was raining kisses on her face: kissing her eyes, kissing away her tears. She let her arms slide round his neck and clung to him blissfully as he whispered, 'You're a torment to me, day and night – a beautiful, terrible torment, and I can't resist . . . ' He trailed off, pursuing a tear to the corner of her mouth, and she heard him gasp. For an instant his parted lips touched hers – and then his hands were suddenly brusque as he took her head between them, and pressed her face quickly against his shoulder. For a moment she could still feel him breathing fast; then he stroked her head slowly and gently, as if to calm both of them down. 'My brave girl,' he murmured finally, in a matter-of-fact voice. 'You've had a nasty fright, and so have I. Come – we need a little cognac to fortify us.' He released her and stepped back, giving her a smile in which she could detect a hint of evasiveness. 'And besides,' he added, 'this isn't at all the right setting for our first kiss.'

'He was so detached and inhuman,' Chloe said, looking down for a moment at de Malebois and then straight at de l'Epinay, to make sure there would be no misunderstandings over her momentary yielding to him. 'Whatever I'd felt about him, I could never . . . '

'En effet,' de l'Epinay murmured with another smile, dry and wary, as he turned away.

142

Was he Scorpio? Probably not, Chloe thought, but all the same he was incorrigible.

De Malebois stirred and moaned again. De l'Epinay put out his foot, and pushed the prone man's arm until the handkerchief still clutched in his hand was resting against his nose and mouth. 'Sweet dreams!' he murmured. Then, holding out to Chloe the phial of opium, which he must have taken from de Malebois' pocket while he was examining him, he added casually, 'By the way, I believe this belongs to you.'

Eleven

THEY WERE BOTH SILENT as they followed the great white marble flight of stairs down and down through the dark house, Chloe carrying the candle and de l'Epinay his pistol. Chloe's mind was racing. How much did de l'Epinay know about her mission? Could he have returned to the house quickly enough to reach the attic and eavesdrop on her conversation with de Grismont? It hardly seemed possible. Perhaps he had merely guessed that such a mission was bound to be assigned to her. Or perhaps, in spite of his jealous anguish, he had been able to deduce it from her whisperings with de Malebois, although thinking back she was sure that they had said very little, and had not mentioned any name. Yet intuition told her that de l'Epinay knew. Something about the way he'd looked as he'd given her back the phial had conveyed as much. So, even while he had been holding her so passionately in his arms . . . Oh, was there no limit to his astuteness and his duplicity? And when would she remember that it was when he seemed most human, and most to be trusted, that he was at his most dangerous?

He was a few paces behind her as they descended the stairs, and she paused for a moment on one of the turnings to look back at him: a figure as sinister as he was handsome. He was moving with easy, soundless grace in spite of his limp, and his face was keenly alert yet also very calm, his pistol held casually raised in his hand – not pointed at her, but not away from her either. She thought of the amused coolness with which he had given her back the phial of

144

opium, and his significant failure to comment on it. As if reading her thoughts, he gave her an enigmatic smile, and she turned away and walked on. Yes, he was Scorpio, after all. He must be Scorpio.

When they reached the entrance hall, where the black and white diamond tiles seemed to stretch away for ever into the darkness, de l'Epinay guided Chloe through a succession of once elegant but now ruined reception rooms, in the opposite direction from the way she had come in.

'My cousin –' she began, wondering where he was taking her.

'Ssssh!' He put his finger to his lips, then gave her another cryptic smile, motioning her on with his pistol.

Did he realize what she suspected? Her mouth dry, she remembered that she too had said nothing on the subject of the phial of opium when he'd returned it to her: a silence no less significant than his. They continued on through more drawing-rooms and ante-chambers, and then through another maze of dark passages. She listened to his quiet footsteps behind her, with their haunting, faintly uneven rhythm: a graceful lilt, a hesitation, rather than a limp. Was it the last sound she'd ever hear before she vanished off the face of the earth? The last sound General de Bourges had ever heard, and perhaps Trévelan too?

'Mind the step,' he murmured, as the night sky at last glimmered dark blue and starlit beyond the black frame of an open doorway ahead of them. His hand lightly touching her arm, he guided her over and round the motionless forms of two men sprawled on the passage floor just inside the door, one face down and the other face up. There was no time to see whether they were dead or merely unconscious.

They stepped out into a cobbled stableyard. De l'Epinay went across it to an archway opening on to a sidestreet, and whistled softly. In spite of her fear of the unknown future, Chloe stood for a moment looking up in gratitude at the millions of stars, and breathing in the fresh, fragrant night air. A stir of light breeze caressed her face. It was so good to be alive and free, even if it was only for a few minutes.

There was the muted sound of approaching horses' hoofs and carriage wheels out in the street, and a quiet jingle of harness. De l'Epinay beckoned her to the archway, his pistol still in his hand. She went obediently to his side – where else could she go? – and saw a fine carriage drawn up outside. It was the one of the new, very fast cabriolets, drawn by four matched thoroughbred greys. The starlight glistened on the satin-sleek whiteness of their arched necks, and on the blue paintwork of the carriage, with its coat of arms on the door, and its black and silver wheels. The coachman and the guard were dressed in blue and silver livery, and as far as Chloe could tell in the shadows they were dark-skinned and sloe-eyed, as if they might be Levantines. De l'Epinay murmured something she didn't catch to the coachman as he handed her up into the interior, which was deeply padded in soft grey or grey-blue suede with silver studs.

'Where are you taking me?' she asked, catching her breath at a sudden memory of the mural in the Café des Artistes. True, Pluto's carriage had been gold, and drawn by black horses, but all the same . . .

Swinging himself up beside her and closing the door, de l'Epinay didn't answer. He tapped lightly on the panelling with the head of his cane, and the cabriolet set off at a breathtaking speed.

'Where are we going?' Chloe asked again, keeping her voice level with an effort. The carriage swayed deeply on its springs as they careered round a corner into a wider street, then went faster than ever.

'Oh . . . just round in circles, for the time being,' de l'Epinay answered. He moved so that he was sitting opposite her, with his back to the horses, deep in the shadows of one corner while the light of the streetlamps they were passing fell on her only. All the same, she saw him give a strange little smile.

'But what about my cousin? He's been waiting – '

'Don't worry about your cousin. I saw to him hours ago.'

'Saw to him?' Chloe turned cold all over.

De l'Epinay watched her for a moment, his face unreadable in the shadows, then he said, 'I sent him a message to say that you'd be delayed. To the best of my knowledge, he's still in the café where you left him, playing *vingt-et-un* with three of my men, who will naturally have discouraged him from risking his life by trying to enter the house in search of you, or from wandering off anywhere. They're also protecting him from being taken by de Grismont's ruffians, and held as a hostage against your good behaviour – a possibility which couldn't be ruled out. Whatever did you think I meant?'

Chloe understood well enough that Philippe was under a very polite and veiled form of arrest, and wondered if he realized it. But she said, in a helpless, shaken voice, not difficult to assume, 'I don't know ... I didn't mean anything. But if you won't even tell me where we're going – '

'But we're already there,' he said softly.

The cabriolet crossed the Place St Germain, turned into another sidestreet by the church, and slowed down under the massive medieval walls of the notorious Abbey Prison – notorious for the massacres committed there during the Terror, and rumoured now to be where the Secret Police interrogations were carried out. Fortunately Chloe was too numb with fear to cry out and betray herself completely, for the cabriolet drove on a little way, then turned into the forecourt of a big house on the opposite side of the street.

A great linden stood in the centre of the forecourt, its leaves a dark flicker against the gold globes of the lamps beneath it. The warm light of chandeliers also spilled out from many of the windows, and Chloe could see that both the courtyard and the house had been restored to their *ancien-régime* elegance. The lighted windows gave glimpses of rich curtains and beautiful furniture within. It was de l'Epinay's town house, of course, and it was true that they had driven almost in a circle; on foot, via a maze of narrow alleys, it probably was only a stone's throw from the house they'd just left.

She supposed she should have known he'd bring her here, now that he'd guessed that she scarcely had any choice but to become his mistress. Hadn't he said, in that sordid, looted room where de Malebois lay unconscious, 'This isn't at all the right setting for our first kiss'? And hadn't he placed Philippe under guard, telling him that she would be delayed?

She looked at him in trepidation, but also in a melting, traitorous thrill which wouldn't be suppressed. Yet he only continued to lean back motionless in his shadowy corner, watching her with that same strange, faint smile.

And afterwards? She looked out through the arched entrance of the forecourt at the grey prison walls across the street, their bleak height unrelieved even by any barred windows; only by dark cascades of creeper here and there, like something dripping. How easy for de l'Epinay to have had an underground tunnel excavated under the street, leading from his own cellars to those of the prison. Thus he could come and go undetected; thus visitors to his house, if occasion required, could vanish after they had been entertained. She wondered if de Grismont had ever thought of it.

As she gazed, a figure in a black soutane separated itself from the deep shadow of the creeper on the prison wall, and slipped quickly away along the street. Gone to report to de Grismont, she supposed, that she was already carrying out her mission.

The front door of the house had opened, meanwhile, and a liveried servant came down the steps. As he approached the carriage window, Chloe saw that he too was a Levantine. She supposed de l'Epinay employed them because they were more discreet.

'Cognac, and two glasses,' de l'Epinay said; and then, to Chloe: 'Are you hungry? I dare say there's some cold pheasant or something.'

She shook her head.

'Just the cognac, then.'

'*Oui,* Monsieur le Comte . . . You mean out here, Monsieur le Comte?'

'Yes, out here.'

The man retreated without a flicker of expression on his smooth, olive-skinned face. But he must have been used to de l'Epinay's coming home now and then with some pretty waif or stray from the boulevards, his guest for a night, or for an hour.

'It's late, and I mustn't keep you,' de l'Epinay explained casually, after the man had gone. 'And I have much to do . . . It's only a shop-front, really,' he added, seeing Chloe's eyes travel over the lighted windows of the house. 'I just camp there, rather like de Grismont. There are hundreds of rooms I've had to leave locked up.' He put his head out of the window and murmured to the coachman, 'Just move forward a pace or two . . . Good! You two can go in and have a drink yourselves. Send a lad to hold the horses, and be ready to come when I call you.'

He relapsed into his corner, which was darker than ever now that the carriage had been moved forward a few paces, while the glow from the lamps under the linden fell full on Chloe's face. Why didn't he want her in his house? He had made too many excuses, of course, so there was some other reason which he was concealing. Because Trévelan still lay hurriedly stabbed or strangled there? Or perhaps still under guard, awaiting his fate? There was no sign of him through any of the windows. The manservant returned with the cognac and the two glasses on a silver tray, and Chloe watched de l'Epinay pour their drinks with his calm, black-gloved fingers, then lean back again in his corner. And why did he want to be in the darkness? Why didn't he even take off his gloves and his black silk scarf? Nothing could be seen of him now but the faint gleam of his hair, and the subtle dark lustre of his eyes. It was as if for some reason, though he wanted her to be with him, he craved total invisibility.

'I doubt I shall be able to see you for the next two days,' he said eventually, and something in his tone told her that he had been contemplating her during their quite long silence. 'I can't neglect . . . Trévelan can't be left alone; it's

149

something of a contretemps. And there's that shipment of arms arriving . . . In short, there's too much happening at once.'

It was the first time Chloe had ever heard him sound so ruffled and uneasy; and there was an undertone in his voice which suggested that he had more causes for disquiet than he had named.

But could he be telling the truth about Trévelan? If he was . . . Oh, if only she could have some proof, one way or the other, about de l'Epinay!

'You're not really going to blow up the Opera?' she asked, to try to make him say more.

'Not I. But Trévelan will – under my tuition. I see no choice. One can minimize the damage a great deal, of course.'

Chloe thought fleetingly of how quickly her fire at the Tuileries had been put out, and a panic discreetly prevented by those polite-faced, dark-clad men.

'But couldn't you send him to England, if he's in such danger?'

'That has its hazards too. Most of the *émigrés* there are extremists, and now that he's declared himself against them . . . Or I could spirit him away into hiding here in France – I've places where that can be done. But then there's a risk . . . Well, it's a long story. Everything will be all right if he just does as I tell him at the Opera.'

' – You'll be there?'

'Of course.'

It all sounded too involved to be a fabrication. If there really was an explosion at the Opera in two days' time, and she saw Trévelan afterwards, alive and free, then she might after all believe . . .

'And you think he'll do it?' she asked aloud.

'If I can persuade him to trust me. At the moment I've even had to lock him in his room. He's having an attack of Celtic second sight, if you remember.'

'Ah yes,' Chloe said, with a smile, wishing the lamplight wasn't falling so directly on her. She daren't even swallow, for fear he'd see her throat move. Could he have made that remark just so that he could study her reaction? Was that why he had placed her where the lamplight fell, and himself in darkness? – so that he could carry out the most subtle and veiled inquisition?

Not too quickly, she took refuge in her cognac, and a silence fell. Still he said nothing about her mission; nor did she. Every continuing second of her silence about it, she knew, was telling him what it was. But although she couldn't see him, she could sense a palpable and growing disquiet in him. If he could play on her nerves by remaining silent, so could she play on his.

'You haven't much to say,' he murmured finally, with a little laugh.

'Well, I can't see you.'

'True.' He took her empty glass from her, though without emerging from the deep shadow, and their gloved fingers touched. 'You're not very visible yourself tonight, though, are you?' he added, and she supposed he was referring to her black lace pelisse, which shadowed her face and veiled her *décolleté*, as well as to her long gloves. He withdrew his fingers from hers only slowly and caressively, and she thought she detected a faint tremor in his voice.

A passionate thrill swept through her, taking her unawares. Her head swam at the memory of his hard, lithe body against her only a little while ago, and the touch of his parted lips on hers. Another moment, and she could have run her fingers through his hair, and put her fingertips in his ears, and drawn him closer still to her, and he'd have been overwhelmed, he'd have lost his head entirely . . . It was like a beautiful pain, just the thought of it.

He had leaned back abruptly into his dark corner, but she sensed that he stirred, in a movement of anguish and stealth, like a writhing. She supposed he could tell from her face what she felt, and if she wasn't careful . . . Yet to become his mistress: mightn't that be her one chance of survival, if he was Scorpio? And she would find out the truth about him. And if she yielded to him now, mightn't

151

he at last admit that he was in love with her, and capitulate to her for ever? If he had stopped himself from kissing her, if he had failed to invite her into his house, if he lurked so warily in his dark corner now, wasn't it because he knew that it was so?

She moistened her lips tentatively, and in a sudden swirl of urgent movement he seized her hand and unlatched the carriage door. One of the cognac glasses, overturned by him, fell out and tinkled into fragments on the cobblestones. He gazed down at it for a moment, motionless. Then he slowly closed the door again, released her hand, and leaned back once more into the shadows. After a while he gave a soft, humourless little laugh, and murmured, 'You'll be my downfall!' And then: 'What were we talking about?'

'Trévelan.'

'Ah yes. You see: I'm becoming forgetful – not thinking what I'm doing.' And then he added quietly, 'This can't go on.'

Chloe said nothing. His hand was still resting on the rim of the open carriage window, and she realized with a remote feeling of horror, looking at his still, black fingers, how close her own aroused passions had brought her to self-betrayal – and would again, if she let them. Who knew what terrible things he might have done, and might still do?

And yet . . .

'Do they always kill agents who fail to carry out a mission?' she asked.

His fingers tightened on the rim of the window, then drummed lightly, as if to disguise that involuntary movement. 'Usually,' he answered. 'Unless I intervene. I've a particular place of safety – only there's no coming back . . .' He trailed off, perceptibly disquieted again, and she wondered if he meant the prison across the street, or perhaps his château in the Forest of Fontainebleau. He drummed his fingers again indecisively, and murmured, half to himself, 'I must think, think . . . '

Chloe thought she understood his dilemma. Whether he became her lover or took her to his 'particular place of safety,' he would be ensnared by her, and she would learn the whole truth about him. If he did nothing, she would die.

He left the carriage abruptly, kicked the broken glass to one side, and whistled for the coachman and the guard. 'Allow me to have you and your cousin conveyed home,' he said, in a tone of distracted courtesy, closing the carriage door and only then raising her hand to his lips through the open window. 'But if you'll excuse me, I have so much to see to . . . '

The coachman and the guard approached across the forecourt, wiping their mouths on their sleeves.

'Did you make any arrangement to see de Grismont again, or contact him?' de l'Epinay asked casually.

'Yes, I'm to report to him three days from now.'

'So soon!' He glanced absently round the forecourt, but smoothed back his hair. 'Well, I'll see you before then – I expect – somehow.'

He nodded to the coachman, and stepped back. As the cabriolet drove out through the archway of the forecourt and turned beneath the prison walls, Chloe caught a last glimpse of him, still standing in the dappled lamplight beneath the linden tree. His dark, motionless figure suddenly seemed strangely lonely; fatally irresolute.

Twelve

A THOUSAND RED STARS burst into flower against the darkening sky above the gardens of the Palais-Royal, and the long 'Oooh!' of the onlookers mingled with the sighing of the great chestnut trees, as their leaves stirred in the first breath of cool night air after the long heat of the day. 'I'm winning, and he'll be mine!' Chloe thought, in a wave of passionate triumph and longing, as she watched the glowing stars fade into darkness above the trees; and then she shivered, telling herself, 'I can't still want him – how can I still want him? – if he's Scorpio.' Nor was it so certain that she was really winning.

Two days had passed without a glimpse of de l'Epinay, or a word from him; but it was true that he'd warned her of that. Two uneventful days, sewing *petit point* and taking music lessons in the gloomy, pompous appartement near the Palais du Luxembourg. At first she had felt as strange there as a visitor from the New World or the Antipodes; and then, gradually, it was her evening in the Faubourg St Germain which had faded until it had seemed no more than a dream, and she had begun to wonder, in a first flutter of panic, if she would ever see de l'Epinay again. The priest strolling in the gardens opposite her window, reading his breviary, had been almost a reassuring sight during the first day; but on the second – today – as she'd watched his shadow lengthening during the afternoon, and there'd still been no word from de l'Epinay, that long dark shape, sliding over the lawns and the beds of geraniums, had become menacing. What if he abandoned her to the Marquis de Grismont?

Now, under the chestnuts of the Palais-Royal, in the gathering dusk, the lawns were still pale, glistening like velvet where the gowns of strolling ladies of fashion, on the arms of their uniformed escorts, drew trails through the freshly fallen dew. There was a whoosh and a bang as another rocket soared up and burst. 'Magnificent!' murmured Monsieur Turgeon, on whose arm Chloe was walking, her own white muslin gown trimmed with silver as lustrous as the dew itself. Every bursting rocket made her start, and she wondered if the explosion at the Opera would be audible here, several streets away. Philippe had thought it would. And it was tonight, and it was time. Turgeon, instead of offering to take them to the Opera in General de Bourges' place, had suggested an evening here at the Palais-Royal, almost as if he'd known what was to take place. 'And that's why I haven't seen de l'Epinay – because of the explosion at the Opera,' Chloe thought. 'But once it's done, he'll come to find me. He won't be able to stay away.'

Turgeon's thick spectacles glinted opaquely in the dusk. Of course he would know about the explosion at the Opera, if he was one of de l'Epinay's lieutenants; if de l'Epinay was Scorpio. If he was. If he was.

She looked round in a torment of uncertainty, her gaze falling for a moment on Philippe, and then travelling on over the arcades which bounded the gardens on three sides, while the palace itself closed it on the fourth. Before the Terror, it had been the palace of the Duc d'Orléans, and here once the voice of moderation in French politics had murmured amongst the fountains and rose-gardens. Philippe, who seemed a little better disposed towards de l'Epinay now that Chloe had told him more, had wondered if he might have been of the Orléanist party; if he might still be a moderate, constitutional monarchist after all. The three men who had kept him company in the Café des Artistes – all wellbred young Army officers – had seemed to hint as much when he'd tried to find out from them. Yet why, then, did de l'Epinay give the impression of having something to hide even from Chloe? They had talked it over and over during the past two days, whenever they had been alone together. And they had always come back to the same point: the total absence of proof one way or the other; the vital need for proof. Philippe had agreed that the reappearance of Trévelan, safe and free, would make it very difficult to go on suspecting de l'Epinay. But if only they could uncover some final and truly unambiguous clue!

There was another loud bang, and Chloe started again. But the sky above the chestnut trees was only filled with frivolous, slowly falling purple balls of fire. Surely the explosion at the Opera ought to have happened by now? Or could something have gone wrong?

'What a dear nervous child!' Turgeon said, patting Chloe's hand in what seemed to her a slightly too familiar manner. He had been rather more in evidence than usual during the past few days, calling frequently at the appartement, and behaving towards Chloe with a certain sly assurance which her uncle and aunt, disappointed and vexed at de l'Epinay's continuing absence, had done nothing to discourage. They were uneasily silent now, scarcely remembering to utter the appropriate Ooohs and Aaahs at the exploding pyrotechnics. Turgeon had finally told them in confidence, over dinner in one of the restaurants under the arcades an hour ago, that General de Bourges had, indeed, been misappropriating Army funds; that he had been caught in the very act of paying into his own secret bank account thousands of francs which had been destined for the purchase of boots and blankets. Could the story be true? It was never possible to tell from Turgeon's face. But the General had been under suspicion for some time, he'd added; and so had Uncle Victor's colleague at the Tuileries, a Monsieur Durand, who had proved to be the General's accomplice.

'Trophime de Bourges, whom we would have trusted with our very lives – just fancy!' Aunt Eugénie murmured, for what seemed the hundredth time, fanning herself agitatedly as they strolled past the fountains in the centre of the gardens. 'But of course we should have realized. I always did think his eyes were a little too close together. And then his having a carriage, and a box at the Opera, and those grand, fashionable rooms overlooking the Seine, right opposite the Tuileries – all on the mere pay of a General! Of course we should have smelt a rat. But being honest, simple folk – '

' – Satisfied with our humble, hard-earned lot ... ' murmured Uncle Victor, stepping aside to make way for a pair of flamboyantly uniformed dragoons and their be-jewelled and be-feathered ladies dallying beside the fountains.

'Quite so, quite so,' Turgeon said soothingly, his spectacles glittering in the reflected brilliance of the fountain-spray, which was like a rain of diamonds in the light of the lamps nearby. 'The temptations of high office, alas! And even quite junior officials, sometimes, inflated by social ambition – '

'A remarkable coincidence, that!' Uncle Victor said with a nervous laugh, running his finger round inside the top of his tight cravat. 'I mean that I was only talking to Durand after a meeting at the Tuileries a week or two ago ... I don't know if anyone noticed. Just passing the time of day, of course. Hardly knew the wretched fellow.'

There was a gleam of fair hair in the shadows beyond the fountains, and an instant's silence fell. But it was only a young hussar, his golden-brown curls momentarily gilded by spray and lamplight.

'Quite so,' Turgeon murmured again, silkily; and then, with a little smile, pressing Chloe's arm against his side: 'Ah, dear me, the folly of chasing rainbows!'

Chloe withdrew her hand sharply from his arm as they strolled on. His presumption was intolerable, and so was his secretly sneering manner. For wasn't he sneering at her, and at her adoptive family, for entertaining hopes about de l'Epinay? But why? Was he fatuous enough to imagine that he had some chance with her, just because of de l'Epinay's elusiveness as a suitor? Or had he some reason for believing that de l'Epinay's absence was permanent?

They walked slowly up the wide stone steps to the arcade. Chloe fell back to stroll beside Philippe for a moment, and whispered, 'What's the time?'

'Half past eight.'

'Then the explosion should have happened an hour ago!'

'Yes.'

'And even if we hadn't heard it, there'd have been news of it by now.'

'Yes.'

'Something's gone wrong, then!'

Pausing at the top of the steps, Turgeon glanced back at them, smoothing his grey silk gloves and ignoring something Uncle Victor was saying to him.

'He definitely knows something,' Philippe whispered, bending his head and pretending to adjust his fob-chain. 'Can't you try to get him talking? Heaven knows, from the way he keeps pawing you . . . '

'Ugh!' Chloe answered with a shudder. 'And besides . . . ' She glanced up the steps and gave the still waiting Turgeon an icy smile. His thick spectacles flashed blankly in the lamplight, and his clever, pallid, thin-lipped face was as expressionless as ever. There scarcely seemed any point in trying. 'Well, if the occasion presents itself,' she conceded reluctantly.

They rejoined him at the top of the steps, and Chloe coolly took his proffered arm again. Uncle Victor and Aunt Eugénie had strolled on a little ahead. It was so crowded under the arcade, with ladies in their long, high-waisted gowns of silk or muslin garlanded with flowers or a-shimmer with sequins, and officers in their gold-braided coats and white breeches, it was impossible to walk more than two abreast. Uncle Victor and Aunt Eugénie continued to stroll ahead, and Philippe fell a few paces behind. Now and then a glimpse of a dark green cavalry officer's uniform, amongst all the other uniforms, made Chloe turn cold, but it was never the Vicomte de Malebois. Perhaps he was still recovering from the blow de l'Epinay had dealt him; but in any case she supposed that de Grismont would have ordered him to keep away from her, at least till she'd had time to carry out her mission. After that, if de l'Epinay chose not to protect her . . . Meanwhile it was difficult not to flinch at every movement of the shadows.

It was as they strolled along a darker stretch of the arcade, Uncle Victor and Aunt Eugénie out of sight in the crowds ahead, and Philippe several paces behind, that Turgeon murmured, 'How changed you are, if I may say so, chère Mademoiselle, just in a mere fortnight! Such a wild, independent creature you were then – quite the little tomboy, in your misguided longing for adventure! – whilst now you start and tremble at every shadow. So much more feminine! Ah, it's only when a young girl has, how shall I say, played with fire and burnt her fingers – ' he gave her a secret little smile – 'that she realizes her frail vulnerability, her need of truly reliable masculine protection – something very different from the dazzling promises of philanderers and adventurers, here today and gone, rather suddenly, tomorrow – and becomes that most divine of beings: weak, helpless, palpitant woman! I flatter myself,' he continued, drawing her hand closer under his arm, and pressing it in his own silk-sheathed fingers, 'that I have your uncle's tacit consent – '

'Perhaps, but you haven't mine,' Chloe said sharply, withdrawing her hand again. 'And if you take any more liberties with me, sir, be sure that I'll slap your face, here and now.'

The swinging doors of a gambling-saloon they were passing burst open, and two green-uniformed officers reeled out. One, clinging round a dark stone column, made a lurching grab at Chloe. Philippe stepped quickly forward, but Turgeon was quicker still. Holding her by the upper arm now, in a cold, tight grip, he propelled her on and away, his spectacles glinting in the light of a jeweller's shop they were passing, though whether in anger or in secret amusement it was impossible to say. 'Ah, these cavalry

159

officers!' he murmured after a moment. 'But perhaps their attentions please you?'

'There are moments when even they seem all sweetness and light,' Chloe answered stingingly, but she turned her face away, her heart beating fast. Was there anything he didn't know? And what was it he was hinting about de l'Epinay – 'gone, rather suddenly, tomorrow.' Had something happened to him?

Another bursting rocket cast a flickering, bluish light under the arcade, fleetingly penetrating even the deepest shadows. Chloe's heart almost stopped as she glimpsed a familiar figure huddled in a dark doorway: a slender, black-haired, black-eyed lad in a grimy white shirt and torn velvet breeches. Trévelan! The blue flicker of light faded, and darkness reclaimed him, but not before Chloe had seen that he was pressing himself back into the doorway, panting for breath, and that his eyes, darting frantically to and fro, were wide with terror.

Breaking away from Turgeon in the crowd, Chloe turned to run back to Trévelan. But even as she did so, he suddenly started out from his hiding-place, dodged wildly away amongst the chattering strollers, and disappeared down a flight of wide stone steps into the darkness of the garden.

What had happened? Had he run away from de l'Epinay at the Opera? And why? Because he hadn't believed that the explosion would be so carefully timed and controlled that it would do no fatal harm? Or had he seen or heard something in de l'Epinay's house which confirmed his terrible intuitions? And who was he fleeing from in such terror? De Grismont and his men? Or could it be de l'Epinay himself who was ruthlessly hunting him down?

She became aware that Turgeon was speaking to her, but for a moment her ears were so singing with shock and horror that she could scarcely hear him.

' . . . Must remind you that my position in the Administration is such,' he was murmuring with a thin-lipped smile, close to her ear, gripping her coldly by the upper arm again, 'that a great deal of secret information – about

the private activities of certain individuals, for instance –
comes to my notice. You have only myself to thank, you
know, for your having remained at liberty thus far. What a
pity if I felt provoked into withdrawing my protection.'

'You'll be telling me next that you're Scorpio himself!'
Chloe managed to say with a contemptuous laugh.

'There's many a true word spoken in jest, my dear.' And
then, when Chloe gave him a glance of scathing disbelief,
he elaborated, 'What may not be true today, may well be
true tomorrow. Mistakes may be made; accidents may
happen; powerful men may face sudden ruin or even
sudden death. And alas! even a Chief of Secret Police may
have his, how shall I say – ' he gave one of his secret smiles –
'his Achilles' heel.'

Chloe walked on at his side in a frozen silence for a few
moments, Trévelan forgotten. That last remark was the
clearest possible hint that de l'Epinay really was Scorpio.
'Oh, let him be lying!' she thought in anguish. After all, he
knew that if she were ever sure that de l'Epinay was
Scorpio, she could no longer be in love with him. And he
had always hated de l'Epinay. And she remembered too,
with a sinking heart, de l'Epinay's enigmatic smile as he'd
said in the palmhouse, 'No, Turgeon isn't Scorpio, but
he'd like to be.'

But she wouldn't let Turgeon believe, from her silence,
that he would gain any advantage by saying such things.
Rallying, she said with a stinging smile, 'Well, allow me to
wish you well, Monsieur, in the post you're hoping to
acquire. That code-name, Scorpio, certainly might have
been chosen with you in mind, it fits you so perfectly. One
instantly pictures something skinny, cold, poisonous, and
utterly repellent.'

A pattern of glittering emerald green stars writhed in the
dark sky above the chestnut trees as another firework
burst, and there was a long, sighing 'Aaaah!' from the
crowd. For a moment the livid glow turned the big leaves
and the lawns beneath an unnatural, vivid jade, with deep
violet shadows under the trees; and it seemed to Chloe, as

the great green stars fell through the sky and faded, that she could see dark figures darting swiftly through the deepest shadows. Was that a flash of fair hair? For an instant she was almost sure of it; then the last of the green stars was extinguished, and there was nothing to be seen but the darkness.

Turgeon smiled, but Chloe could see that his pallid face had turned a strange, almost luminous white. 'Aren't you afraid of death, you silly girl?' he asked softly.

'No,' Chloe said, wishing it were truer than it was. 'I believe in something greater than death. But you'd never understand.'

He smiled again, and murmured, 'It isn't always quick.' And then, as Philippe happened to approach within a few paces of them, he continued smoothly, 'And as for that name we were discussing: it comes, as a matter of fact, from the device on a signet-ring worn, though not in public of course, by the present bearer of the sobriquet – '

'A signet-ring!'

' – Which he uses to seal his orders, and so on. It's Egyptian, and of great antiquity. I understand he found it in the sand near the Great Pyramid.' Turgeon's face glowed again with a peculiar, unearthly pallor. 'Undoubtedly it has a profound occult significance, quite lost on its present wearer. The high priests of that cult, with its ritual of human sacrifice – '

A scream – a woman's piercing scream – rent the air: a scream of such blood-chilling horror that a deathly hush fell on the whole crowd. For an instant everyone stood as if turned to stone; then there was a surge of movement out from the arcades to the many flights of steps leading down to the gardens. From the deep gloom beneath the chestnuts, where the scream had come from, the figures of two dragoons emerged, supporting a half-fainting lady in a yellow dress. There were shouts of 'A body – a dead body – in there, under the trees! Stabbed through the heart!' A dozen officers ran towards the trees from different parts of the arcade, drawing their pistols, and the crowd surged out across the lawns.

162

Carried forward in spite of herself by the throng, and separated from both Philippe and Turgeon, Chloe gazed transfixed as the officers re-emerged from the darkness under the trees, carrying a limp, lolling figure like a rag doll. As they approached across the grass, she could see the slender limbs of a boy; soft dark curls; a white shirt; torn velvet breeches. The silent procession passed close by her, where she stood alone amongst the great arching sprays of rose-trees in bloom, and she saw that the white shirt was stained crimson in a large patch on the breast, with the hilt of a dagger still jutting out. Trévelan's eyes, wide, black and sightless, seemed to gaze into hers as he was carried past, as if telling her some terrible truth.

The silent crowd followed, eddying back from the lawns to the arcade. Alone, Chloe turned and wandered blindly away, deeper amongst the rose-trees and their shadows, seeking the refuge of solitude and darkness. Now and then a spray of roses showered her with damp petals, or tore threads from her muslin gown, and the dew soaked through her silk slippers, but she was heedless of that. Nor did she ask herself where she was going, though she was dimly aware that she was wandering deeper and deeper into the thorny, fragrant darkness. All too soon, anyway, she seemed destined to follow Trévelan, wherever he'd gone. Poor Trévelan! Was it true that there was something beyond death, something greater than death? Suddenly she doubted it; although, through her grief, it was almost as if she could feel its presence stealing over her, as though each invisible rose, pouring out its scent into the darkness, were intimating to her that it was immortal. The moon was rising white above the trees, and she paused to watch one bloom, untouched even by the moths, collapse silently into a scattering of petals, like drops of blood on the pale grass. Was that rose immortal? Yes, yes, it was, if she could only understand . . . But she couldn't think about it now. And anyway, what use would such understanding be if de l'Epinay . . . 'Oh, let it not be true about him!' she prayed in anguish. 'Let it not be him who murdered Trévelan!'

She wandered on, and found herself at the edge of a circle of lawn in the midst of the roses, where the pale glimmer of a marble statue stood framed by the profound blackness of a group of ornamental cypresses. For a moment, through the shimmering of her tears, it seemed to her that the statue moved, white stirring stealthily against black, and she drew back involuntarily amongst the roses. Then, with a deeper flutter of her heart, she made out a snowy shirt-front, a black velvet coat and breeches, a gleam of fair hair, the fainter gleam of a silver-headed cane. He was leaning against the statue, one black-gloved hand covering his face, in the attitude of a man utterly and darkly spent. He didn't glance up, and Chloe realized that he was unaware of her presence. She supposed she must have approached very silently in her silk slippers, and in the moonlight her white and silver gown must have been lost against the dew-drenched grass and the pale roses surrounding her. All the same, it was very unlike de l'Epinay to be so unguarded, and she wondered if he had ever been watched before by an invisible witness, as he had so often watched others. Was his attitude one of grief and exhaustion, or one of guilt? It would have been unwise anyway to startle him; and she thought, 'I'll watch, and then, perhaps, at last I'll really know the truth about him.'

For a long moment he remained motionless. There was a time for Chloe to notice his dark footprints in the dew, leading through the rosarium to where he stood. They came from the direction of the chestnut grove, it was true; but they were not the straight, blurred streaks that running feet would have made: only clearly etched, separate prints, following a meandering course amongst the roses, as if he too had wandered here slowly and gropingly, seeking the sanctuary of solitude and darkness, and its mysterious power to console.

'It wasn't him,' Chloe thought, breathing a silent sigh of gratitude, and beginning to back inobtrusively away. But just then he stirred, moving his hand wearily over his face. His black fingers passed across his eyes, began to lace through his already ruffled hair – then froze. Abruptly he uncovered his face and examined his palm and fingers in the moonlight. Only the subtle lustre of fine leather gleamed in the white radiance; but on his other black-gloved hand, when he lifted it, there were patches of something still stickily liquid and glistening. Chloe saw a quiver or a shudder run through him as he wrenched the glove off his hand, and tossed it, with its pair, deep into the impenetrable shadow under the roses. Swiftly he examined his white shirt-front and the white lace at his cuffs; then, reassured, but with another faint but visible quiver through his nerves – of guiltily superstitious horror, or of a last, subsiding thrill of a killer's after-pleasure? – he relapsed against the statue again and closed his eyes.

He had done it, then. He had murdered Trévelan. He was Scorpio.

Minutes must have passed, though she couldn't have measured them, any more than she could move. As if in a trance, she stood gazing at him, knowing that she could never again love a man as she'd loved him, though it was all over now. How elegant and graceful his figure was, even in exhausted repose! And his fair hair was so silkily fine, and his sensitively chiselled face so beautiful, she felt her heart would break. And yet he was evil, depthlessly and irredeemably evil; and it began to seem to her now that his beauty itself was sinister, since it had concealed the truth about him.

She knew that if he became aware of her presence he would almost certainly kill her, because of what she'd seen; yet she remained unable to move, even when he opened his eyes again. But there was something blind and empty in his gaze as he looked slowly about him, as if he saw nothing: not her; not the roses lustrous with dew and caressed by large, pale moths; not the holy beauty of the night. There was only an infinite bleakness in his eyes, often glimpsed before behind the ironic gaiety of his social manner, but only now so clearly and chillingly unveiled. It was the gaze of a man who believed in nothing; who had long since lost his soul. Deep within the mesmerized horror which kept her standing there motionless, Chloe even felt a remote stirring of pity for him.

Moving aimlessly over the roses enclosing the clearing, his eyes came to rest on her, still glazed; then abruptly they were sharp and alert. Before she could even catch her breath for flight there was a swift flash of movement, and she saw a pistol in his hand. For a moment he levelled it at her; then he slowly lowered it and murmured, 'Ah, it's you.' He gave an unsteady little laugh, and added, 'You frightened me. I thought you were a vision or something.'

Or a ghost? His words seemed an involuntary admission of guilt, just as his impulse to draw his pistol against the world of the spirit seemed an involuntary admission of soullessness.

'How long have you been there?' he asked, in a not entirely successful attempt at a casual tone. He straightened up and smoothed back his hair, in an effort to regain his social poise, but he didn't approach her.

'Only a moment,' she managed to lie, her heart beating fast.

He glanced round, as if absently, his pistol still in his hand. 'Are you alone?'

'Yes.'

She thought, 'He knows I lied – that I saw the blood on his gloves.' Yet still she was too stunned with horror to move. But he only said, replacing his pistol in his coat pocket, 'You shouldn't be alone here. De Grismont and his bunch of assassins may still be about, and if de Malebois is with them ... '

He believed her, then; believed she'd seen nothing. And oh, how skilfully he was already beginning to spin his tale, that it was de Grismont who had murdered Trévelan. Yet he still, mercifully, made no attempt to approach her, and his poise seemed very tenuous as he said, 'You know Trévelan's dead?'

'Yes.'

'Yes, I ... ' His voice shook, and he broke off. Then,

mastering himself, he said in a too matter-of-fact tone, 'I'm afraid things went very wrong.' He began to pace to and fro beside the statue, turning at every third step, in a slow, graceful but tortuous weaving like that of a tightly caged wild animal. 'You don't approach me, I see,' he remarked, giving her a brief glance in passing. 'But it's true – it's all my fault. I hoped and believed, against all reason ... But he never even began to trust me. And at the Opera ... At the Opera I saw a girl in a red dress, high up on one of the balconies overlooking the foyer. I knew it couldn't be you, and yet I thought it was. She vanished, and I was waiting for her to reappear ... And that's when Trévelan slipped away. De Grismont's spies were there, of course, and they had just a few seconds' start on me. And how could I save him when it was me, most of all, that he was running from?' He stopped pacing abruptly and stood facing her, still several paces away, his fingers laced distractedly through his hair, and added, 'I said you would be my downfall. Perhaps you will be yet, but meanwhile it's poor Trévelan who's paid the price.'

In silence, Chloe gazed at him, distantly marvelling at the deviousness of his nature, as endlessly and meaninglessly complex as a labyrinth. His distress seemed so genuine, and his story so plausible, she would have believed him if she hadn't with her own eyes seen him hurriedly get rid of those bloodstained gloves. And perhaps his distress really was genuine, in a way, welling up from some dark and convoluted recess of his nature which she would never understand. He was Scorpio, and he had murdered Trévelan; and yet his whole attitude, as he stood facing her in silence, seemed to be a plea for her forgiveness.

As if in a dream, she still couldn't speak or move, and she seemed to be watching from a great distance as he caught at a rose from a trailing spray, and began to shred its petals wretchedly between his fingers. 'You're winning, you see,' he murmured, after a while. 'You called me cynical, and it's true that the life I've led ... Well, that's another long story, and some of it I could never tell you, but I regret it now –

167

oh, more bitterly than I can say. And there's no hope for me, unless you . . . ' He let the mutilated rose fall from his fingers, and met her eyes. 'Only you can help me.'

He had never let her glimpse his real feelings before, and in the moonlight there was a dark, elemental power in his gaze which seemed to cast a spell over her. Struggling against it, she thought, 'But how can a man without heart or soul be in love?' Yet he was; in his own way he was in love with her, and he was telling her so. Was it just a morbid intensity of physical desire, which had become an obsession? Or an impossible longing to be redeemed by her, and by her faith in life, which perhaps he could sense? . . . An impossible longing? Desperately she caught at the sudden, insidious slide of her feelings towards the impulse to save him.

Without knowing it, she must have retreated a step. There was a flicker of acutely sensitive awareness in his eyes; then he smoothed back his hair again and adopted an attitude of formal elegance, both hands resting on the head of his cane. 'I see,' he murmured gently. 'It's too late, I suppose. So much for my sense of timing. But unfortunately, if you're to report to de Grismont tomorrow, as planned. . .' He drew a random pattern in the dewy grass with the tip of his cane, irresolute. 'There's much I have to decide, but if . . . '

It was only a hint, but it was his first tacit acknowledgement of what her mission was, and Chloe felt her heart give a sinking, traitorous flutter – of fear, yet not only of fear. But he had trailed off, suddenly alert; and after a moment her senses, less keen than his, caught the sound of footsteps approaching across the grass, and the rustle of sprays of roses being brushed aside. A voice called her name, and then, an instant later, Philippe appeared at the edge of the clearing, followed by her aunt and uncle, and then Turgeon.

'Chloe! We've been looking everywhere for you! You frightened us, disappearing like that!' Philippe said, hastening to her side and putting his arm tightly round her.

168

Chloe said nothing, and de l'Epinay murmured, 'I think she's still rather dazed.'

Philippe gave him a level glance. And even Uncle Victor's bow was perceptibly stiff as he said, 'Oh, it's you, Monsieur de l'Epinay. Good evening.'

'We were both wandering about, bemused, and came upon each other here,' de l'Epinay explained, slightly fumbling a situation which he would usually have carried off with effortless panache. Turgeon's spectacles glittered in the moonlight. 'No wonder he's becoming so ambitious,' Chloe thought, as they started back towards the arcade, she walking on Philippe's arm in the midst of her family, while de l'Epinay and Turgeon fell behind. The indecision and distractedness she had first glimpsed in de l'Epinay two nights ago were becoming increasingly perceptible, as if everything was beginning to slip dangerously from his grasp. From his unguardedness now, she supposed that he must have kept Trévelan in view throughout his flight, and seen that he'd had no chance to tell anyone whatever it was he'd found out. And he could tell the royalists that he'd killed the boy because he'd tried to defect. They might not entirely believe his story, but yet again they'd be without a shred of real evidence against him; he remained unmasked. But for how long? If he made one more mistake . . . And what was so frightening was that although he was Scorpio he was her only protection – not only against de Grismont and de Malebois, but now against Turgeon too – at any rate as long as he was in love with her. 'That's the only reason I care,' she told herself, forcing herself not to look back at him. 'After what he's done, there isn't – there can't be – any other reason.'

They emerged on to the open grass. The fountains were still playing, flashing in the lamplight; more fireworks burst against the dark sky; and an orchestra had been brought out from one of the restaurants and was playing a gay serenade by Mozart. Probably Trévelan's body had been taken away to the morgue. Couples and groups of strollers paraded along the gravel paths, chattering and laughing as if nothing had happened. Chloe was almost glad to be in the midst of such heartless frivolity, as if it might aid her in her struggle against her terrible thraldom to de l'Epinay. She glanced back at him in spite of herself. He was still several paces behind, and seemed deep in conversation with Turgeon, despite their differences. The lamplight caught them as they emerged from the rose-garden, illuminating the poised and impeccable elegance of de l'Epinay's figure, very aristocratic in white lace-trimmed lawn and black velvet, and with not a strand of his fair hair out of place. The sight of him seemed to pierce Chloe's heart. He looked more composed, which was reassuring in a way. Yet how could he look so composed, so intact, after what he'd done? And why did such a perfect face and form have to conceal such evil?

'. . . But fancy his saying "*Tonnerre* – by thunder!" like that!' murmured a lady in a pink gown to her escort, as they passed close to Chloe and Philippe, who were walking a little ahead of Uncle Victor and Aunt Eugénie. 'He was one of those Breton royalists, I heard someone say, and you know what devout Catholics they all are. You'd have thought he'd have found something better than "*Tonnerre!*" to say with his dying breath. And to a lady of easy virtue, too!'

'Well, he couldn't help whose arms he fell back into, there in the bushes, could he?' said her escort reasonably, as they strolled slowly away towards the fountains. 'When you've got a knife between your ribs, you know, you can't pick and choose.'

'Ah no, I suppose not.'

'And anyway, she was frightened out of her wits – you heard the scream she gave. She probably misheard him.'

'Ah yes, I dare say . . . '

The voices faded away across the grass, and were lost in the warbling of the orchestra's woodwind and the murmur of the fountains.

Irked by the banality of what she'd overheard, yet obscurely disturbed by it, Chloe glanced back again at de l'Epinay, still strolling some way behind with Turgeon. What could Trévelan really have whispered as he died? And had de l'Epinay heard him? *Tonnerre . . . Tonnerre . . .* The word seemed to tease elusively at her memory.

'Has there been much talk about this?' she asked Philippe, in a disquieted undertone.

'Oh yes. The woman kept babbling about it, up in the arcade, most of the time you were missing.'

'And you didn't notice . . ?' Chloe lowered her voice still further, feeling another inexplicable chill. 'Do you think you'd have recognized de Grismont, if you'd seen him?'

'Yes, I thought I did catch a glimpse of him, in the crowd nearby.'

Chloe bit her lip, then asked, 'And did Monsieur Turgeon hear what the woman said?'

'Yes, yes. Everyone did.'

Chloe glanced back once more at de l'Epinay, half reassured. Perhaps it wasn't important anyway. But if it was, and he didn't know about it, Turgeon had had ample opportunity to tell him.

Aunt Eugénie had also glanced back more than once, and now she paused, smoothing her gown: more ready than Uncle Victor, it seemed, to forgive de l'Epinay his continuing failure to call on them, and his having been found alone with Chloe in the rose-garden.

' . . . Tonight,' de l'Epinay could be heard saying, as he and Turgeon approached within earshot. 'There's too much at stake. And I've had enough, after what's just happened . . . ' He trailed off, gave the Lenoirs a debonair smile, and murmured, ' – A fine night for a shoot, I was just saying.'

'Ah yes . . . in the Forest of Fontainebleau, you mean?' Aunt Eugénie said. 'I suppose you could be there well before dawn, if you've a good carriage. And as you say, after what's just happened – in a public garden, of all things; in a place of the highest fashion! – one feels quite sick and tired of the capital, and longs . . . '

'Far better to wait till the new moon, if you'll take my

advice,' Turgeon murmured smoothly, at de l'Epinay's elbow. 'It's only another week or so, and then you'll be sure of a really complete bag.'

'How extremely kind of you to take such an interest in my affairs!' de l'Epinay said with a stinging laugh. 'But you quite miss the point, my dear Turgeon, which isn't surprising. I'm overrun by vermin,' he explained to Uncle Victor and Aunt Eugénie, scanning the crowds with a keen but apparently casual gaze as they strolled on. 'That's what comes of neglecting one's estate. In another week or so there may be no deer or pheasants left. And besides,' he added, pausing at the foot of a flight of stone steps leading up to the arcade and turning to face them, his hand resting on the balustrade, as if to take his leave of them, 'How do I know where I'll be, a week or so from now?' His glance passed briefly over Turgeon. 'One must act while one can.'

Chloe understood. De l'Epinay sensed danger. From the absence of firm decision in his manner – his willingness to debate the point – it was perhaps no more than an intuition; but he was in half a mind to abandon his original plan to wait for the shipment of arms and money from England, and to arrest all the royalists tonight, before some dimly guessed-at disaster could occur. Tonight? Would that mean that she too would be arrested? Since he'd rejoined them, Chloe had felt chilled and deeply disturbed by his close proximity, though he hadn't looked directly at her; and now, more than ever, she had to resist a desire to shrink away from him.

'Our dear Chloe's always longing to go to the forest, for a walk or a picnic,' Aunt Eugénie said. 'But as you so rightly say, Monsieur de l'Epinay, one must wait for the occasion to present itself. Without a carriage, you understand . . . And then one worries rather about the brigands. I quite fancied for a moment, when you mentioned vermin . . . '

'Ah yes, alas, we haven't all had Monsieur de l'Epinay's advantages in life,' murmured Turgeon, looking up at the moon. 'Still, benighted townsman that I am, I too – we all – may have our little flights of poetic fancy, laugh at them as you will, sir. Here is this moonlight, this dew, this divine scent of roses . . . and such stillness, such tranquility, even here in a public garden! Look at the trees! Not a leaf stirs; nothing whatever troubles their serenity. Ah, perhaps if there were a storm brewing, or even a little breeze and a few drops of rain, one might sympathize with your impulse, my dear sir. But to choose a night of such profound and perfect peace to go blazing away at everything! – and just on a mere passing whim, just on a mere unfounded *frisson* of the spirit! You must allow us honest burghers, counting ourselves fortunate if we own so much as a window-box, to find your remedy for jangled nerves a trifle extravagant.'

De l'Epinay had scanned the arcades and the gardens again while Turgeon was talking, then his gaze had returned to rest attentively on Turgeon's face. Now he drew idle, abstracted, indecisive patterns in the gravel path with his cane, and murmured finally, 'Perhaps you're right.'

Again Chloe thought she understood. Turgeon had persuaded de l'Epinay that his intuition of danger was unfounded, and that he should continue with his original plan and make no arrests tonight. She only wondered why Turgeon, turning away, should seem to be concealing a private smile.

' . . . Must visit me at my house in the Faubourg St Germain,' de l'Epinay was saying, as he bowed over Aunt Eugénie's hand. 'You must come one morning in the very near future, and take luncheon with me. I'll send my carriage for you.' His eyes met Chloe's and held them for a moment as he took her hand, and she realized with a shock what he was really saying. She was to go to his house tomorrow.

The sudden, secret passion in his gaze was like a dark whirlpool, dragging her towards him, dragging her down. What if she couldn't resist his terrible power over her feelings? And if she could resist, what then?

He raised her fingers to his lips, and then, his eyes still dwelling on her, stepped back and rested his hand on the stone balustrade, where the lamplight fell. Trying to

173

escape his power, she lowered her gaze; but all she could see was a minute speck of blood like a pinprick on his lace shirt-cuff, and that subtle, polished indentation on one of his fingers, left by the Egyptian signet-ring he wasn't wearing.

Thirteen

COLD AND HEAVY IN EVERY LIMB, she lay on a marble bier in a dark garden. Above her, the whole night sky was filled with a vast constellation of glittering stars in the form of a triumphant scorpion poised to sting. She tried to stir, but the powerfully seductive fragrance of roses and lilies all about her deeply pervaded her senses, drugging her, and she knew that she could never move again.

'Chloe! Chloe! Wake up!'

With a violent effort, Chloe turned her head on the pillows and opened her eyes. There really were white lilies and red roses beside her, in a large, trailing bouquet on her bedside table; but beyond the mass of nodding, fragrant blooms she could see the figure of Aunt Eugénie holding out a glass of orange-blossom water, as well as that of the maid in her white, lace-fringed apron and mob-cap, opening the windows and throwing back the shutters with a clatter. Sunlight streamed into the room.

'How you've slept! It's nearly mid-morning already!' Aunt Eugénie said. 'I thought I'd let you sleep on, you seemed so dazed and shaken last night, after that poor boy...' She went to the mirror and tweaked her curls carefully into place while the maid latched the shutters back, but Chloe could see that she was secretly all agog about something. 'But I had to wake you now because of what's come for you,' she went on in an excited whisper, rushing back to Chloe's bedside as soon as the maid had left the room. 'Look, they're from the Comte de l'Epinay! Addressed to me, of course, as is right and proper, but you know and I know...'

Chloe lifted the gleaming, ivory-white calling-card out from amongst the flowers. On one side was printed, in a neat italic script without flourishes, *Lucien St Clair Ferrier, Comte de l'Epinay*, and on the other side, in a swift, graceful hand quite unlike the precise and courtly style of the first royalist message she'd received: *In the most heartfelt anticipation of your coming visit.*

'– But he doesn't mean for us to go today,' Aunt Eugénie said, her excitement momentarily a little clouded. 'His coachman delivered the flowers, and I saw a blue cabriolet with four greys out in the street, with a coat of arms on the door and everything, but – '

'When was this?' Chloe asked in alarm, gulping down her orange-blossom water. The clock on her mantelpiece said ten to eleven, and she hadn't even decided what to do.

'Oh, just this instant. But calm yourself, it isn't today. The coachman – a very swarthy fellow, by the way, a Mameluke I shouldn't wonder – said the Count had a very important prior engagement this morning. And there's nothing on the card about when we *are* to go, as you can see, but I suppose these real aristocrats . . . and he seems to be a very busy man. Still fighting a bit shy, I suspect, too,' she added archly. 'The coachman said he just happened to be passing this way – going to the blacksmith's just round the corner from here, as if there aren't plenty of black-smiths in the Faubourg St Germain! – but just look what the Count's written here: *Heartfelt. In the most heartfelt anticipation . . .* That's practically a declaration. And I saw the way he looked at you last night. "Something'll come of it yet," I said to your uncle only this morning, before he went off to the Tuileries. "Never mind Monsieur Turgeon and his hints – trust a woman's intuition." Because he's been dropping hints, you know: that the Count wasn't above seducing young girls of good family, and that wild horses would never drag him to the altar, and so on, but I thought all along it was probably only jealousy. And there you are: *Heartfelt*. And these cool, collected, clever sort of gentlemen, like Monsieur de l'Epinay – ' she leaned confidentially closer – 'when they do fall in love, you know, it's a grand passion, it's something quite out of the ordinary. You can tell that just from the flowers he's sent. Look at them!'

Chloe turned her eyes towards the great sprawling bouquet of white lilies, streaked with pale green and spotted with crimson within their deep trumpets filled with golden pollen, amongst which nodded mossy blood-red, deep pink and pale pink roses, and damask roses slashed with white and purple, all entwined with yards and yards of red silk ribbon. 'Something out of the ordinary'; Persephone's flowers; flowers of both love and death. Sometimes Aunt Eugénie stumbled closer to the truth than she could ever know. And in the next street, just round the corner – she'd understood – de l'Epinay's carriage was waiting for her. And the clock on the mantel-piece was ticking on, ticking towards eleven, ticking its whispering tick. He'd expect her at noon. What was she to do? As she gazed at the bouquet there was a faint stir of warm air from the window, and pollen trickled stealthily from the lilies' trumpets. The wave of heavy, passionate fragrance seemed to bring back all the horror of last night, all the horror of her dream, and her head swam.

'Yes, they're lovely,' she managed to murmur, falling back on her pillows. 'But I feel a little giddy. The scent, I suppose.'

'Or the weather. It's rather sultry, and Philippe's got one of his headaches coming on, so there'll probably be a thunderstorm later.'

Tonnerre . . .

Chloe closed her eyes, haunted by some elusive thought or memory which the word stirred in her mind. *Tonnerre* . . . *Tonnerre* . . . Still achingly tired in every limb, she was only dimly aware of Aunt Eugénie's voice and footsteps fading away out of the room and into silence. That dark garden she'd been lying in, how had she got there? Hadn't she been led there down a long dark tunnel under the . . . ?

'Philippe!'

177

She leapt from her bed and ran to the door in her nightdress, her heart beating wildly.

'Philippe! Are you there? Are you up? Oh, come quickly!'

Pale, but fully dressed, Philippe appeared in the doorway of his room across the narrow corridor. Aunt Eugénie could be heard talking to the maid in the dining-room. Swiftly Chloe drew her startled cousin into her room and closed the door.

'Listen! Oh Philippe, listen!' she whispered, her hands to her head in appalled realization, heedless of her long, tangled black ringlets and her muslin nightdress half-slipping from her shoulders. 'Trévelan didn't say "*Tonnerre*" – he said "*Tunnel*"! There must be a tunnel leading from de l'Epinay's house to the Abbey prison – I thought there might be – and Trévelan must have discovered it somehow. And de l'Epinay doesn't know. I mean, he knows that Trévelan found the tunnel, and that's why he murdered him, but he doesn't know that Trévelan's given him away. He'd never have sent these flowers and his carriage and everything if he knew – he'd be making his arrests. After all, Trévelan only whispered that word as he died, and de l'Epinay must have had to take cover quickly, because of the prostitute, and he didn't hear. And Monsieur Turgeon... Oh, I was in a daze last night, but now I understand it all! Turgeon didn't tell him. De l'Epinay sensed danger, but Turgeon persuaded him that there wasn't any. No wonder he smiled to himself – that horrible snake in the grass! Because de Grismont was there, you say. And if I can work out what Trévelan really said, and what it means, then so can the royalists. *Tonnerre – tunnel*. It's easy, when you think of it. Perhaps they've already guessed. Oh Philippe, what are we to do?'

' – Do?'

Philippe was gazing at her in bewilderment. She had told him last night, only half-coherently, about the blood on de l'Epinay's gloves, and about everything Turgeon had said to her; but she could see that even with his logical, lawyer's mind he was having difficulty in catching up with the wild

178

pace of her thoughts. His pallor had given place to a distracted flush, too, and she moved away from where the sunlight was streaming through her muslin nightdress, and sat down in the shadow on the edge of her bed, twining her hair into a long, loose braid over one of her shoulders with as much patience and calm as she could summon.

'But surely, if you're right, his other agents will have warned him by now?' Philippe objected finally.

'Oh, but don't you remember what Uncle Victor told us?' Chloe whispered, twisting her hair round and round her fingers in agitation. 'Almost no one, even in the Secret Police, knows who he is. Perhaps just a few of his lieutenants. And Turgeon could easily be pretending to them that he's already been warned, and doesn't want to be disturbed, or something.'

'But you know how astute de l'Epinay is. He'll have guessed somehow.'

'He didn't seem very astute last night. He seemed . . . ' Chloe gave an oblique, involuntary glance at the headily amorous bouquet of flowers beside her, with their secretly passionate message, and felt giddy again, remembering the irresistible intensity of de l'Epinay's gaze at her in the rose-garden, and again when he'd said goodnight. 'He seemed . . . well, quite different.'

Philippe gazed at her in silence for a moment. Then he whispered, 'But you surely can't mean you want to warn him yourself?'

'No no! No!' Chloe leapt to her feet, then sank down again limply at the far end of her bed, though even there the sinister fragrance of the flowers still pervaded her senses. 'Of course I don't want to! I never want to see him again, after what he's done. But what choice is there? I'll have to go to his house this morning anyway – I can't see how to avoid that.' She kept her eyes lowered as she spoke, fixed on the glossy black tresses of hair she was braiding. She had told Philippe only a half-truth about her mission: only that she was to encourage de l'Epinay in his courtship of her. 'And if he . . . if he were killed, there'd be no one to protect me from Turgeon, or from de Malebois, would there?'

'I'll go out and buy a pistol now!' Philippe burst out, in a fiercely intense whisper.

'Oh Philippe, I know you'd do anything for me – I know!' Chloe whispered back helplessly, dwelling on his mop of pale, soft hair, his white face, and his still boyishly slight frame. 'But you're only seventeen, and you don't even know how – '

'We could leave Paris. We could hide somewhere.'

'Leave!' Chloe found herself glancing involuntarily at de l'Epinay's flowers again. She shivered and turned her eyes quickly away, whispering, 'But how can we leave, or hide, when all the time . . . Is that priest out there in the palace gardens?'

Philippe went to the window, and admitted, 'Yes.'

'Well, there you are, then!'

Philippe leaned in the window-recess and gazed at her in silence again for a long moment. She stopped braiding her hair, aware that her fingers were visibly trembling.

'But he's Scorpio!' Philippe whispered finally.

She shut her eyes and said, 'I know.'

'And he murdered that boy.'

'I know, I know.'

'You'd be changing sides, if you warned him. You'd be betraying the whole royalist cause. You'd be working for Bonaparte!'

'How can I help that? I wasn't really interested in politics anyway. I believed . . . ' Chloe opened her eyes, found herself gazing mesmerized at the bouquet once again, and averted her eyes with an effort. 'That wasn't what I believed in.'

There was another moment's silence.

'But how can you warn him without revealing how much you know?' Philippe reasoned eventually. 'He'll listen, and then he'll thank you politely, and then he'll politely usher you down his tunnel, and you'll never be seen again!'

'I'll think of a way,' Chloe said, leaping to her feet again

180

as the stealthy scent of the lilies stole over her. She went to her wardrobe and began searching through it with fumbling, trembling hands, choosing a dress. 'I could give him a hint, for instance, whilst making it seem as if I don't know anything. I could talk about Trévelan – that wouldn't seem at all unnatural – and just mention in passing what he's supposed to have said, and that de Grismont . . . It won't really be difficult. And I'll only stay a moment. But you'll have to come with me, otherwise Aunt Eugénie . . . Can't you take a little laudanum? But I promise I'll only stay a moment, just to warn him, and then I'll never . . . '

' – See him again? Chloe, you're not thinking! He's too clever – he'll guess how much you know. And even if he doesn't he'll have you arrested with all the other royalists. What else can happen?'

'I am thinking,' Chloe said, returning slowly towards the bed with her chemise, pantelets, silk hose, and her newest crimson and pale rose-striped dress over her arm, its wine-coloured silk sash trailing. For a moment she felt almost calm as the realization struck her. 'I think de l'Epinay ought to have guessed long ago that I suspected what he really was,' she said. 'Perhaps even the first time we talked together.' She was thinking of their assignation in the palmhouse nearly two weeks before, which she'd still never dared tell Philippe about. 'I had a strange intuition about him from the beginning, like Trévelan, and he ought to have sensed that. But I think he doesn't want to realize. I think he hopes I'll never know what he is or what he's done. And he isn't planning to arrest me with the others. He's planning to leave me free, and come back to me after it's all over, pretending – perhaps even to himself – and trying to forget, because . . . '

She broke off as the trailing hem of her garments brushed against the bouquet, and one rose collapsed into a scattering of petals on the lacquered cabinet.

'You're still in love with him,' Philippe whispered bitterly. 'Even now, knowing what he is, knowing what he's done! You're more in love with him than ever.'

'No I'm not! I'm not!' Chloe whispered back in panic. 'I couldn't be! I admit I was – a little. But not now. Not after what he's done. And even if I still feel . . . It'll pass, because I could never pretend, or forget . . . And I'll just stay a moment, and warn him – about Turgeon too – and then I'll be safe. And afterwards I'll refuse to see him again. He needn't ever know why.'

'Well, nothing can have happened yet,' Philippe murmured, as they left the house most of an hour later. In the palace gardens opposite, beyond the black wrought-iron railings, the priest only glanced up casually for a moment from reading his breviary, lifted his broad-brimmed black hat to scratch his head, then paced on through the deep shade between the beds of geraniums. A nearby church clock struck noon, its chimes dull, flat and tinny in the airless heat. Chloe had bathed, dressed and put up her hair faster than she'd ever done before since she'd attained the age of young womanhood, but they were inevitably a little late. But not, it seemed, too late. 'Perhaps they haven't guessed what Trévelan really said after all,' Philippe added, as they both turned and waved at Aunt Eugénie's figure high above on the dining-room balcony. She thought they were going out in search of air, and shade, and perhaps ices in some café where there were tables outdoors under the trees. But in fact the glaring, breathless, late August heat, bouncing off the walls of the houses and the bald grey pavement, could hardly have been worse for poor Philippe's headache. Chloe herself, after her heavy sleep fraught with nightmares, and her inability to swallow even a morsel of breakfast because of her coming interview with de l'Epinay, was beginning to feel limp and dizzy again by the time they reached the corner.

'And you know – I've been thinking,' Philippe went on valiantly, as they turned down the sidestreet. 'Even if they do guess that Trévelan must have said "tunnel", it still doesn't give them conclusive proof against de l'Epinay.

182

They'd have to get into his house somehow and find the tunnel, wouldn't they? And it must be very cleverly concealed. It's a wonder Trévelan managed to find it.'

'Perhaps Turgeon called at the house and dropped a hint to him, just as he dropped hints to me. He obviously hopes the royalists will kill de l'Epinay.'

There was no sign of the blue cabriolet in the long street ahead of them, but the nearest blacksmith was round the next corner, a hundred paces away. The street was deserted, except for a small, elderly nun in a black habit, who was approaching them slowly along the pavement, carrying a large black bag.

'And they've broken into de l'Epinay's house and searched it before,' Chloe continued, lowering her voice as the nun drew closer. 'But of course they didn't know what to look for then. They were probably just rifling through his papers.'

'Yes, but what I mean is,' Philippe whispered, 'they can't search his house while he's there.'

'No, that's true.'

The street was entirely shadeless, and so hot that mirages like sheets of water or polished metal shimmered in the air. The nun had paused on the pavement a few paces in front of them, and seemed to be looking for something in her voluminous black bag. In spite of the stifling heat, Chloe felt an inexplicable shiver run through her, and the blazingly white street suddenly seemed like a long dark tunnel. Dizzily she watched the figure of the nun swim forward out of a haze of rising, quivering mirages, smiling at them for some reason with bad, brownish teeth, like a phantasma from another nightmare.

'And he won't go out all the time he's expecting you to come, will he?' Philippe continued to reason in a low voice, walking with his head bent to shield his eyes from the glare.

'No, that's . . . '

'One moment, if you please, *mes chers enfants*,' said the nun, barring their way. She smiled again, and lifted her hand just far enough out of her bag for them to see the dark glint of a pistol levelled at them. Chloe clung to the railing of the house they were passing, feeling more than ever as if she was living in some evil world of dreams, and Philippe stood with the last trace of colour drained from his face. What terrible trap had they walked into?

'In a moment you'll continue on round the corner to where de l'Epinay's carriage is waiting, and I'll follow you,' the nun said – not that she was a real nun, Chloe was sure. She had the cold, hard, mercenary eyes of the old women Chloe had sometimes glimpsed inside the open doorways of brothels at the Palais-Royal, sitting at tables counting money. Yet anyone glancing out of a window in one of the overlooking houses would have taken her for a Sister of Mercy asking her way, or perhaps begging money for some charitable cause. 'But you won't go to de l'Epinay's house,' she went on, still pointing the half-concealed pistol at them. 'You'll order the coachman to drive you straight to the Pont des Arts, where you'll be given further instructions. In the meantime you're on no account to try to see de l'Epinay or to communicate with him. And his coachman's in our pay, by the by, so don't think you can get any message to de l'Epinay through him. Now on your way – walk! And if you try any tricks, be sure that I'll put a bullet through your pretty little head.'

Could the royalists have guessed that she'd planned to warn de l'Epinay of the danger he was in? But how? For a moment longer Chloe still clung giddily to the railings, but she managed to say lightly, 'I don't understand. My orders from Monsieur de Grismont – '

'That's all changed. Something came to light that makes it look as if de l'Epinay might be Scorpio himself, no less. But we need to get into his house and search it to be sure, and I dare say you'll have some role to play in that manoeuvre, or you wouldn't be wanted at the Pont des Arts.'

'I'll be only too glad to help,' Chloe said, with a bewildered smile. 'But why the pistol? After all, if he's really Scorpio, I'll naturally do everything – '

184

'He's also a handsome devil. We've seen the way he looks at you, and we've also seen the way you look at him – especially last night at the Palais-Royal – and we've a shrewd idea of what you might naturally do.' Within the frame of her wimple, the woman's sallow face creased into a suggestive leer. 'Sorry to disappoint you, dearie, but we're taking no chances. De Grismont always was a fool where women are concerned. Now walk!'

Chloe swung round on her heel in pretended anger, but her mind was numb with shock as she and Philippe walked on towards the next corner, with the false nun a few paces behind them. What could save de l'Epinay now? And what could the royalists want with her at the Pont des Arts?

They turned the corner, and came almost immediately upon the blue cabriolet with its four matched greys, waiting at the kerb. The coachman glanced at the clock on the church tower further down the street – it was already almost a quarter past noon – and the guard jumped down from his high perch. There was nothing in either of their smooth, olive-skinned, sloe-eyed faces to show that they were even aware of the black-robed figure standing at the corner a few paces away, one hand inside her half-open bag. Was the coachman really in the royalists' pay? There seemed no way of telling.

'Please take us straight to the Pont des Arts,' Chloe said in a clear voice, watching the man's face closely. Was that a faint flicker of surprise in his black, almond eyes, or a fleeting look of secret triumph? Whatever it was, it was gone in an instant, and his face was only impassive again as he touched his whip to his blue top hat. The guard handed her up into the grey-blue suede and silver-studded interior; Philippe followed; and they drove off at a brisk trot. Still standing at the street-corner, grinning after them, the figure of the false nun receded rapidly behind.

'She might have been lying about the coachman,' Philippe whispered, after they'd stared at each other for a few moments in a stunned silence.

'I know,' Chloe whispered back. 'But how can we be

sure? And if he really is in their pay, and I give him a message warning de l'Epinay – '

' – They'll know for certain that you've changed sides, yes. No, you can't risk it.'

'Anyway, whether he's in their pay or not, we'll be watched all the time,' Chloe said, gazing out of the window in despair. Already, through the sultry haze of heat, a black barouche had become visible not far behind them; and although the cabriolet travelled swiftly down the long, wide avenues leading towards the Seine and the centre of Paris, the black hood of the barouche remained always in sight a little way behind. Two noblemen wearing low-brimmed hats and mounted on dark horses emerged from a side-turning and cantered along, as if by chance, beside them. Here and there, amongst the strollers and shoppers on the pavement, a priest turned his head to watch them pass. Even if the cabriolet had slowed down or stopped for a moment, so that they could have jumped out, there was no hope of escape, nowhere to go. Their only safety, if it could be called safety, lay in de l'Epinay, and no house in Paris would be more closely watched than his.

'They just want de l'Epinay to go out,' Philippe whispered, in a brave attempt to reassure her, though he himself was as white as a sheet. 'That's the only reason why they've stopped you from going to his house. They probably thought you'd stay there all afternoon.'

'Yes, but why do they want to see me at the Pont des Arts?' Chloe whispered back, shivering at the thought that de Malebois might be there.

Even Philippe could find no answer to that, and only stared helplessly at his hands.

Sick and giddy from fear, and from the thundery heat, Chloe leaned back in her corner. Every street they drove down now, whether darkened by great chestnuts and lindens, or glaringly shadeless, seemed like a tunnel, and every window seemed blinded or shuttered. Decapitated statues at crossroads stood like the most ominous of signposts, and here and there the word *'Liberté'*, scrawled

186

on a wall, mocked at everything she had believed in. They crossed the wide parvis of the massive, gloomy church of St Sulpice, which had been pillaged and turned into a pagan temple during the Revolution, but was now reconsecrated. The words 'Temple of Liberty' were still chiselled into the stone above the heavy pillars of the portico and the great black doors, and two priests stood motionless on the steps, watching them pass. Real priests? It scarcely seemed to signify. Nearly all the clergy were royalist sympathizers anyway, and what did politics lead to but corruption and murder? And de l'Epinay was the most evil of all of them, and she could no longer love him, so there was nothing left.

The church clock boomed out the half-hour as they passed, and a flurry of pigeons whirred up from the cobblestones and the trees round the fountain in the centre of the parvis, their grey and white wings whirling round the cabriolet like snow.

Chloe relapsed in her corner, closing her eyes and running her fingers over the soft suede of the padded seat, trying to suppress the returning whisper in her memory: 'Something greater than death.' Why should those words keep recurring, deep in her mind, when they no longer held any meaning?

Soft, grey-blue suede . . . In his house, only a few streets away now, de l'Epinay would be pacing ever more restlessly. What plans had he made for her visit? To entertain her with his wit, keeping his elusive distance, but to detain her long enough to deceive the royalists, and then to send her away to the Pont des Arts with some carefully ambiguous false clue to pass on? Or to take her in his arms and confess the truth to her between kisses – not the truth of what he was, of course, but the truth of what he felt? . . Oh, what deep, fatal trance had he fallen into, to imagine that he could deceive a woman who loved him – had loved him – as to his true nature; to imagine that a great love could grow and thrive out of such a lie; that the bleak despair in his soul, however well concealed behind gaiety and elegance, could ever have an end, after the things he'd done? And not even to realize that he had been betrayed; not even to glance out through the half-shuttered windows and see . . .

The cabriolet reached the Place St Germain, but turned away along the boulevard instead of crossing the open, cobbled space by the church, where it would have passed within sight of de l'Epinay's house. Perhaps that proved that the coachman really was in the royalists' pay; yet there was another reason, sound and perfectly innocent – a busy fruit-market in the narrow streets between the Place St Germain and the river – to explain his making this detour. And the black barouche was still behind them, the two noblemen on dark horses still riding casually at the cabriolet's side. There was time, before they turned away from the Place St German, for Chloe to see a priest standing at the corner, as if waiting for the diligence; two more apparently deep in conversation in the shadows of the church porch; a fourth walking inobtrusively away down the Rue de l'Abbaye, close under the ivy-hung prison wall opposite de l'Epinay's forecourt. And somewhere out of sight nearby, no doubt, Turgeon was also watching like a vulture. Oh, why didn't de l'Epinay look out through the shutters and see that he was surrounded by betrayal and death? Was it contrition, useless contrition, for his murder of Trévelan which had plunged him into such doomed abstraction? Or a final and total loss of belief in life itself? He must know – he was too keenly intuitive not to know, deep within himself – that he couldn't have deceived her for ever, or even for long; that he could never have her; never change. The Place St Germain fell away out of sight behind them, but his words, lightly-spoken yet prophetic, seemed to follow her like an echo: 'You'll be my downfall.'

And what of her own fate? She and Philippe hadn't dared exchange any more whispers during the journey, with those two noblemen riding so close to the cabriolet's open window. But they exchanged a look of helpless dread now, as they neared the end of a long, narrow, deeply-shadowed street and glimpsed the flash of the river, and the gay colours of the flower-stalls on the Pont des Arts.

Fourteen

NO FLICKER OF EXPRESSION stirred in the guard's black Levantine eyes as he handed Chloe down on to the cobbled quayside; nor in the eyes of the coachman as she murmured to him, 'Please wait for us here.' The two anonymous noblemen in their low-brimmed hats had dismounted casually a few paces away. The Seine rippled oily-olive and oily-grey under the leaden, thundery haze which was spreading out over the sky. Taking Philippe's arm, Chloe stepped on to the bridge. The two noblemen followed a few paces behind.

It was a pretty wooden footbridge, decorated with boxes of heliotrope, roses, mignonettes, jasmine and orange blossom, and crowded with flower-vendors, hawkers of singing canaries in wicker cages, and pedlars of silk ribbons and other knick-knacks, as well as with numerous fashionable strollers, undeterred by the breathless, stifling heat and the ominous sky. The lavender-seller, Chloe knew – she supposed numbly that her final destination was there – always sat near the far end of the bridge, close to where the lines of young plane-trees and the bright parasols of café tables broke the monotony of the long façade of the Palais du Louvre.

In silence, they passed stalls of roses; women with baskets of marguerites and sweet william; pedlars with trays of Egyptian trinkets made of bronze and cornelian and amber, decorated with arcane designs of scarabs, cats, or human figures with narrowed, heartless eyes. Then a stall of death-scented lilies. Everything seemed to speak to

Chloe of death: her own death, and the death of de l'Epinay. The lavender-seller came in sight. On the quay beyond, the small, grey-haired figure of the Marquis de Grismont paced back and forth in the shade of the plane-trees. A priest sat on a bench nearby, reading his breviary. And at a café table, making Chloe's heart almost stop within her breast, the green-uniformed figure of the Vicomte de Malebois sprawled gracefully, smiling to himself. Chloe glanced round, but the two noblemen were still following. The dark thunderclouds crept over the sun; the surface of the river seemed to turn to marble; the caged birds fell silent.

'You'd better not come any closer,' Chloe whispered to Philippe; and he nodded, white-faced, and paused beside a pedlar, as if idly examining the trinkets in his tray, while Chloe went forward alone.

The gipsy woman was dressed in grimy, brightly-coloured rags, her seamed brown face shaded by the black, low-crowned, broad-brimmed Spanish hat she was wearing, and veiled by the smoke from her white clay pipe. Sprigs of fresh lavender, and little muslin bags filled with the dried flowers, were displayed on her garishly-painted tray, slung from her neck by a red cord.

'Buy yourself some sweet lavendar, darlin',' she said, in a harshly cajoling voice, as Chloe hesitated beside her. 'Make your pretty clothes smell nice.'

'I was really planning to buy some lilies,' Chloe managed to murmur in an almost steady voice, bending over the gipsy's tray. The smell of unwashed clothes and cheap tobacco overwhelmed the fragrance of the lavender, and her head swam.

'Lilies?' The gipsy smiled, though her eyes remained beady and malevolent under the shadow of her Spanish hat. 'Well, well. And you'll pay for them with a gold louis, I dare say!'

'Naturally,' Chloe agreed, guessing that the words 'a gold louis' were part of the royalist code.

'Vive le roi.'

'*Vive le roi.*'

The gipsy took her clay pipe out of her mouth and spat a jet of brownish liquid over the parapet into the river; then she contemplated Chloe slyly for a moment. 'So you're what all this fuss is about today. The nemesis of Scorpio himself, no less!' She looked Chloe up and down insolently from head to foot, then conceded grudgingly, 'Yes, a juicy little plum! Dark and juicy, and you've gone to his head – he can't get enough of you, can he? Our friend Monsieur le Comte de l'Epinay, who always promised me no woman would ever catch him. "A beautiful woman is just a beautiful trap," he used to say to me. And for once he never spoke a truer word, the devil, though he's yet to realize that.'

'What do you mean?' Chloe whispered, a terrible suspicion beginning to dawn on her.

'Well, you *are* slow!' the gipsy said, spitting over the parapet again. 'Still, as de l'Epinay said to me once, "A woman who's being made love to as she should be – and that means day and night for at least a week, and better still a fortnight – becomes a water-nymph, like the legendary nymphs who haunt the pools in the Forest of Fontainebleau: a woman all secret shadows and deep green dreams, a woman living underwater." We always used to have an exchange of that sort when he was passing – after all, it's everyone's favourite topic, isn't it? – and he could be quite poetic sometimes. Especially just lately,' she added with a sly smile, 'though you haven't had your whole fortnight, have you, poor darlin'? And now you're never going to, sad to say.'

'Get on with what you have to tell me!' Chloe whispered sharply, though she was rather glad that Philippe was out of earshot. Not that there was any truth in the gipsy's insinuations . . . Which suggested that the royalists didn't know everything, she reflected absently, in passing, her mind half-numbed by the knowledge of what she was about to hear.

'Oh, quite the little countess *manquée*, aren't we?' the

gipsy said with a jeering laugh, beckoning her still closer with a grimy forefinger, so that Chloe was obliged to pick up one of the muslin bags of dried lavender and hold it to her nose. 'In a moment I'll slip you a little muslin bag, like these others here, but inside it you'll find notepaper and an envelope, folded up small, and a stump of lead pencil. You're to go to one of those cafés there on the Quai du Louvre – not the one where Monsieur le Vicomte de Malebois is sitting, but another. And you're to write a note to de l'Epinay, saying that you were prevented from going to his house this morning by your young cousin there – ' she jerked her thumb towards Philippe – 'but that you can meet him secretly this afternoon. Give him a definite time – half-past two or three o'clock would suit us – and think of some nice lonely spot. And be sure to make your invitation as tempting as can be, because we want to be certain that he keeps the appointment. Not that *you* will, of course,' the gipsy added, with an evil grin visible under the shadow of her hat. 'A dozen or so of us'll do that for you.'

Chloe straightened up and looked slowly round. Under the luridly thunderous sky, not a leaf stirred, not a bird fluttered, and the dark river was like glass as it flowed swiftly under the bridge. She should have known all along. They were going to use her not only to lure de l'Epinay from his house; she was to lure him to his death.

Beneath the dark surface of the river, a few strands of weed, like tendrils of green hair, floated by under the bridge and were gone, and a half-thought stirred deep in her mind. 'What lonely spot am I to invite him to?' she asked.

'Where you've met him in secret before would be best – he'll never suspect a trap then. Where was it? And don't try to pretend you've never met him secretly somewhere. He's a devil to follow, but we're sure of it.'

Chloe looked round once more at the ominously darkening scene. Under the great forbidding façade of the Louvre ahead of her, all sounds seemed to echo: the ring of footsteps on the cobblestones; the voices of departing strollers. Now there could be no turning back. 'You mean the Jardin des Plantes?' she whispered, with simulated reluctance.

'Ah, so that's where it was!'

'Yes.'

The Jardin des Plantes was a large botanical garden out on the eastern fringes of the city: a fashionable spot for riding and strolling, but with many sequestered glades and arbours.

'Where in the Jardin des Plantes? There's acres of it, and it's like a labyrinth.'

'The palm-tree grove.'

'Ah, very romantic, to be sure! Well, off you go, then, and write your little *billet-doux*. And when you've done it, leave it unsealed, and give a sign to Monsieur de Malebois. He'll come over to you, as if just to pay his respects in passing, and take the letter away. Unsealed, mind you – we'll want to make sure there's no trickery in it. Now be gone with you! Time you made yourself a bit useful to us.'

Chloe gazed down for a moment longer at the dark water below the bridge, telling herself, 'Everything I'm about to do is only to try to save myself. It isn't because I'm still in love with de l'Epinay.' But the river seemed to glide like silk, like cold glass, like the gleam of a private, vengeful smile, deserving death, as she murmured, 'Oh, but I had some information for you, about Monsieur Turgeon. Still, since none of you seems to trust me . . . ' She shrugged, and made as if to turn away.

' – What information?'

'Oh, only that he's definitely a senior member of the Secret Police. He didn't say who Scorpio was, but he did tell me that if a change of leadership was necessary for any reason, he himself would immediately assume command.'

'He told you all that? Outright?' The gipsy stared at her open-mouthed.

'Yes. He tried to make advances towards me, I told him I found him repellent, and he lost his temper and threatened me with torture. I'd have told you before, if I could have got a word in edgeways.' Chloe gave the gipsy a stinging little smile, beckoned to Philippe, and walked on towards the Quai du Louvre, holding her head high and not looking back.

'Come buy! Come buy my sweet lavender!' the gipsy sang out in a sharp, urgent tone behind her. The small, shabby, grey-haired figure of de Grismont jostled rudely past on the narrow bridge, just as Chloe stepped down from it on Philippe's arm.

'What's happening?' Philippe whispered in alarm.

'I can't tell you now.'

From the secluded café table Chloe led him to, de Grismont could be seen leaning over the parapet of the now almost deserted bridge, a pace or two away from the lavender-seller, who seemed to be absorbed in counting her money, her lips moving. After a few moments de Grismont walked slowly on, like a vagrant with nowhere to go, then leaned over the parapet again a pace or two away from the two noblemen in low-brimmed hats, who were standing as if lost in contemplation of the view. After a while they walked casually but swiftly away towards the far bank of the river, growing smaller and more anonymous than ever in the distance, till they were lost amongst the last of the dispersing strollers on the Quai Malaquais.

The heat was still stifling, and so humid that mysterious circles of moisture appeared on the marble top of the café table, as if oozing from the air itself, though no rain was falling. The leaves of the plane-trees overhanging the table were lifelessly limp. Yet the marble felt chill to Chloe's arms as she gazed blindly across the dark water to the far shore. Somewhere over there, soon, in some shadowy alley or unfrequented courtyard, Turgeon would be found lying with his blank, pebble eyes staring up at the sky, eternally glassy and inscrutable, and it would be she who had killed him. He ought to have realized that she might betray him, but perhaps he had been too intent on bringing about de l'Epinay's downfall to think of it. Perhaps he had been mad. 'And now I'm no better than de l'Epinay,' she

194

thought. And then: 'But I didn't do it for him. I did it to save myself, and I had no choice.'

From across the water, faint, hollow and echoing, there drifted the single chime of a church bell: one o'clock. More than two hours, now, since de l'Epinay had sent his carriage to fetch her. What if, disturbed or just impatient, he left his house to go in search of her? – not stealthily, by some secret side-entrance, but impulsively and unaware, running down the front steps. Rather than risk his disappearing into the maze of the city, mightn't the royalists shoot him down then and there in his own forecourt? There was no time to lose. Rousing herself, she gulped down half the iced orange-flower water Philippe had ordered, then opened the little muslin bag the gipsy had given her, and laid the notepaper, the envelope and the pencil on the marble table before her.

'Whatever's happening?' Philippe whispered again.

'Hush! There's very little time, and I must think.'

'But de Malebois – '

'Hush! I know.'

She was all too well aware of the gracefully sprawled, green-uniformed figure not far away beyond the screen of limp plane-tree leaves, watching her with cold dark eyes and the faint curve of a patient, calculating smile. No doubt he'd been promised that later that day, when it was all over . . . But she mustn't think about it; she must forget he was there. Every word mattered; de l'Epinay's life and her own hung on the nuance of each word she wrote.

'Look away – don't watch what I'm doing,' she whispered to Philippe as she took up the pencil. Further along the quayside a black barouche stood waiting. 'I'll explain afterwards.'

'Lucien mon chéri, mon amour . . . '

So she began, then paused. They had never once called each other by their first names; never spoken to each other using the intimate *tu*. But the royalists believed they were lovers, and to cast any doubt on that assumption might be fatal. And de l'Epinay, reading such words from her, would

195

surely guess at once that something was amiss; that they were only written to deceive the royalists; that she didn't really mean them. Why, then, did her fingers tremble so much that she had to pause?

'*All I want is to be in your arms*,' she wrote on, after a moment. '*And I feel desolate, because Philippe's so jealous, and he prevented me from coming to you this morning. Please don't be angry, don't disappoint me, but come to me at our own secret place at three o'clock this afternoon – I can slip away then. And wear your sea-green suit and your turquoise cuff-links, just for me. The turquoise so brings out the colour of your eyes, mon beau Lucien, even in those deep green shadows, and it was what you were wearing the first time that you caressed me – though I thought it was a palm-leaf then, you know – and told me how much you wanted me, and we both knew . . .* ' Her fingers trembled again, and a damp circlet formed on the notepaper. '*. . . And we both knew in our hearts that we were meant for each other, though so much – too much – has come between us. And I'm in despair, for without you there's nothing but death.*'

She signed her name, then slowly folded the letter and slipped it into the envelope. It was done. If he read between the lines, she had told him everything: that she did really love him, but that she knew what he was, and that she was saying goodbye. Would he understand? Would he even wake from his trance and guess that he'd been betrayed? There was so little she'd dared say, for fear of discovery. Or would she have to meet him in the palmhouse and warn him to his face? If either of them was still alive by three o'clock; if the royalists didn't see through her subterfuge.

She looked up. The sky was a menacing purplish-black, and the scene was deserted but for her motionless watchers. Only a few lads played tag along the quay, their screams echoing eerily under the long façade of the Louvre. She turned her head and met de Malebois' dark gaze for a moment, then took refuge in sipping the rest of her orange-flower water.

The ring of footsteps, slow, stealthy and prowling, came

closer across the cobblestones; then there was a rustle as a spray of leaves was brushed aside. The footsteps came to a halt, and although there was no sunlight or shade, it was as if a cold dark shadow fell across Chloe's whole being. She raised her eyes reluctantly. In unsmiling silence, de Malebois bowed and held out his hand for the letter. It seemed to Chloe that she had never seen anything so deadly as his black expressionless gaze.

She gave him the letter. He only said, very softly, '*A bientôt* – until soon.' Then he bowed again and walked away.

With Philippe she watched him stroll gracefully across the quay and along the Pont des Arts. He passed de Grismont, who could be seen a moment later reading the letter as he leaned over the parapet. He read it once, twice, three times. Then he put it back in the envelope and called to one of the lads playing on the quay. The boy ran to him. The letter changed hands, and there was the glint of a coin; then the boy sped away over the bridge towards the far bank, where a patch of blue against the grey and white houses showed where de l'Epinay's cabriolet was still waiting.

De Grismont, de Malebois and the priest all walked quickly away in different directions without glancing back. The gipsy closed the lid of her tray and gathered up her folding stool. With an echoing rumble of wheels under the dark façade of the Louvre, the black barouche approached along the quay.

Fifteen

THE QUARTER-HOUR CHIMED. A quarter to three. Chloe
wandered distractedly from room to room in the silent,
shadowy appartement. Philippe and Aunt Eugénie were
both asleep; Uncle Victor wasn't expected home from the
Tuileries till the evening. It was so still that her carefully
muted, slippered footsteps sounded loud to her. She could
hear her own breathing, and seemed to hear the rapid
beating of her own heart.

Never had the appartement seemed so close a prison.
The false nun who had brought them home in the black
barouche, her pistol on her knee, had forbidden them to
go out again for the rest of that day, and the guard had been
doubled. In the deserted palace gardens, under the heavy,
motionless trees, the usual priest paced slowly to and fro
opposite Chloe's bedroom window, reading his breviary;
but from the dining-room balcony a second priest was now
visible, sitting at one end of a long green bench beside the
entrance gates. She ought to have known. If de l'Epinay
came to the palmhouse, she wouldn't be able to go to him
and warn him. Unless, wearing her grey pelisse and running
like the wind through the blinding downpour when the
storm finally broke . . .

Under the ominous, purple sky, the trees and grass in the
palace gardens were a lurid jade, and the air was as dark as if
it were already dusk. There was not a soul to be seen but
the two priests. But not a leaf stirred; not a drop of rain fell.
If was as if the storm would never break. And even if it did,
she'd be seen; she'd be shot down as she ran; and she'd have

betrayed de l'Epinay's whereabouts.

Amid the cold white marble and the dark panelling of the dining-room, the whispering tick of the ormolu clock seemed to echo faintly. Ten to three. De l'Epinay was usually early for his appointments. Perhaps he was already there in the palmhouse. But how could she even know if he was there or not?

Helplessly she wandered back along the dark passage to her bedroom. Was there any hope that de l'Epinay would have guessed from her letter that he'd been betrayed? It hardly seemed possible. But would he have been alerted enough, at least, to have left his house unobserved? Or, still in his trance, would he have set out so openly – perhaps even in that distinctive cabriolet – that the royalists would have been able to follow him to the palmhouse and shoot him down there? Shoot him down? She thought of de Grismont's malicious little smiles, and his way of playing idly with his knife all the time, gouging small holes here and there with the point of it, and she shivered. No, he'd have de l'Epinay taken alive. And she'd never even know. She'd only know tonight, or tomorrow, when de Malebois, with his polite curve of a smile, and his level, deadly dark eyes . . .

Five to three. The air seemed darker than ever. It was the last day of August, she remembered irrelevantly, as she moved like a sleepwalker towards her window again. The last day of summer; Persephone's last day above the ground.

In the tense gloom under the trees in the palace gardens, the long avenues were still deserted, the lawns and gravel paths still dry. Only the priest had stopped pacing, and was sitting at the foot of a great linden, his head tilted back against the trunk and his broad-brimmed black hat over his eyes. His breviary lay carelessly open on the grass beside him. His attitude was hardly priestly, but no one was about, and she supposed that he wasn't a real priest anyway. Perhaps even he had finally wilted under the oppressively thundery atmosphere, though no doubt he was still watching her carefully from under the brim of his hat.

She turned away, and resumed her helpless pacing. As she wandered back along the dark passage towards the dining-room, the ormolu clock chimed three, cold and final. Yet it was more than ever impossible not to wander compulsively on through the shadows; not to be drawn yet again, futilely, to look out of the window.

On the long green bench by the entrance gates to the gardens, the second priest lay stretched full length on his back as if staring up at the sky. There was a first mutter of thunder, and a few big drops of rain pitted the dusty ground beside the bench, but he didn't stir.

Chloe flew back on tiptoe to her bedroom, and looked out through the window. The first priest hadn't moved either, though large, scattered raindrops were falling on the open pages of his breviary. As she watched, he slid slowly sideways like a propped-up doll until he was leaning at a drunken angle, his head lolling back. His hat fell off and rolled away across the grass. Drops of rain fell on his upturned face.

De l'Epinay! Only de l'Epinay could have approached so invisibly, despatched two men within sight of the windows of a hundred appartements unseen, then as stealthily vanished again.

He knew, then. He knew that something had gone badly wrong. Perhaps he even knew that his identity had been discovered; perhaps even that she herself was aware that he was Scorpio. So why had he still come? Why was he waiting for her – at this very moment – over there in the palmhouse?

The trees swayed and seethed suddenly in the palace gardens, and in her room, almost as dark as night, the sinister, passionate fragrance of the roses and lilies by her bedside stole over her with deepening seductiveness, making her head swim. There was a vivid bluish flash, and a loud rumble of thunder from all round the house, reverberating down the long avenues of trees in the gardens. *Tonnerre – tunnel.* It was like the sound of the ground opening up.

200

She sped down the dark passage towards the front door of the appartement. Philippe murmured something weakly, perhaps in his sleep drugged with laudanum, as she passed his door, but she didn't answer. Nor was there time to dwell on the heavily scrolled white and gold furniture and potted plants in the salon as she ran past its open door, or on the memory of her warm, rose-patterned nest of a bedroom behind her, or think, 'I'm never coming back.' She flew down the three flights of stairs, then down the long straight street towards the palace, just ahead of the sweeping curtain of torrential rain. She didn't even ask herself why she was going there, running to de l'Epinay. It was as if the pursuing rain drove her to him; as if the earsplitting crash of thunder all around her opened up the way.

As she flung open the door of the palmhouse there was a flash of fair hair and a flash of turquoise, and then she was swept up into his arms and carried away deep into sea-green darkness. Rain hissed as it sluiced over the glass roof and walls, and flickers of lightning silhouetted sinuous trunks and arching sprays of interlacing palm-fronds; then there was only the dark again, and the swift caress of his lips, now burning like fire, now thrilling like rivulets of cool water, now drinking deeply and delicately from her mouth until she thought she'd die blissfully from lack of breath. And then his voice, part of the sob and murmur of the rain washing over the glass and the sigh of the leaves: 'I love you . . . I love you . . . ' And then: 'So you love me too?'

'Yes.'

'And you're mine now. Say you're mine.'

'Yes.'

'Say it!' His teeth nipped the lobe of her ear. Palm-trunks and black slashes of foliage leapt into stark and quivering life in another flash of lightning.

'I'm yours.'

'For ever?'

Wheeling precariously, he was carrying her at random from clearing to clearing, deeper amongst the dense groves of tropical plants. The lightning zigzagged down the length of the palmhouse, down its dark green tunnel ahead of them.

'Yes,' she whispered at last, under the crash of the thunder, closing her eyes. And she thought, 'But there's no for ever now. No life together. Only dying together perhaps, and then hell, or nothingness. But that's for ever too.'

'For ever, then!' he whispered, still wheeling, a dark force like a whirlpool. 'I want nothing else now. Nothing. Nothing.' Lightning fleetingly lit up his face, frighteningly beautiful, frighteningly lonely and intense. 'Why did you hesitate just now, before you answered? You don't know what I've been through – how I've nothing but you now. And last night, when you seemed so remote . . . And when you didn't come this morning. But then your letter . . . ' Warm wet leaves caressed them as he swayed deliriously, dangerously. 'Say it again – how you began it.'

'Lucien.'

'And then?'

'My darling.'

'And then?'

'My love.'

And then only silence and darkness, and the haunting, lilting rhythm of his steps, making her cling the closer, lacing her fingers through the cool silkiness of his hair and pressing his head to her breast, lost in hopeless, helpless love of him. But the thought drifted into her mind and dwelt there: he was still in his trance; he'd understood nothing. And somehow she had to warn him.

'But do you know,' she whispered, 'that I wrote that letter at – ?'

' – The Pont des Arts? Yes of course. My coachman told me.' Still carrying her, he began sipping stealthily at the drops and trickles of rainwater or condensation on her throat and her bare shoulders and the upper curve of her

202

breasts. 'But let's not talk politics, now or ever again.'

'Your coachman?' She closed her eyes in relief as well as in thrilling pleasure. 'They said he was in their pay.'

'So he is.' De l'Epinay's soft murmuring was intermittent: rapid, casual snatches of phrases between searching sips. 'It's convenient, you see, that they should believe' – sip – 'that one of my servants is working for them.' Sip. 'I can control what information's acquired about me then, true or false' – sip, sip – 'and it stops them from trying to bribe anyone else in my service. But I'd have known anyway, because your letter was all too well scented with cheap tobacco as well as with lavender. De Grismont never seems to learn . . . But let's not talk.'

Chloe opened her eyes again, listening to the drumming of the rain on the glass in the green darkness, but listening, too, to the memory of de l'Epinay's words. That indifference, that dismissive contempt: was it the tone of a man secure in his supremacy over his enemies, or of a man who was no longer thinking at all; who no longer cared? 'But you didn't come here in your carriage just now? she asked, suddenly frightened at the thoughtless risks he might have taken.

'No no,' he murmured, his lips following a last rivulet of moisture to where it trickled down between her breasts. 'I only use it when I want to advertize my activities, which this morning – '

'Because it was meant to be a trap. They wanted – '

'Oh, a trap,' he said impatiently, as if traps were laid for him every day, as perhaps they were. 'De Grismont and his wretched traps . . . Why do you keep on about it? I'd know how to stop you talking, if there were only . . . ' He wheeled round swiftly in a complete circle as lightning lit up the whole palmhouse for an instant. 'But you see how it is – we're plagued by inconvenient settings. There isn't even one of those wrought-iron garden sofas, although that wouldn't have been the perfect answer either. What am I to do with you?' He whirled her round again, a branch snapped, foliage rushed up past them, and they lay sprawled along the slanting trunk of a palm, so closely entwined that it was as if she could feel every vein in his lithe, powerful body pulsing against her. Gently he drew her dress off her shoulder, and his parted lips moved down over her breasts. She put her fingertips in his ears, she ran her hands through his lovely hair and nursed his head to her, she gasped aloud with bliss; she couldn't stop herself. Lightning lit up urgent, devious, writhing shapes like snakes. Shaking, he scooped her closer still as they began to slide, then rested his dewed brow against her breast with a sound like a sob or a soft laugh, or both, and was still.

'Well, this is delightful, in a way,' he murmured after a few moments. 'That you wanted to see me again at all, and in secret . . . And I'm even wearing the cuff-links you asked for, and everything. But the truth is that we can't consummate our love here, either on the floor, between two of those anonymous puddles, or up a tree. It might be what I feel like doing, but it wouldn't be at all chivalrous. So let's go.' He rested his lips lightly against her breast again for a moment, then eased the neckline of her dress gently back into place. 'Let's go to Fontainebleau. And be married. And never come back. And forget everything, and not think – not think any more. You won't need your clothes, or anything – I'll dress you in gold and silver. So come.' He stepped back from her, taking her hand. 'Come with me now.'

There was another rumble of thunder, but already further away. Chloe dwelt on de l'Epinay's face. For all the apparent practicality and light-heartedness of some of his words, there was still something fatally trancelike in his eyes and in his whole manner. And although he seemed to know most of her letter by heart, what of her words, 'Too much has come between us'? It was if he hadn't taken them in; as if he'd skipped them quickly, in dread of what they might mean – in dread of their stirring and waking the truth lying hidden deep within him: that it wasn't possible to forget all the things he'd done, and escape with her for ever into a dreamworld. Not far from them, a spray of leaves like a black hand glistened wet in a faint wave of light, and drops of moisture on the mosaic floor gleamed palely like sightless eyes. He wanted to carry her away into dream-world, and yet . . .

She broke free and walked a few paces away from him. Through the screen of tropical leaves and the wet glass wall beyond them, the palace gardens loomed dismal and deserted under the dark sky. The lawns and gravel paths were flooded, the geraniums had been battered flat, and rain was bouncing off the seats of the little iron chairs and pouring off the long green benches in ragged silver fringes. A wooden toy soldier floated abandoned in a wide puddle, staring blindly upwards. Oh, why had de l'Epinay murdered Trévelan? Anything else she could have forgiven. Perhaps it was even contrition about the boy which had plunged him into such a trance, the memory of what he'd done mesmerizing him so that he couldn't even see the danger he was in. And only her forgiveness could wake him from that trance and save him. She longed to forgive him – forgive him anything . . . She leant against a palm-tree, still turned away from him, tears streaming from her eyes. But how could she? How could she ever forget – ever share her life with him, daring to forget – that he had cold-bloodedly murdered that innocent boy, hardly more than a child?

'What is it? Why have you gone away from me?'

There was a catch in his soft voice, as of pain, or of nameless fear, and she heard a sigh of leaves as he spoke, as if he was turning away, not wanting to hear her answer.

Somewhere nearby, sounding as if it were chiming underwater, a church clock struck the half-hour. Half past three. How long would it take de Grismont and his men to realize that she'd deceived them about the Jardin des Plantes? How long before her references to palm-trees, and to slipping easily away, would suddenly fall into place in their minds, and lead them here?

Dashing the tears from her eyes, Chloe turned to face de l'Epinay. His figure was so motionless and solitary, so pale and unreal, it was as if it were his ghost she was seeing.

'It's about Trévelan,' she said, turning away again,

fearful that a flash of lightning or a break in the clouds might reveal some telltale expression in her face. Her heart was beating fast. How could anything she said now be made to sound casual or ingenuous? And how much dared she say? 'I've kept trying to warn you, but you wouldn't listen. Trévelan said something before he died. That woman – the woman who screamed – was telling everyone about it while you and I were in the rose-garden. And Philippe said to me afterwards that de Grismont was there in the crowd. The woman thought Trévelan had said *Tonnerre*, but I . . . but some people thought he might have said *Tunnel*. And this morning, at the Pont des Arts, they seemed very sure that it meant . . . that it meant something. They wanted me to arrange to meet you somewhere out of the way this afternoon, so that they could search your house.'

There was a deep silence, a deathly stillness. Not daring to glance round, Chloe ran her trembling fingers over the cold, moist glass of the palmhouse wall. How close was he behind her? She knew how soundlessly he could move. And who could tell what he might do, if he'd realized how much she knew about him? He'd been strangely attached to Trévelan, for some reason – even de Grismont had said so – and yet . . .

A fingertip traced the line of her neck and shoulder, and she almost screamed aloud, but his hands were as gentle as they were urgent as he turned her to face him. 'You haven't answered my question – why you've become so remote from me again,' he whispered. 'As for what you tell me – don't worry – they won't find anything, least of all a tunnel. So it doesn't matter about . . . ' He closed his eyes for a moment, and she thought he shivered. 'So we needn't think about Trévelan, or anything, but it's all the more reason to go to Fontainebleau. So come with me. Don't ask me to explain, but I can't stand any more. Come with me now. Please.'

Chloe shut her eyes briefly in her turn. There seemed nothing left now but to tell him at least half the truth. 'I can't come with you,' she said. 'I love you, but I'd never be able to forget that you killed Trévelan.'

De l'Epinay backed slowly away from her, silent. For a moment the green dusk in the palmhouse lightened fleetingly again, and because of the glass awash with rain, or because of her tears, the tropical trees seemed to sway and blur like submarine weeds. De l'Epinay too, standing motionless a pace or two away from her, seemed to grow pale and sway in the watery half-light.

' – Killed him?' he said at last, almost inaudibly. 'But I didn't kill him.'

'Don't lie!' Chloe cried out, her fear almost forgotten in her sudden anger. 'There isn't time.'

'I'm not lying. I'd never lie to you about such a thing.' He came closer to her, his face passionately appealing in the renewed and deepening dusk. 'How could you imagine . . ? I didn't kill him, I swear to you.'

'I saw you!'

'You didn't! I didn't kill him. I was trying to save him. He – oh . . . ' De l'Epinay suddenly bowed his head, lacing the fingers of both hands through his hair, and gave a muffled exclamation which might almost have been a sob. 'There are things I can never tell you, but oh, if you knew . . . '

'I saw the blood on your hands.'

'Blood?' He raised his head, looking bewildered. If she hadn't known the depthlessness of his duplicity – his hypocritical gentleness towards General de Bourges at the Tuileries ball; the many times he'd enlisted her complicity as one of his own spies, under cover of wooing her: but the examples were numberless and without end – she might have been taken in by him now. His face cleared a little in comprehension, and he said, in seeming grief, 'Ah . . . But if you care for someone, you can't prevent yourself – even if it's too late, and there's no hope . . . ' He lifted his hand, as if to touch her, then let it fall, perhaps seeing the disbelief in her eyes. Then he asked softly, searchingly, leaning closer in the deep shadow, like a man waking unwillingly from a long dream, 'If you love me, why are you so ready to believe the worst about me? I'm not sure if I quite understand.'

There was nothing left to lose, Chloe thought. Nothing mattered any more. And it would be a relief to have the truth finally in the open between them, whatever it cost. 'Well, I know, you see . . . ' she whispered. 'I've felt it from the beginning, only now I'm sure. I know that you're Scorpio.'

Sixteen

In the green, striped dusk, very still, de l'Epinay gazed at Chloe without a flicker of expression in his face. Only the faint gleam of his fair hair caught any light amongst the deep shadows of the palm-fronds, and the ice-clear blue of his eyes. All spellbound dreaminess, all passion, even all trace of ordinary human feeling, had abruptly left his face, and he looked as he had when Chloe had first seen him in the shadows at the Tivoli Gardens: ruthless, calculating and sinister. It had been necessary to wake him from his trance, necessary that the truth should be out in the open between them, and she had known that it would be frightening. But to this degree? She leaned back against the cold glass wall of the palmhouse, hoping he couldn't see that she was trembling, though he was very close to her.

'So that explains it all,' he said at last, speaking very softly, as if to himself. 'Your remoteness, your believing that I could have killed Trévelan . . . And of course you'll never take my word for that now. I suppose I should have guessed. But I hoped, dreamed, beyond all reason . . . ' There was a sudden wince of anguish in his eyes, and he covered his face with his hands, and murmured, 'Still, that's all over now.'

There seemed nothing Chloe could say, and after a moment he backed away from her, letting his hands fall. Gone was that inhuman iciness, which had perhaps only been a mask anyway. As he retreated further, there was a brief, wan wave of light between the leaves, dimly illuminating his honey-coloured hair, his darkened grey-blue eyes and his clear olive skin, and all the handsome elegance of his face and figure, all the ineffable solitariness and emptiness of his soul. Chloe felt as if her heart was breaking. How could all those dark things be true about him? If only they weren't true! And yet they were. He hadn't even tried to deny that he was Scorpio.

The light quickly faded again, the deep shadows returned, and he stepped still further away from her, a veil of formality and remoteness seeming to descend over him as he merged with the gloom. 'Well, this is no time for explanations – supposing you even wanted to hear them,' he murmured, his voice only courteous and matter-of-fact now, speaking out of near-invisibility. 'On the contrary, you had better enlighten me about what's been happening. I can imagine that, believing what you believe about me – about Trévelan – the last thing you want . . . But your own safety may depend on it. And I haven't had my mind on things – there's much that I don't understand. For instance, it's true that there's a tunnel leading from my house to the Abbey prison, but the entrance is perfectly invisible, no different in appearance from the rest of the stone wall in the cellar. Trévelan . . . Well, perhaps you won't believe this either, but he couldn't possibly have discovered it. And I was careful not to use it while he was there, so I'm mystified. Someone must have betrayed me, but I can't plan anything – there's no safety anywhere – until I know who it was.'

Chloe said hesitantly, 'I wondered if Turgeon . . . He gave me some very clear hints about you at the Palais-Royal last night, and talked as if he was expecting to take over your role.'

'Did he indeed? Yes, and he could have told Trévelan about the tunnel. He often came to the house, and they may well have been alone together for a few moments now and then. No wonder the boy fled from me!' There was a note of bitterness in de l'Epinay's voice, then a sudden stillness in the deep shadows where he was standing. 'And Turgeon called in this morning, while I was waiting for

210

you, and then went across to the prison, through the tunnel. He could easily have left the door open – I never thought to go down and look. So . . . ' Beginning to pace, de l'Epinay became visible again, turning on his heel in a deeply-screened clearing amongst the tropical plants, his light eyes as alert and level now as a tiger's. 'And they'll have found it by now. Well, they could hardly have more conclusive proof than that.'

'But didn't you ever think that he might betray you?' Chloe asked in despair.

'There was always that possibility. But he chose his moment well,' de l'Epinay murmured, moving stealthily closer to the glass wall to survey the drenched palace gardens, careful to keep behind a screen of leaves. 'He'd never have outwitted me at any other time. And of course he had more to gain than usual by my removal from the scene, or hoped he had.' He gave Chloe a brief, preoccupied glance, and added, 'That rose-coloured gown you're wearing's rather eye-catching. Keep well away from the glass, and stay where the leaves and shadow are darkest, while I think what to do.'

'But why did you employ him at all?' Chloe asked, bewildered, as she obeyed him. 'It was always obvious that he hated you.'

'I had no choice,' de l'Epinay answered absently, prowling behind the screens of leaves and scanning the open stretches of lawn outside, and the sombre groves and avenues of trees. 'He was blackmailing me . . . But that's a long story. Fortunately he failed to report to me this afternoon, just before I came out, or he'd know where I am now. Presumably – '

'Listen, I . . . '

'Later. Presumably de Grismont and his friends weren't expecting me to come here?'

'No, to the Jardin des Plantes. They seemed to think we'd been meeting in secret somewhere – '

'Yes, I had my coachman put that story about, because of your mission.'

' – But they didn't know where, so I told them it was at the Jardin des Plantes.'

'At three o'clock?'

'Yes. But listen, I ought to tell you. I guessed what Turgeon had done – and anyway he threatened me with torture – so I betrayed him to the royalists at the Pont des Arts this morning.'

De l'Epinay glanced up calmly from his fob-watch, which he was holding to the little light there was. 'You were condemning him to death, you know. Did you realize that?'

'Yes. But he wasn't – '

' – An innocent child,' de l'Epinay finished for her, with a stingingly bitter little smile. Then he turned away and continued his stealthy prowling, studying the surrounding gardens from every angle. 'The trouble is,' he went on after a while, in a more casual but very remote tone, 'I had only two other lieutenants besides Turgeon who even knew who I was, and I haven't seen either of them since early yesterday evening. I suppose Turgeon was keeping them away from me. But the result is that I haven't a single man to deploy, never mind the score of men I need, unless we leave here and I can get a message to one of them.'

'But why don't we leave?' Chloe asked. She had been surprised that he hadn't made a swift decision to leave instantly, perhaps abandoning her here, or perhaps questioning her while they made their escape. Why delay here at all, where they were cornered with no second exit, and where the royalists were most likely to come in search of them?

'A good question,' he murmured, still stealthily scanning the gardens. 'Here we are, virtually in a glass case – not at all the venue I would have chosen. And it's my fault entirely – I wouldn't listen when you tried to warn me – but I fear it's too late to leave here. They've had most of an hour, you see, and it wouldn't have taken them long to think of looking here. And if they've found those two so-called priests in the gardens, they'll know this is where we are. It's all too likely that they've already got us surrounded, and would shoot us down the moment we emerged. That they're just keeping out of sight and waiting. It's what I'd do in their position. They can't miss, you see.'

He walked soundlessly towards the only door out of the palmhouse, disappearing into the shadows. There was a long silence, as if he were listening. Chloe visualized the wide straight corridor beyond that door, leading to the rest of the palace, and remembered that there were no alcoves, pillars or statues along it, no doors opening off it into other rooms; no cover at all. De l'Epinay was right. If the royalists had already got into the palace – and de Malebois in particular, as one of Bonaparte's equerries, would have had no difficulty – then it was true; they couldn't miss.

'I think they're there,' de l'Epinay murmured, materializing out of the shadows near her, his silver-headed cane gleaming in his hand, though he hadn't been carrying it earlier. Chloe supposed he must have retrieved it from somewhere near the door, where he'd flung it in order to catch her in his arms when she'd burst in as the storm broke. 'It's difficult to be sure, because of all the other noise,' he added, 'but I thought I heard whispers, and footsteps.'

Chloe watched the rainwater streaming down the long glass panes between the iron arches forming the structure of the palmhouse. 'Couldn't we break the glass and escape out into the gardens?' she whispered. 'The spaces between the girders are easily wide enough.'

'They'll have thought of that, I'm afraid.' De l'Epinay moved covertly closer to the glass again. 'We'd have a wide stretch of open lawn to cover, and in every one of those groves and shrubberies, unless I'm much mistaken . . . Ah!' He breathed a stealthy, predatory sigh, like a hunter sighting his quarry, even though it was he himself who was at bay.

'What is it?' Chloe whispered. 'Did you see something?'
'Yes. One of them moved.'
He returned to her, murmuring calmly, 'So . . . It's all

just as I thought.' Watching him approaching, Chloe saw how elegantly smooth, swift and silent his movements were, and how keenly alert his face, with his eyes a piercingly light grey-blue even in the deepest shadow. Even if he had murdered Trévelan – and somehow she half-doubted it now, although how else was his tormented ambiguity about the boy to be understood? – she was suddenly very glad of all those qualities in him which she had found frighteningly sinister from the start: his detached and calculating mind, his stealth, his hunter's and killer's singleness of purpose. He was even smiling faintly to himself.

'What are we going to do?' she asked casually, determined to match his unruffled calm.

'Fight it out with them here – there isn't much choice. And this place does have one or two natural advantages, you know. If we can't get out without being shot, neither can they get in. And at the moment it's lighter in the gardens than it is here. They can't approach without my seeing them, while they won't be able to see me.' He watched with narrowed eyes as the sun, already quite low in the sky, showed for a moment beneath the ragged hem of the dark stormclouds, illuminating some distant *faubourg* of the city, or the outlying countryside, with a few brief rays of theatrical dark gold. 'It's best not to delay,' he added. 'I shall take them by surprise, I think, by opening hostilities.'

He had taken a slim black case out of an inside pocket of his coat while he was speaking, and counted the bullets in it. Now, as he met her eyes, there was no trace of a smile on his face. 'It's only fair to warn you,' he told her quietly, 'that we're very unlikely to win. There'll be at least twelve of them, perhaps twenty, and I've scarcely a dozen bullets – and this, for what it's worth.' He indicated his silver-headed cane, and Chloe realized that it must sheathe a rapier. 'But I haven't made a career of flashing swords about, like de Malebois. And with an unreliable foot too ... Well, we must hope it doesn't come to that.

There's the very remote chance that my coachman, who knows I came here once before . . . But I gave him the afternoon off. I'm sorry. For myself, I can't say I care much. I've precious little to lose now.' He averted his eyes, loading one of his two pistols. 'I'll kill as many of them as I can first, and then . . . But there's you.'

Chloe said nothing. She had glimpsed the bleakly resigned loneliness in his averted eyes, and her heart bled. If only he hadn't murdered Trévelan! Or if only she could see any other reason for his haunted and anguished obsession with the boy's death. It would never have been easy to understand how such a finely aristocratic man could have become the parvenu Emperor's hired spy and assassin, hunting down his own kind, but perhaps she could have forgiven and forgotten that if it hadn't been for Trévelan. For if he had killed Trévelan, he was capable of anything, and all the rumours about his inhuman cruelty might be true. So she couldn't say, as she longed to, 'I love you and trust you without reservation, and I'd have come to Fontainebleau with you for ever, if we weren't going to die.' And they couldn't even die together, one in heart and soul; they had to die with this terrible and enduring rift between them.

'Here – take this,' he murmured, holding out the loaded pistol to her, and she noticed that his face was suddenly pale and set.

'Ah, so you'll let me try – ?'

'No. I'm going to hide you in the safest place I can find here, and you're not to move or make a sound, whatever happens. It's that if I'm killed, or wounded badly enough for them to take me alive . . . I can't bear to think what they might do to you. So promise me.' In a faint flicker of lightning, a dew of sweat was visible on his brow, and Chloe could feel how cold his hand was as he closed her fingers round the butt of the pistol. 'The surest way is to – is to put the barrel in your mouth and point it upwards.' He closed his eyes for an instant, then added, 'It'll be quick, at least. So promise me, Chloe. Please.'

'I promise you,' she whispered.

'And you've only one bullet, so don't use it on anyone else, however tempted you are.'

'No. But what about you?'

'Hush now. If I'm to be killed, my only regret is that I shan't be able to take de Grismont with me, as I had a particular score to settle with him. And to rid the world of him – all that he is – would have given some little meaning and value to my life, which otherwise I can't find in it. But there it is. He only kills the helpless and unarmed, and he'll keep well out of the way until it's all over. But hush now.'

Taking her free hand, he led her quickly and silently through the deep shadows towards the door. There was a shallow alcove there in the stone wall dividing the palm-house from the rest of the palace, screened both from the door and from the nearest glass wall by dense clumps of tropical plants. Chloe could see the comparative safety of it. No one would expect either of them to be so close to the door. And unless the weather lifted, no one would be able to see her from more than a pace or two away, within the palmhouse.

De l'Epinay kissed her hand, pressed her fingers briefly to his chill, dewed brow, then stepped back from her with a trace of a smile. He motioned to her to huddle down on the floor of the alcove, then turned away. In an instant he had melted invisibly into the shadows.

In the waiting silence and stillness, broken only by the incessant hiss of the rain, Chloe was haunted by all that had just happened: by de l'Epinay's horror at the thought of her blowing her brains out; by his having given her one of his precious pistols, leaving himself only half-armed; and by the deep, silent love expressed in the way he'd pressed her hand to his brow as he'd said goodbye. She guessed that if he'd been alone he'd have used up all but one of his bullets on the royalists, then shot himself. As she was there, he would fight on, if necessary with his rapier, protecting her for as long as he could, with the terrible risk that he would be captured alive; she hadn't been taken in

216

by his evasiveness on that subject. Far from killing her, then, because she knew he was Scorpio, he was making every possible sacrifice for her sake. And he truly loved her. How could the same man have murdered Trévelan? If only there was more time – time to think, to look into his eyes, to question him and to listen, to try to understand. But it was too late now.

In the dense foliage and shadow close to the glass wall some way down the tunnel of the palmhouse, she could just make out the faint gleam of de l'Epinay's hair and the glint of a pistol, deathly still. It was where he had been standing a little while ago, when he'd glimpsed one of de Grismont's men moving, perhaps in a shrubbery some hundred paces away. There was a sudden sharp report, a tinkle of broken glass, and then, only an instant later, from out in the gardens, a scream of pain, dying quickly away into silence.

For a second, for two, three, four seconds, the silence endured, as if the royalists were stunned by this turn of events. Chloe glimpsed de l'Epinay's silhouette fleeting swiftly away through the shadows towards the far end of the palmhouse; then he vanished, as if perhaps he'd dropped flat to the floor. A hail of bullets suddenly smashed into the palmhouse from all sides with an explosion of breaking glass. Bullets and glass splinters whined in all directions. With a loud sighing of leaves, a long stem of a palm sank slowly to the floor, and in the brief ensuing silence the sound of entering rainwater became audible, pattering down on the mosaic floor and the litter of broken glass. There was no sign or sound of the palace guards, but they were really only footmen with muskets, not professional soldiers as at the Tuileries, and it would have been easy enough for de Malebois to convince them that he had been sent with a contingent of men to arrest a group of Jacobins who had been using the palmhouse as a meeting-place.

The stillness in the shadows where Chloe had last seen de l'Epinay was only momentary; with relief she saw that he too was unscathed. Within seconds, she glimpsed his dark figure stealing towards the glass, the barrel of his pistol gleamed, and then there was the crack of a shot, followed by another trailing cry out in the gardens, and another hail of bullets, this time sustained. De l'Epinay was just visible in flashes, firing, zigzagging swiftly away through the shadows, then firing again, now from one side of the palmhouse and now from the other, but always keeping his distance from the door, so that scarcely any bullets whined in Chloe's direction. But he, encircled now by constant fire: it seemed a miracle that he had survived even for a few minutes. And they were getting closer. The door from the palace had been kicked open, and there was firing from there too. And now and then, from the gardens, a dark, anonymous figure loomed up suddenly large, close to one of the places where the glass had been blasted away in a gaping hole, then fell back again as de l'Epinay fired point-blank at him. Chloe almost screamed as she saw a man slip into the palmhouse through the door close beside her – then he reeled and sprawled out on the floor, staring sightlessly into her face. The gold braid and epaulets of a military uniform gleamed in the shadows, but it wasn't de Malebois.

From somewhere far back in the corridor, out of sight and out of de l'Epinay's range of fire, de Grismont's waspish voice became audible, raised in anger: 'Stop those damn fools! Vincent, you silly hot-head, stop those damn fools from blazing away like that! I want de l'Epinay alive.' De Malebois said something in answer, much closer to the open doorway, there were shouts, and the shooting gradually died away to silence.

Under the pattering of the rain, and the distant mutter of thunder, Chloe could hear de l'Epinay panting. Had he any bullets left? She had tried to keep count of the times he'd fired, amongst all the other shooting, and she thought it could hardly have been less than ten or twelve shots. And although he had killed or wounded half a dozen men for certain, and perhaps more, how many royalists were left? There might only be de Grismont and de Malebois in the corridor, and four or five others in the gardens, surrounding the palmhouse, or there might be twice that number. There was no hope, then. There had never been any hope. Lightning flickered over the broken glass and pools of rainwater on the mosaic floor, littered with smashed palm-fronds, and briefly lit up de l'Epinay's figure, leaning against the sloping trunk of a tree. With horror, Chloe saw that he was clutching his right shoulder, and that dark trickles were running down from inside his shirt-cuff and over the back of his hand and the silver hilt of the rapier he was now holding. His pistol lay empty and useless amongst the broken glass at his feet.

'De l'Epinay!' de Grismont called out in the silence, with a needlingly triumphant note in his voice. 'Or should I say Scorpio? How very absent-minded you've been lately, since you became involved with that Lenoir girl! Or is it because of that little tragedy last night at the Palais-Royal? I know all about that, you see – I've been putting two and two together. No wonder you were so exercized about that boy. And by the way, we found your tunnel a little while ago.'

De l'Epinay remained silent, leaving Chloe to wonder what de Grismont could have meant about Trévelan.

'Come now – you're wounded, aren't you?' de Grismont continued. 'And you've no ammunition left. And you're going to die anyway. We'll let the girl go if you give yourself up.'

'I wish I could believe that,' de l'Epinay murmured from the shadows.

'I give you my word.'

'Ah, your word!' de l'Epinay answered, with a soft, scathing laugh, but Chloe thought she could hear a catch of pain or despair in his voice. The air had lightened a little outside in the gardens, and with a sinking heart she counted no less than seven dark figures surrounding the palmhouse, pointing their muskets in through the broken glass. Two or three of them were standing ready to rush in where the holes were large enough. The faint light glistened on de l'Epinay's pale, dewed face as he added, 'In any case, it's too late. You won't find her alive now.'

In her hiding-place, Chloe half opened her reticule, where she had secreted the loaded pistol de l'Epinay had given her. Her fingers trembled, for she had understood the real meaning of his words. It was time for her to keep her promise. It could only be a matter of minutes now – seconds – before he was overwhelmed and captured by de Grismont's men.

'Go in and get him,' de Grismont ordered the dark figures surrounding the palmhouse. 'But make sure you take him alive.'

Her hand frozen on the cold pearl handle of the pistol in her reticule, Chloe watched the dark figures, as in a nightmare, edge in through the gaps in the shattered glass. Silently, in a circle, they closed in on the deep shadows where de l'Epinay had been dimly visible a moment before. Yet there was nothing: only the dripping and trickling of the subsiding rain, the grate of heavy footsteps on broken glass, and the sigh of palm-leaves as muskets pushed the great fronds aside.

'He isn't here,' a puzzled voice said. There was a crashing and ripping of palm-leaves. 'He's nowhere in this – '

'Look out!' another voice shouted in alarm. In the darkness behind the backs of two or three of the searchers there was a long flash of steel, and then a cry, and the snapping of branches as a man fell. Lightning flickered, illuminating de l'Epinay in a clearing several paces away, spinning on his heel, his rapier lifted, and a faint, unearthly smile on his face. With more crashing of foliage his assailants quickly surrounded him, but they kept warily out of range of that swift, lethal rapier; perhaps out of range, too, of the elemental, angel-of-death intensity of a man who had nothing to lose.

'Leave him to me,' said a drawling voice close to Chloe, and de Malebois stepped quickly and gracefully in through the doorway, his own duelling rapier flashing in his hand. 'And when I've disarmed him, which won't take a moment, be ready to seize him and tie him up. What a long, pleasant evening we're going to have, back in the Faubourg St Germain,' he went on, with a graceful, mocking bow to de l'Epinay. 'Such a lot of old scores to settle, at our leisure. Not to mention certain attentions which remain to be paid to Mademoiselle Lenoir – who is still alive, I don't doubt, and hidden away in a corner here somewhere. Find her,' he ordered, glancing at one of the other men, 'and tie her up.'

De l'Epinay had been standing motionless, his rapier still warily lifted and his left hand nursing his bleeding shoulder, absorbing de Malebois' taunts in a bleakly indifferent silence. But now he stirred and murmured casually, 'You people never did investigate your agents properly – I always had to do it for you. She's the grand-daughter of an English baron, and her name isn't Lenoir, it's Culverwood. Or rather it was,' he corrected himself, with a slight unevenness in his voice. 'I told you, you won't find her alive.'

He didn't glance in her direction but Chloe knew that he was telling her again, urgently, to fulfil her promise to him. And she knew that it was true: even without his wound, he stood no chance against de Malebois' famed swordsmanship. Yet she couldn't do it – she couldn't abandon him. Not yet; not just yet. The man who had been sent in search of her had moved away towards the far end of the palmhouse, beating at the undergrowth with his musket as he went, and she guessed that her actual hiding-place close to the door was the last place where he would look. It would be a few minutes, then, before he began to approach dangerously close to her.

De Malebois gave de l'Epinay another mocking bow, touched the hilt of his sword to his forehead, then pointed its shining tip at de l'Epinay's heart with an ironically formal *'En garde!'* From his easy arrogant stance in the dim, fitful light, Chloe could visualize the cold, level blackness of his eyes, and the politeness of his smile. De l'Epinay, by contrast, was pale and deadly calm as he faced him. His lips only moved once, framing the single word 'Now!' as he

221

looked past him in Chloe's direction: a word which de
Malebois might well have understood to mean 'At last!' –
that the bitter rivalry of so many years was at last to be
fought out to the death between them. Chloe's hand
tightened on the pearl butt of the pistol in her reticule
again, but she still couldn't bring herself to obey de
l'Epinay – to abandon him.

'Steel rang on steel as the two rapiers flashed and
clashed in the half darkness, de Malebois attacking with a
lightning succession of swift, deft thrusts, moving as
gracefully as a dancer. There had never been any man in the
whole French officer corps to match him, in the public
fencing tournaments on the Caroussel or at the Champ de
Mars, and it seemed that it could only be a few seconds
before de l'Epinay was defeated and disarmed. Yet despite
his limp, despite the wound in his right shoulder which
made him wince at each impact of steel on steel, despite his
earlier disclaimers about his own swordmanship, de l'Epinay
was holding his own. Parrying each flickering thrust of de
Malebois' rapier, he was backing deeper into the shadows,
until scarcely anything was visible but the bluish flash of
steel. Chloe guessed that he was taking advantage of the
darkness which had become his natural element. Now and
then, vanishing and reappearing, he even darted in to the
attack, and it was de Malebois – only the trace of a
mechanical smile still on his lips as the lightning lit him up
– who had to whirl round and parry the rain of glittering
blows.

Motionless, the dark figures of the other royalists stood
watching in a silent circle. In the doorway stood the small,
shabby, grey-haired figure of de Grismont, half out of
sight. In despair, Chloe saw that de l'Epinay was tiring.
Now and then, as the lightning flickered over him, she saw
how deathly pale he was, and how profusely the blood was
trickling down over his right hand and the hilt of his rapier.
Once, parrying a blow and stepping back deeper into the
shadows, he swayed and almost fell.

De Malebois darted after him. In the darkness the steel

rang and echoed, and then, suddenly, in a flicker of lightning, de l'Epinay's rapier was flying up into the air in a transient, shining arc, and de Malebois was stepping back and bowing with a mocking laugh, lowering his own sword to his side. 'And now, gentlemen,' he murmured, glancing round at the dark, waiting figures, 'If you have your ropes ready . . .' Chloe scarcely saw what happened next: only a swift upward leap in the darkness, a flash of fair hair, a flash of steel. For a moment longer she still couldn't grasp what had happened, though de Malebois continued to back slowly towards her, while de l'Epinay stood motionless and half visible, his rapier in his hand again.

Slowly de Malebois stumbled back against a clump of tropical plants, then slid to the floor, his head almost in Chloe's lap. For a moment his handsome face had a look of appealing boyish bewilderment on it, while the blood spread out over his white lace shirt-front, and his lips moved in smiling protest. Then he sighed, and the look of bewilderment faded into the remote of peace of death.

'A kind of justice,' de l'Epinay murmured under his breath, as if to himself, and Chloe could see a strange, distant look of grief in his face. Perhaps de Malebois had been his boyhood friend as well as his brother officer, his fellow aristocrat, and his rival in love. Or perhaps he was reliving the death of Trévelan. But what had he meant by those strange words? – 'A kind of justice . . .'

There was an earsplitting bang. Chloe didn't know for a moment what it was or where it had come from. Nor, for an instant longer, did she understand why de l'Epinay spun round as if caught in some invisible whirlwind, then reeled against the trunk of a palm. Then she saw the figure of de Grismont in the doorway, a smoking pistol in his hand, and saw that his hand was shaking.

For a moment de l'Epinay clung round the palm-tree, his hand to his face and blood coursing down between his fingers. 'Promise . . . You promised . . . You . . .' he murmured, as if he was talking in his sleep; then he slid slowly to his knees and fell forward, face down on the wet mosaic floor. Beside his head, a pool of rainwater slowly turned pink, then red.

Chloe walked towards him as if in a dream. Her promise, yes – but later. She sank to her knees beside him. He wasn't breathing, and she could feel no pulse in his cold wrist. His fair hair was turning wet and red with blood. She laid her hand on his head: not knowing where the bullet-wound was in it, not wanting to see what had happened to his face, knowing there was no hope; but as if touching him might bring him back.

'First the son, then the father. And now you,' said a dry voice.

Chloe looked up to see de Grismont approaching from where de Malebois lay dead. His normally greyish face seemed ashen, and there was a curious twitching tic at the corner of his mouth. Chloe supposed distantly that in his own perverse way he had loved the handsome cavalry officer. She noticed, too, as if from a long way away where nothing mattered any more, that his pistol was still in his hand.

'What do you mean?' she asked, looking at the blood on her fingers. What was it de l'Epinay had tried to say to her, about Trévelan? 'If you care for someone – even if it's too late, even if there's no hope – you can't prevent yourself . . . '

'What do I mean? That I'm going to kill you, of course,' de Grismont said. 'You'll pay for all – '

'No no,' Chloe said impatiently. 'You said "the son, and then the father." What did you mean by that?' But she thought she already knew.

'Why, that Trévelan was de l'Epinay's natural son. It was a very well-kept secret – the cuckolded husband was rabidly pious – and even the boy himself didn't know, but I'm sure of it. I know de l'Epinay had a love-affair with Vicomtesse Trévelan at Versailles, before the Revolution – he was just a young cadet at the Military Academy then, and she wasn't more than seventeen either – and then there was the way it took him: the boy's death. He'd never have admitted it, for the sake of the boy's name – not even when the boy was dead – but I'm sure of it.'

'So am I,' Chloe said, stroking de l'Epinay's blood-drenched hair. And in her mind she said to him, 'Forgive me. Oh Lucien, forgive me for not believing you, and for letting you die so terribly alone, rejected by me. Now–now that it's too late – I know how deeply true and good you were, in your own way.' Useless tears trickled down her face and made little fair splashes on his hair. Then she looked up at de Grismont and said, 'So it was you who killed Trévelan?'

'Naturally. He refused to carry out a mission – he betrayed the cause. Just as you, to a far more treacherous degree . . . '

Slowly Chloe opened the reticule still hanging from her wrist. 'I'm breaking my promise to you,' she told de l'Epinay in her mind, 'but there's different kinds of honour; you know that. You said your life had been empty and meaningless, although you shouldn't have felt that, when you were so brave and true. And you said that killing de Grismont would have meant that you hadn't lived in vain. So help me, Lucien, wherever you are now. Help me not to miss.'

Still kneeling close beside de l'Epinay, she took the pearl-handled pistol out of her reticule, pointed it at de Grismont, and pulled the trigger. There was a scream, and she shut her eyes and blocked her ears, but it went on, on and on, only very gradually fading away into some far, far distance. Somewhere very far away, and very dark.

But why was it so dark here too? She'd thought the storm was over, but it was getting darker and darker. 'Lucien, where have you gone?' she cried out. Anonymous figures surrounded her, melted away, returned again. A polite-faced man in a dark suit tried to take her arm, and she understood. 'It's too late,' she told him, freeing herself and stumbling away. 'Lucien, they've come – your men have come – and I suppose I'm safe now, and you must be glad of

225

that, but it's too late now. I don't want to live without you.'
The scent of rain-drenched earth and leaves came over her
in a wave, and she called out, 'Lucien, let me come with
you! I know it's all free and light and gold where you are, so
let me come too!' But the tunnel seemed endlessly long
and dark and lonely as she wandered on, and there was only
her own voice echoing back to her, never answered: 'De
l'Epinay! Lucien! I can't live without you! So wait for me,
please! Please don't leave me behind!'

Seventeen

THE DARK TUNNEL went on for ever. She wasn't always wandering down it alone, calling in vain to de l'Epinay, though often she was. Sometimes there were dark figures at her side, and sometimes it even seemed to her that she was being carried, wrapped in a blanket. Sometimes, too, they went very fast, and it was as if there was the lullaby swinging of a carriage, and the drumming of horses' hoofs, and a sighing like the wind in great trees on either side, as though the tunnel led on and on through an endless forest. Once it seemed to her that great courtyard gates were being opened, and light was dazzling out from the open door and the many windows of a dream castle, and then that she was being carried up the long, wide, graceful sweep of a flight of stairs. And then whispers, curtains, strange servants, and being laid to rest. But all that must have been only a dream, for the dark tunnel went on again, even darker and more endless than before, and she had to struggle on alone, her brow burning and her limbs aching, and every breath a stab of pain. With the last of her strength she still called out again and again, 'De l'Epinay! Lucien! Don't leave me! I know now that you didn't kill Trévelan – de Grismont told me it was he who did it – so please, let me come to you, wherever you are!' For a long time there was no answer. But then at last he seemed to come to her, invisible in the darkness but wonderfully loving and soothing, cradling her in his arms, and kissing her, and endlessly stroking her hair, so that she sank down and down into peace, peace, peace . . .

Sunlight filtered through her lashes, and she opened her eyes. For a little while she gazed at the pattern of the gold-embroidered drapes and coverlets of the wide bed she was lying in. Never had she lain in a bed so deeply soft, or between sheets so fine and smooth, scented with sunlight and fresh air and roses.

She sat up. She was in a large bedroom, carpeted from end to end with oriental rugs. The furniture was of the last century, elegantly simple and in a rosewood inlaid finely with pearl and gold. The chairs had seats of yellow damask silk, and yellow silk curtains stirred lazily at the open windows, through which sunlight, dappled with leaf-shadows, streamed low and mellow. Everywhere in the room there were vases of yellow, white and pale pink roses.

There was no one in the room; no sound anywhere but the singing of wild birds.

She slipped out of bed, stood swaying for a moment, clad in a white lace nightdress finer than any she had worn before, then walked to one of the windows. There she stood gazing out over a paradisaic vista of velvet lawns, rose-gardens and orchards, and beyond that a lake where a solitary swan floated motionless under the trailing green veils of a little willow-fringed island. And beyond that, encircling the gardens and holding them in a bowl of gold leaves and early evening sunlight, miles and miles of forest stretched away in every direction to the horizon, touched with amber and copper. But there wasn't a soul to be seen.

Was it Fontainebleau? It was how she had always imagined it, only even more beautiful. But it had been the last day of August, she remembered, when she had run through the storm to find de l'Epinay in the palmhouse, yet here it was late September, or perhaps even early October. The leaves were turning, and there were red apples in the orchards, and ripe peaches on the espaliered trees along the warm sandstone walls.

Yet how could it be Fontainebleau? Who would have brought her here, and why? She remembered how de l'Epinay had seemed to come to her, and hold her soothingly in his arms, and at the memory of it tears stung her eyes. That had only been a dream – the cruellest of dreams – for she knew that he was dead.

Out of the sunlit silence, drifting elusively to her like the scent of the roses, coming and going magically like the sheets of enamelled gold on the surface of the lake, there came the faint murmur of a sweetly familiar voice, and a soft laugh, light-hearted and elegant. To her swimming head, it seemed to her that it came from everywhere and nowhere: as if he were invisible, or as if his voice were the scent of the roses and the light on the water, tantalizingly distilled into momentary sound. But now and then, as her head cleared, it seemed to come from somewhere below – perhaps from a terrace screened from her sight, or perhaps through the open windows of a ground-floor room, or perhaps from somewhere in the gardens. She bit her lip in an agony of trepidation, turning round to face the room and searching with her eyes for clothes, a hairbrush, water to wash with. Was it the cruellest yet of all illusions, or was de l'Epinay really there?

She stood for a moment at the top of the main staircase in her white muslin gown, with its silver and opal clasp just beneath her breasts, and her silver and opal necklace and bracelets. She had found many of her own clothes and other belongings in the bedroom: the least of many mysteries yet to be explained.

She glanced round. On either side of the head of the stairs, polished galleries hung with oriental tapestries wound away, deserted, silent and gleaming, into the shadows, and in the great empty entrance hall below, as she went slowly down, the Persian carpets seemed to shimmer like mirages in the sunlight streaming in through the many windows and open doors. There was no sound; nothing to tell her that she wasn't entirely alone in the whole breathtakingly beautiful château. The pier-glasses she passed, and the great gilt-framed mirrors at the turns of the stairs, offered her back the gliding image of an evening ghost, slender and pale, with the large, darkly lustrous, secret eyes of a woman rather than of a girl; and her hand trembled on the bannister with the fear that she was only dreaming.

Downstairs, every pair of interconnecting double doors was open, and so were the french windows of every room she wandered through, though there was still no sight or sound of any human soul. The sunlight glancing off the surface of the lake filled the rooms with mysterious ripples and shimmers. Was that a flash of fair hair? She spun round. No; only the light fleetingly catching the surface of a mirror, brightening as the sun sank lower. And that keen, grey-blue gaze? She turned swiftly round again, but it was only a portrait, which she had glimpsed reflected in another mirror: the portrait of an army officer in the uniform of a hundred years before, gazing at her with de l'Epinay's eyes. And – her head swam as she spun round again – that suddenly lengthening shadow in the french windows . . .

Slowly her vision cleared. The marble console she had clung to for support was cool and real against her hand. And the elegant figure standing before her, his fair hair stirring slightly in the first breath of evening breeze, and his grey-blue eyes smiling as they returned her gaze?

'Are you real?' she managed to whisper.

'I hope so,' he said, with a laugh. 'And you? Aren't you too beautiful, too brave and too loyal to be true – to be mine?' Then he held out his arms to her. 'Come – there's only one way to find out.'

'So now you'll never leave me?' he murmured, a little later, at the dinner table, reaching for her hand.

'Never!'

'And we'll be married?'

'Yes.'

'And live here?'

'For ever!'

They were sitting close together at one end of the long, darkly polished table, which was a-glitter with silver, crystal, crested porcelain, candles and bowls of white roses. There were more lighted candles in silver candelabra and more bouquets of white roses all about the room, multiplied in the many mirrors like an infinity of gold blooms of light and white blooms of fragrance.

'I thought you were dead,' Chloe said, kissing his hand. 'I thought we were both dead.'

'I too,' he said, kissing hers. 'When I first regained consciousness, I lay there wishing I'd died, because I thought that you . . . ' He closed his eyes for a moment, briefly reliving a long, dark nightmare of his own. 'And then they told me – told me that you were alive, and that you were calling for me; that you knew the truth about Trévelan.' His glance flickered away from her with what seemed a hint of reluctant evasiveness, as he lifted his wineglass to his lips. 'I mean that it wasn't I who killed him.'

Chloe studied him for a moment. Many questions had been answered, and mysteries explained. He had told her, for instance, that though he really had been shot in the head, the wound had only been a graze, just above his temple – albeit deep enough to have sent him into a coma, which was why he had seemed to have no pulse or breathing. And the wound in his shoulder, for all that it had bled so profusely, had only been a flesh-wound. He was still a little pale, and a little thinner, it was true, but otherwise there was nothing to show that he had been within an inch of his life. He had even been up and about again for the last week or more – long before her, who had had pneumonia, brought on by shock according to the physician. De l'Epinay's lieutenants, alerted by his coachman, had rescued them from the palmhouse and brought them here to Fontainebleau for safety while the last of the royalists were rounded up. Uncle Victor and Aunt Eugénie had been told that she'd been interned for a short while, just as a

231

formality, on account of her being half-English; and as it was well known that the interned English nobility were living in fine style in various châteaux throughout France, entertaining one another with games of charades, and balls, and of course proposals of marriage, they hadn't been unduly alarmed. Only Philippe had been told the truth.

But there were other truths; other things which remained unsaid, and perhaps always would. Chloe noticed that de l'Epinay had avoided any reference to the men she had killed, or had seen killed: Turgeon, de Grismont, de Malebois. Perhaps he feared that the stirring up of such memories might be too much for her, after her illness; and perhaps he was right. Nor, except for that one evasive flicker of his eyes, had the truth about Trévelan – that he had been his son – been touched on. Should she tell him that she knew? Or should she wait for him to tell her in his own time, if ever? She couldn't yet decide. But meanwhile there was still so much else: all his life, all the mystery of the work he'd chosen to do, all that lay behind the name Scorpio . . .

'Explain,' she'd said.

The sun had gone down behind the forest, the dew was falling, and the candlelight was beginning to outshine the long gold afterglow lingering in the gardens. Still they sat over the remains of their meal, balloon glasses of cognac cupped in their hands. From the walls, as if out of the hazy, mirrored infinity of candle flames, the family portraits looked down on them: de l'Epinay's sisters, three rosy little girls laughing and tumbling in the long grass and wild flowers at the margin of the lake; his severe, blond father, with whom he'd quarrelled bitterly from boyhood about the treatment of their servants and tenants; his adored, dark, beautiful mother, who had spoiled him and laughingly encouraged his early amorous adventures. Her portrait was behind de l'Epinay, and to Chloe it was eery to see how

Trévelan, with his fine, imperious, sensitive features and intensely dark colouring, seemed to look out of her face. But then, now that she knew the truth, there were frequent glimpses of the boy in de l'Epinay's face too. Hadn't she thought at the start that Trévelan resembled him? It was just that the striking contrast between de l'Epinay's fair hair and grey-blue eyes, and the boy's extreme darkness, had blinded her to the truth; that and the improbability of a man of de l'Epinay's age having an adolescent son. His early amorous adventures . . . He touched on the subject briefly, then it was gone, without any mention of Trévelan.

And then the Revolution, which he had believed in ardently at first, knowing the burning need for reform and justice in a still feudal France, where it was a common thing for peasants to starve in hovels hardly better than mud huts, five hundred paces away from palaces. Reform, yes. But then the Terror. He had returned from fighting in the civil war in the west of France, a twenty-year-old captain in the republican army, already sick at heart from killing his fellow Frenchmen, to find his home looted, and his entire family gone to the guillotine: his father, his mother, and his three sisters. And then the hiding, the lying, the bribing, the continual switching of allegiances, just to stay alive; just to see France stagger on through year after year of civil war, famine, and a succession of ephemeral governments as weak as they were corrupt. By the time he was twenty-five, fighting in the Italian Campaign, it had seemed to him that there was nothing left to believe in.

Briefly he had believed in Bonaparte: Bonaparte the man of the centre, the man of fire, the national hero. Who else could have united the country, and brought law and order and internal peace to it? Deeply bitter and lonely after so much disillusion and personal loss – even if he had tried to conceal that from himself and others by a kind of levity – de l'Epinay had been all too ready for the work Bonaparte had offered him: to live alone in the shadows, close to death. And for five years that faith in Bonaparte, the murkiness of that work, had seemed justified. But now . . .

233

'Emperor!' de l'Epinay said scathingly, draining his glass. 'Conqueror of the world! Living in a palace and spitting on what he calls "the rabble"! Plunging us, I predict, into another decade of war. How the wheel keeps turning full circle! I'd gladly assassinate him myself tomorrow, but what would happen? We'd have civil war again between the royalists and the Jacobins, and another Terror, and another famine, and then, I suppose, another Bonaparte. Oh, I've seen too much, and I think too much, but I can't help it: I despair.'

He gazed out at the falling dusk over the rim of his empty glass, and Chloe saw again the ineffable bleakness in his eyes which she had seen so often before. But now she understood it. And she remembered that in the rose-garden at the Palais-Royal, at the nadir of his disillusion and grief, he had said, 'Only you can help me.'

'But you only feel despair because you still really believe in something, surely?' she murmured.

He roused himself from his empty gazing out into the dusk and glanced at her. 'Do I?'

'Well, you care. About France, about ordinary people – about life itself. You feel like this because you care so much.'

'Ah, perhaps,' he said, taking her hand, his own fingers not quite steady, as if from the sudden hope she'd given him. 'But how . . ? Still, Bonaparte can't last for ever. He'll try to invade Russia – he'll over-reach himself.' He watched a single petal fall from a white rose, fluttering down like a flake of snow. 'And meanwhile, if a new generation of lads like your cousin, like . . . like other young boys I know, or used to know . . . ' He trailed off for a moment, gazing at the dying flame of one of the candles, and Chloe silently shared his grief with him, stroking his hand. ' . . . And we must try to learn from England,' he went on, collecting himself with an effort, 'where they've had political stability – reform and moderation together – for hundreds of years. I've always felt that. It was why I sent them there, or sent them back. To be educated.'

'Who?' Chloe asked, bewildered.

'Ah, so Turgeon didn't drop any hints about that? He found me out – that's why he was blackmailing me. Otherwise I'd have been court-martialled and shot out of hand. I've smuggled many of my royalist prisoners back to England, you see. Not the hard cases and the professional murderers, of course – they went to the execution they deserved – but the young, the merely misguided, the natural moderates. Marignac, for instance – he's there by now.'

' – With the invasion plans? You really meant them to reach England?'

'Of course.'

So he had, after all, been a kind of double agent. Chloe shivered, thinking of the solitary, dangerous game he'd been playing.

There was a silence. The candles were burning very low now, casting large, dark shadows over the walls and ceiling. She had asked de l'Epinay earlier if she could see his signet-ring, and it still gleamed forgotten on his finger, broodingly sinister with its scorpion poised to sting. She knew now that there had never been any torture, other than in the wishful thinking of Turgeon; and de l'Epinay had told her too that General de Bourges, who really had been embezzling Army funds, had only been sent to America. Yet the scorpion, though it was beautiful in its arcane way, sent another shiver through her as she gazed at it. It was de l'Epinay himself now that she feared for: not only because of the terrible dangers of his work, but because of the way that work was poisoning and destroying his spirit. Didn't scorpions often end by stinging themselves to death?

'And will you go on?' she asked at last, in trepidation. 'Will you go on being Scorpio?'

Following her gaze, he slid his signet-ring off his finger and weighed it thoughtfully in his hand; then he only said, 'Let's go down to the lake.'

It still wasn't dark outside, for a pearly glow lingered in the sky, mirrored by the dew and by the lake, so that the roses all about them were visible, browsed upon by large, pale moths. It was like the garden at the Palais-Royal in a way, where she had first known for certain that de l'Epinay was in love with her; only now they were separated by nothing, two souls becoming one soul. True, he hadn't told her about Trévelan, and perhaps he never would. Perhaps he had given the boy's mother his word of honour that he would never tell anyone, for the sake of the boy's name; and death wouldn't end that obligation but only deepen it. She was sure it must be something of the kind, to have made de l'Epinay risk losing her rather than tell her, and to cause him to bear his grief in silence now, unshared. Well, let it be so. The men who had heard what de Grismont had said in the palmhouse were almost certainly dead now, executed, and de l'Epinay's secret was entirely safe with her. Perhaps in time, realizing that she knew the truth, he would come to tell her the whole story. Only one thing troubled her a little, meanwhile: that there might be others besides Trévelan.

'Well, how many children have you, scattered about France, Italy and the Levant, after all your love-affairs?' she asked in a half-joking tone, as they reached the edge of the lake.

'None.'

The surface of the water was motionless, except for an occasional silvery ring where a fish touched it.

'I had a son,' de l'Epinay said, after a while. 'But he died.'

She took his hand, kissed it, and said, 'I'm sorry.'

He said nothing more for a few minutes; and then, softly: 'What is it you believe in? I've always felt – known – that you believed in something.'

Chloe looked slowly about her. The roses grew right down to the water's edge and were mirrored in it, and their scent filled the still air. Again they told her that they were immortal – even those which collapsed into a scattering of pale petals as she watched. One spray, overhanging the water, dipped and touched its own dim and mysterious reflection, like time and timelessness meeting in a kiss and becoming one.

'Love, I think,' she answered at last. 'It's difficult to put into words.'

'But you'll show me?' de l'Epinay said, drawing her into his arms. And then, his lips against her hair: 'And you'll give me another son?'

'Yes, but sons need their fathers – '

'I know.'

' – And you haven't answered my question about your work.'

He flung something far out into the centre of the lake. There was a brief flash of gold, a tiny splash, and a slowly widening ring of ripples – widening and widening until the surface of the water was motionlessly smooth again. 'There's my answer,' he said.

'And Bonaparte – ?'

'He'll survive for a while. All the royalist ringleaders have been caught, and my lieutenants can manage perfectly well now without me.'

'Yes, but will he let you go so easily?'

De l'Epinay shrugged. 'Why not? He never has time, you know, to visit men who have been wounded or maimed in his service. He was told I'd been shot in the head and the right shoulder, and that I'd be incapacitated for a long time – which the doctors believed at first. There's no need to correct that impression. And in a year he'll have forgotten about me.'

'And what will you do instead?'

'Have sons,' he said, taking her chin gently in his hand and lifting her face to receive his kiss. 'Sons and daughters, and a happy home for them to grow up in – a home full of love and belief in life: isn't that where it all begins, all hope for the future? And a well-run estate. And good friends – friends who think and feel as I do, and with whom I can work and plan behind the scenes, for when the moment comes. And you, above all. You, you, you.' Gently he kissed her brow, her eyes, and her lips. 'You'll be the heart of it all.'

She slipped her arms round his neck and he cradled her close, stroking her hair. A flock of wild waterbirds, tiny specks at first in the pearly oneness of lake and sky, spiralled down and settled for the night in the shadowy reeds at the margin, underlining the silence for a moment with their soft and drowsy cries.